A disturbed girl's guide to curing boredom

James Howell

AMYGDALA PRESS

First published in the UK in 2011 by
Amygdala Press
42 St Mary's Road
Southend, Essex, SS2 6JS

www.amygdala-press.com

ISBN: 978-0-9569260-0-5

Typeset in Palatino Linotype 10/14
by Talisman Communications
Printed and bound in Great Britain
by Lightning Source UK Ltd

Acknowledgements

Hannah's story has taken a long time to write, and there have been many amazing people along the way who have helped, supported, inspired and encouraged me.

It first came to life at Martin and Noi's tranquil Rainbow Bungalows resort on Koh Phangan in Thailand, where I bounced ideas off Katie Knowles, Naomi Good, Kat Storey, Hannah Tierney and Andy Leppard. Through this Thailand gang, I was lucky enough to meet Pandora Male, my beautiful Shunt buddy.

Love to the Southend crew as always: Alan and Jane Pearce, Spunky Jay, Czuba and Jen, Tim and Sharon Baker, Helen Sealey, Lisa Nice, Paul and Anne Jenkinson, Dean and Kerry Wastell, Big Stu (Treacle), Amy and Katy Perry, Annie Pearce, Pete and Caroline Sartain and Ray Longdon.

Also shouts to my family, Laura Holland, Paul Davison (Yeti), Sarah and Matt Laing, Mark Dinning, Elaine Morton and Jaime Sandall.

Thank you to Rachel Miller for helping and supporting during the early days.

Special thanks to Gemma Carmody and Becca Sprowles for proof-reading and encouraging me, and my gratitude to Mandy Sullivan and Daniel Harding at Amygdala Press.

Finally and most importantly, love and thanks to my wife Tina for putting up with me and enduring the moods and vodka binges while I got to grips with the book.

And, of course, my thanks to Hannah, wherever the hell you are.

James Howell

Prologue – an introduction by Hannah Harker

My name is Hannah Harker and I am a deeply disturbed young woman. If I was in a special group – perhaps sitting on a plastic chair in a draughty hall – with other disturbed young women, that comment might generate a warm round of applause.

"How brave to admit that!" they might mutter to one another.

I am not in a group. I don't want anyone's applause and I don't expect anybody, you included, to like me. I only admit what I am now because I'm simply too disturbed to conceal it anymore.

Be careful not to jump to hasty conclusions about me though. I don't live in a spooky cottage in the woods with the curtains drawn, rocking back and forth while picking at the stitches in my blanket. I actually live in a large house in a leafy suburb, and I have an incredible job, great wealth and the sort of influence world leaders can only dream about. This enviable position I find myself in came about as a result of me being the only person left alive to describe to the world the most shattering, utterly incomprehensible news event in history.

But, sadly, I'm completely psychotic. Whatever outward shell I portray is completely undermined by the total emotional and mental meltdown of my inner self. Horrors of my own creation dance around my head and no psychiatrist in the world could make them stop. Behind my eyes there is nothing but absolute insanity, and I'm afraid the only way to halt this madness will be to self destruct.

But first I want to tell my story. I want to leave a little confession, because it's not so long ago that I was what you would consider normal. It was only my quest to find a cure for the boredom which plagued me that left me in this ruined state. At least now I'm too insane to be bored.

I have had to enlist the help of another writer to tell my tale because, as you've probably gathered from this short introduction, my mind is not in any state to sit down and compose a structured, chronological account of my journey. I am a journalist of distinction and can write eloquently about all manner of topics, but an autobiographical novel would now be beyond me.

There's no special reason why I chose James Howell to write the book, he was simply a persistent bastard who cornered me in a bar and said he wanted to write my story. He chose his timing well because I was feeling especially vulnerable and sensed that the end was near. I reluctantly decided to allow him into my life for just long enough to record an open and honest account of my rise and decline. The story, therefore, although written in the first person, has been penned by Howell. A few brief sections that I wrote myself, aside from this prologue, appear in italics.

Howell doesn't know that I've written this prologue, and it would probably break his heart if he did because he was in love with me. I have therefore asked the publisher to include this introduction without his knowledge. He has written his own opinions of me in an epilogue at the end, in case you are interested in reading what he thought of me.

When this story is made public the authorities will come for me. I have no wish to spend the rest of my days incarcerated in a secure unit for the insane, barking like a mad dog in a straitjacket as electrodes are plugged into my brain, so I will take my own life as soon as this book goes to print. I'm sure that if I invite him, Howell will join me.

PART 1
RISE

"Since boredom advances and boredom is the root of all evil, no wonder, then, that the world goes backwards, that evil spreads. This can be traced back to the very beginning of the world. The gods were bored; therefore they created human beings." – Soren Kierkegaard

"Sooner barbarity than boredom." – Theophile Gautier

Chapter One

If everybody was somebody, nobody would be anybody. But, if you aren't somebody, you're nobody.

These words from an eccentric but amiable university lecturer came back to me for some reason as I flopped down at my desk at 7.35 on a grey and drizzly Monday morning. I flicked on my PC with blurry eyes and was vaguely aware of impatient voices to my right as the editor, news editor and sub editors of the Rockingsworth Evening Informer tried to rewrite the splash story, which had been hastily cobbled together by a junior reporter on the Sunday shift who was more interested in finishing early so he could catch the start of some football match.

I wandered over to the tea area, grunting brief greetings to a couple of the other reporters, and put the kettle on. I glanced over to where the front page was being finalised as I tipped two large spoonfuls of cheap coffee into my unwashed mug.

"Council U-turn over High Street scheme", was the splash headline on the sub editor's screen.

Christ. The front page story was about the leader of the council taking a call from the disinterested reporter on Sunday lunchtime and telling him that the contract to relay the paving in the High Street would be given to a local firm and not some outfit based in Spain. It didn't matter that the Spanish option had only ever been mentioned once in passing at a council meeting some months back as a cost-saving idea but was never seriously considered as a viable option. Still, my only contribution to that Monday's Informer was a lead on page 17 about residents campaigning for a speed hump outside the local school. "It's an accident waiting to happen," said resident Ted Jarvis, 64, who hadn't seen an accident happen in the 40-odd years that he had lived there.

I grabbed the Sun and the Guardian and took them with the coffee back to my desk. Phil Crichton, the chief reporter, had arrived now and taken his seat opposite mine. Next to him was Jenny Davis, a 23-year-old hypochondriac who would turn the air-conditioning down the minute she walked in and sit at her desk all day wrapped in layers of scarves, sipping

Lemsip and fiddling with a box of tissues.

"How was your weekend?" Phil asked, looking over at me.

"Okay, just stayed in really." I knew if I asked him back he would still be rattling on at lunchtime.

I flicked through the Sun before turning to the jobs section in the Media Guardian. As usual there was nothing of interest, unless I wanted to become a press officer for the National Potato Council or "write informatively and entertainingly about the metal markets for a leading industry magazine."

Despondent, I turned to my emails for inspiration, but all I had was a load of spam inviting me to get a penis enlargement or buy Gucci handbags for $99, a press release from the local horticultural society, a crap joke I'd heard two months previously and a message from news editor Marc Sullivan telling me to cover a hospital trust meeting that afternoon because the health reporter was off sick.

"Hey, Hannah." Simon Maitland took his seat next to mine and gave me a broad smile as he draped his jacket over the back of his chair.

Simon was my best friend at the Informer. We had kissed at the office Christmas party a few months earlier and he'd got a bit heavy after that, but we had a good talk about the situation and now we were able to have a laugh and just be friends.

"Hello, Simon. Did you go out clubbing in the end on Saturday?"

He had phoned me on Saturday afternoon to see if I wanted to go to a club in London. I said no because I knew we'd end up doing a couple of pills, staying up all night and I'd be a wreck for my dad's birthday dinner on Sunday.

"Yeah, I went with Paul and Aaron from advertising. Properly banging, you should've come along."

He gave me a look to say that he'd also taken a bucketful of drugs, but we didn't talk about that kind of thing in front of Phil.

"Sounds like fun," I said. "I had the girls over for some chick flicks and wine. You would've loved it!"

"Awesome," he replied sarcastically. "What are you up to tonight?"

"Nothing much."

"Fancy the pub?"

"Yeah, could do." I had nothing else to do.

"Sounds like a plan to me, Si," Phil butted in. "A bit of team bonding. Shall we make it the Lion for half seven? I'll send an email round."

Simon and I looked at each other with a grimace. Phil was a prick; a 35-year-old bachelor who had done a couple of shifts on The News of the World years ago and now considered himself a former national reporter. He pranced about the office with his sculptured hair and his Pierre Cardin suits, barking orders at the trainees and agreeing obsequiously with anything the news editors or Tina Karageorghis, the editor, said. He thought he was some sort of role model to the reporters under him, but we all just took the piss out of him and hoped he'd leave.

Monday's edition had finally been "put to bed" and would hit the streets about midday, so the news editors were starting to ask for lists of what people were working on for Tuesday's paper. The sausage factory never closed.

My hospital meeting wasn't until 1pm, so I had to come up with ideas. Phoning round councillors was not my cup of tea, there were no stories in the nationals that had a local angle, court would be the usual tedious parade of drink-drivers and town centre delinquents, someone had already checked the fire stations and Detective Inspector Liam King, my best police contact, was on a rest day.

I decided to try the main police switchboard, but knew I'd get offered nothing more than a few shed burglaries. I dialled the number and it rang 12 times before a middle-aged woman answered with a harassed sigh.

"Hi, it's Hannah Harker from the Informer. Can I speak to the duty Inspector please?"

"Oh, nothing's happened. It's been very quiet overnight," the woman replied.

"Can I speak to the duty Inspector, please?" I repeated.

"Just a moment." The woman sighed again and put the phone down without bothering to put it on secrecy. I heard her say to someone "It's the bloody Informer, I'll tell them there's nothing", then she came back on the line.

"I'm afraid the duty Inspector is in a briefing at the moment. Can you call back later?"

"Yeah, whatever." I put the phone down hard. Lazy bitch.

I wandered over to the fax machine and picked up a few council press releases that were spewing out. They would keep me occupied for a while.

Walking back to my desk, I nearly choked on the smell of stale alcohol and cigarette smoke, which signalled the belated arrival of Brian Abbot, the political reporter.

Abbot was a single 50-something alcoholic who seemed to live in the pub and loiter around the town hall thinking he was an "Old School hack". His threadbare and crumpled suits smelt like a pub on Sunday morning, his hair was greasy and lank, his breath reeked and his complexion was so bad that his nose looked like a bunch of raspberries.

"Good morning, Brian," I said. "I've just taken a few council press releases off the fax. Hope you don't mind if I bash them out."

"No, no," he burped. "Help yourself, my dear."

So, I sat down and wrote a page lead about the long-anticipated reopening of the council's botanical museum, a story about an optimistic bid by the council for lottery money to build a community centre and a few "news in briefs" about half-term fun days for children at the local park.

Chapter 2

I got home at 6pm in a foul mood. The hospital meeting had been predictably dire and it was as much as I could do to get one remotely decent story from it. Phil and Jenny had been talking excitedly about the pub when I left work and I had to promise them I would go.

My little house was a 15 minute drive from the office in a pleasant, leafy street in the village of Rockingsworth, some 60 miles south east of London. I didn't have a house-mate, but dad helped with most of the rent so I just about managed to go out occasionally, run a car and buy the odd luxuries with my whopping £14,000 annual salary!

I hung my raincoat in the hall and went up to my bedroom, which was a tip. I put my iPod into its speakers and clicked it onto shuffle then took off my boots and tights. I hung my cardigan and top in the wardrobe and padded through to the bathroom and put the bath on. Downstairs I found the remains of a bottle of Pinot Grigio, which I emptied into a glass and carried back up to the bathroom. The water pressure was low and the bath was taking an age to fill, so I unclipped my bra, took off my skirt and knickers and gave myself a quick examination in the mirror.

I was 26-years-old and pleased with my appearance. Very dark brown hair fell straight against the sides of my face and was cut in a neat line at my shoulders. I had high cheek bones, which I felt gave my face a good shape, and my hazel eyes perched above a long, slender nose. My mouth was quite wide with full lips and good teeth, while my chin was defined without being pointy.

I was just over 5ft 9ins tall and slim. My breasts were a little small but I had a flat stomach and there was no hint of cellulite on my thighs or bum. In fact, the only blemish, apart from the odd mole, was a three-inch crescent-shaped scar just above my crotch, which had been caused by a fall when I was climbing in Nepal during my two-year trip round the world.

I lit some candles, tested the bath water and gingerly lowered myself into the bubbles with a sigh. The heat made my skin tingle and I took a deep swig of wine as my body gradually accepted the temperature and I laid back, closed my eyes and drifted off into a nostalgic daydream.

Hannah Harker. My dad, Peter, a Fleet Street journalist for 37 years, had insisted on the name because he was determined his little girl would become a journalist too and he wanted me to have "a good news name". Dad talked so enthusiastically about his job that even from a very young age I knew that one day I would probably follow in his footsteps. Mum gave me all the encouragement she could while I was growing up, although most of her energies had been devoted to caring for my younger twin brothers, Robbie and Anthony, who were both born with Cerebral Palsy.

I was just four when the twins were born and overnight I went from being the centre of attention to being a virtual outcast in my own family. At such a young age I suppose it was inevitable that I would take it badly, and my dad later told me how I had spent a year screaming, stamping my feet and being spiteful to the babies whenever I thought I could get away with it.

After a while, however, I realised that no amount of petulance and tantrums would bring me the attention I craved. I withdrew into myself, played alone and learned to start enjoying my own company. I then discovered the pleasure of thinking and would lose myself for hours in elaborate daydreams about jet-setting across the globe as a superstar journalist, reporting from the frontline and exposing corruption. My dad had shelves of books about journalism and biographies of fearless reporters, which he would read to me in bed whenever he had the time.

At primary school I earned a reputation for being shy and withdrawn. The teachers encouraged me to get involved with team games and play with the other children, but I was content to read and learn. My reading and writing skills were far better than anyone else in my year group and I easily passed every test and exam they made me sit, so I never got a hard time from the teachers or my parents despite the perceived social inadequacies.

My academic ability ensured that I avoided the local comprehensive and breezed into the best girls' school in the borough. Many of the other girls who joined me went into a panic as the innocence of primary school morphed into a rollercoaster world of bullies, hormones, peer-pressure, identity, boys and exams that really mattered. I, on the other hand, managed to keep a cool head and I developed a dry sense of humour and slightly rebellious streak which ensured that I was generally popular and had a few friends who I could hang out with whenever I decided I wanted to.

I was the first girl in my year to start having periods and thus became something of a mini celebrity. I enjoyed this status and liked having other girls come to me for advice. My natural predisposition to be introverted gave way to cautious extroversion and I suddenly felt like I was a bit special and different to everybody else. I made a conscious effort to avoid peer pressure and cliques, and I made sure I turned my back on anything trendy or popular. If everyone was listening to a new band, I made a point of not buying their album; if a new hit television show became the talking point, I would watch the other channel; if a new hairstyle or fashion item became vogue I would strive to make my appearance the opposite.

My star shone brightest when our school hosted a joint disco between the girls in our year and the same year group from the adjacent boys' school. We were all 14 or 15 and alcohol was strictly banned, but some of the boys managed to smuggle in water bottles filled with vodka and coke cans topped up with whisky. Me and a couple of my friends latched on to these boys and soon found ourselves sitting outside on a grassy hill near the rear of the playing fields. It was the first time I'd ever tried anything stronger than wine and my head was soon spinning and my inhibitions evaporated. One of the boys, Toby Chambers, lit a spliff for me (my first experience of drugs) and I felt his arm slide around my shoulders. We chatted for a while, my head going off in different directions as the minutes passed, and then suddenly we were alone and Toby was unwrapping a condom. I had only just turned 15 but I helped him put the condom on and then reached up my skirt and took my knickers off. I still remember his aftershave and the feel of the prickly grass on my bare skin, but the actual event was mainly a blur. Toby was pissed and couldn't come and as his erection drooped the condom came off inside me. He clumsily fished it out and tried to put it back on, but it was a lost cause. He tried to masturbate himself while roughly fingering me for a while, but then we heard adult voices in the distance and had to stop. He swore as he got dressed, but I was relieved. It had been painful and disappointing and I was desperate to clean up the blood I could feel between my legs.

We had chewing gum to disguise the smell of smoke and alcohol then rejoined the party. The gossip had already started and as I walked in I felt the whole hall turn to look at me. Several of my friends raced over and started quizzing me about what had happened and when I was sure that no teachers could overhear us I gave them an extremely embellished and favourable account of how magical the loss of my virginity had been.

When I walked into school on Monday morning I was a legend and I was only too happy to recount my experience for the other girls in my year. My transformation was finally complete as I went from being the studious loner to being the outgoing storyteller and fountain of knowledge.

Unfortunately, Toby was also a keen storyteller and I earned a less enviable reputation at the boys' school. At that stage however I was so blinded by the limelight and pumped up with my own hype that I saw it as my duty to push the boundaries, and a couple of months after losing my virginity I started sleeping regularly with an 18-year-old Jamaican guy called Carl Lafferty who was studying in their sixth form. Suddenly, the gossip among the girls at my white and conservative school turned sour: a one-night stand with a white boy was cool; an inter-racial underage affair was quite another matter.

My friends shunned me and for the first time in my life I was hurt and affected by the opinions of my peers. The ringleader was a very beautiful and very popular bitch called Ruth Chapman who had become my nemesis. Ruth was tall, blonde, witty and smart. She had a huge circle of friends who were regularly invited over for lavish parties at her parents' sprawling mansion and she became the darling of the playground by buying sweets for everyone from the ice cream van that parked just outside the school gates.

She surrounded herself with flunkies and took an instant dislike to me when it became clear that I was my own person and had no intention of being in her gang. When I started becoming popular myself, her dislike turned into a venomous loathing of me and I realised it was only a matter of time before we came to blows.

She initiated a nasty little smear campaign against me when I started seeing Carl and things came to a head in the school dining hall one lunchtime. I was in the queue minding my own business when she crept up behind me, jabbed a banana up my skirt and whispered in my ear: "Why don't you try this for size, you fucking nigger lover."

In that moment a previously unknown temper was ignited inside me. I spun round clutching a fork and sunk the prongs through her shirt into her upper arm. Before she could register what had happened, I swept her legs from underneath her, pinned her to the floor with my knees and started pummelling her face with my fists. I didn't make a sound and it didn't seem real. I just hit her over and over again until powerful arms reached down and dragged me away. All I remember thinking as I was pulled to the headteacher's office was that I hadn't finished; I had been interrupted before the punishment was complete. A boundary had been crossed and revenge would have to be taken. Ruth Chapman needed to suffer further, and whether it was tomorrow, next month, next year or a decade down the line an opportunity would present itself and I would let her know that by choosing to become my enemy she had made the biggest mistake of her life.

I was suspended from school while the headteacher considered permanent exclusion and Ruth's parents threatened to press charges and sue my parents. During my two week suspension I composed an eloquent defence of my actions, focussing on the racist provocation. I practised the speech in my bedroom and presented it to the headteacher and police liaison officer at my hearing. My defence, coupled with pleading from my father and my own guarantees of guilt and remorse, earned me a reprieve and I was allowed to stay on and complete my GCSEs. From that moment on I took a vow of chastity, kept my head down and eventually got the second best GCSE grades in my year.

I stayed on at the same school to do my A-levels and again excelled. On the summer's day when we collected our results from school a group of us decided to go out to the pub to celebrate. It had been over three years since the incident with Ruth and it had been all but forgotten by everyone, except me. When I saw her in the same pub that night surrounded by her friends, all sloshing champagne down their necks, I knew that the time for revenge had arrived. She was centre stage as usual wearing an expensive dress and I could see that she was very drunk, slurring her words and rocking on her feet. I too was drunk, but there was no doubt that this was the night she would pay for causing me so much grief, for embarrassing my father and for making me tip-toe along a tightrope of saintly behaviour for the past three years.

I knew that Ruth lived very near to the pub, just through a small park across the road, and would be walking home. It was an extremely exclusive area of town and none of her friends lived there, so she would be walking home alone while they went off in the other direction to the bus stop.

At 10.30pm I said goodbye to my friends, announced that I was getting the bus home and then crept across to the deserted park and hid in the bushes. It was a warm night and as I squatted in the dirt my mind took me back to the incident in the school canteen and reminded me of the way she had sneered in my ear as she stabbed the banana up my skirt. Rage started crawling through me and I had to work hard to bring myself under control.

Ruth came stumbling along 45 minutes later. She was sending a text message, mumbling to herself, and was totally unaware of anything that was going on around her.

Perfect.

I waited until she had passed my hiding place, then slipped out from behind the bushes, sprinted towards her in three great strides and cracked her across the back of the head with a heavy stick I had found.

She crumpled to the floor, unconscious.

Shaking with adrenaline, I checked that nobody was around then dragged her into the bushes and smashed her face in with the stick. A force of some kind took control of my arms and I hit her over and over again with strength that should have been beyond me. I don't know how long I beat her for but I suddenly stopped, breathless, and realised I was going to kill her if I continued. The light of the moon illuminated the scene and I was staring down at a deformed ball of meat and hair, with bubbles of blood expanding and bursting from the remains of a once beautiful nose.

I felt ice running through my veins and an unexpected sense of calm.

My plan was to make the attack look like an attempted rape and robbery, so I tore off her dress and underwear, scratched the inside of her thighs and pocketed her purse, watch and jewellery. My fingerprints and her blood were on the stick so I washed it carefully in the park's murky little pond and tossed it into some undergrowth.

I checked that the bitch was still breathing, then took a deep breath of my own and went home. I had a cup of tea, a slice of cake that my mum had left out, then showered and scrubbed away any skin from under my fingernails before sliding into bed.

The next day I woke up early, took a bus 20 miles away to another town and threw a plastic bag containing Ruth's valuables into a deep and dirty canal. On the way back home I called all my friends and cheerfully asked them if they had enjoyed themselves last night and what their plans were for the rest of the weekend. None of them mentioned anything about Ruth. In fact, nobody knew about what had happened to Ruth until an elderly couple found her bloodied and naked crawling through the park later that afternoon.

Her condition was never life-threatening, but she spent two months in hospital undergoing reconstructive surgery on her face while the press ran appeals for witnesses and the police fumbled for clues.

I had braced myself for a knock at the door all throughout this time and fully expected to be arrested as a key suspect, but when she was eventually able to speak to the police, Ruth inexplicably gave them a detailed description of her attacker as a short, stocky Eastern European man in his late forties who was wearing a tracksuit and trainers. I suspected that this was Ruth's pre-programmed stereotype of a rapist and the first image that came to mind when detectives urged her to recall her attacker.

In due course a local alcoholic who vaguely fit the description and couldn't provide an alibi was arrested and charged with attempted rape and assault occasioning grievous bodily harm. He obviously pleaded not guilty and the trial was big news locally, although reporting restrictions meant that Ruth was only ever referred to as "the 18-year-old victim". I was pleased when a few months later the guy was acquitted and, despite protestations from Ruth and her parents, the case gradually slipped down the list of police priorities.

I was never so much as interviewed by police because Ruth had been so adamant about the description of her attacker that the manhunt had been narrow. Besides, my fight with her had been years in the past and it simply didn't occur to anyone that someone would hold a schoolyard grudge for that long.

They were wrong. I hadn't thought about revenge every day, but in the back of my mind I always knew that I still owed Ruth more payback when the opportunity arose. After what happened in the park I felt calm and content, as if a nagging burden had been lifted from my shoulders. I had done what I needed to do to settle an old score and could now put that period of my life behind me. There was certainly no sense of guilt. Ruth would be left with a few physical and mental scars, but they would ease over time. I almost hoped that one day she would realise that it was me who had attacked her; that she would realise that for a few minutes I held the power of life and death over her.

But now I was going off to university, and then to work in the real world, where racial abuse simply wasn't acceptable and where personal disputes were settled by more subtle and insidious means than random acts of violence. At least that's what I thought at the time.

I was coming to the end of my first year at City University, London, where I was studying journalism, when the twins died unexpectedly within seven weeks of each other. Anthony died first, completely suddenly, and we had only just buried him when Robbie also died. They were just 14-years-old and although dad dealt with it pretty well, mum went to pieces and he left his job to be with her. They moved to Brighton and dad started doing a bit of freelance writing and media consultancy work, which ironically earned him a better wage than he ever got working on the nationals.

I was never sure what my true feelings were about the twins' deaths. Of course, I had loved them as any sister loves her brothers and was deeply upset, but I had never really connected with them or spent a huge amount of time with them. When we were all growing up I guess I was impatient and too busy being selfish with teenage girl issues to try and understand their needs and problems. My mum would sometimes try to explain to me what they were going through when she was attempting to put my own dramas into perspective, but it went in one ear and out the other. I suppose I never imagined that one day they wouldn't be around. I thought that when I was older and had more time I would be able to get to know them, talk to them and help them. Now all of a sudden they were both gone and I would never have the chance to know my two little brothers.

Instead of grieving I threw myself into revision for my exams and got very good grades at the end of the first year. The second two years of university were less productive though as I finally rekindled my sex life, and also got into drugs and partying more. I spent more time working behind a bar at a club in Soho than I did studying, but I still managed a 2:1, which was all I had ever been after anyway.

With the money I had saved from my job, student loans and generous contributions from my dad, I had enough money to go travelling after university. My friend Naomi who had been on the same course and had shared a flat with me for the previous two years was keen to travel as well so we bought round-the-world tickets and disappeared for nearly two years: India, Nepal, Hong Kong, Malaysia, Singapore, Thailand, Cambodia, Vietnam, Australia, New Zealand, Chile, Bolivia, Peru, Ecuador, Colombia, Argentina and Brazil. Leaving Brazil was a massive wrench and we had heavy hearts as we flew back to England to begin our careers. Naomi got a job almost straight away as a press officer for a leading humanitarian organisation (central London, £28k, free health club membership) while I, for some reason, lacked any sort of motivation and just did temporary jobs at various brain-numbing companies and toyed with the idea of moving abroad for good, before waking up one morning and deciding to actually put my degree to some use and give journalism a real go. I knew that I was never going to walk straight onto one of the national papers, even with dad's contacts, so I set my sights lower and aimed for the local press to get a foot on the ladder. The Rockingsworth Evening Informer was my first interview and I was offered a junior reporter position the very next day. Tina Karageorghis, the editor, seemed like a nice enough woman and said the paper would train me and help my career along, so I ignored the crap salary and said yes. Dad was so thrilled he bought me a new car and promised to help me with the rent on a house.

The first couple of months had been okay as I got to grips with working in a news room and the pressures of producing a local daily paper, but before long I realised that it was nothing like the glamorous world of journalism I had pictured from dad's books and Hollywood films. Each day we had to scramble around for any snippet of local information that could be classed as news and dress it up into something we could sell to our fast dwindling readership. We'd work flat out until every last inch of editorial space was filled, and then we'd have to come in the next day and do it all again. There was little excitement and hardly anything that could be described as serious investigative journalism. For the most part we were virtually chained to our desks with the phone glued to our ear trying to dredge up fresh angles on the same old tired stories and make insignificant events sound vital.

Pretty much my whole life I had dreamed of becoming a journalist and being like my dad, but after a little over a year in the job I felt like I was already thoroughly jaded with the profession. The other day I had worked out that I probably had something like 40 more years of the same shit until I could retire and that would mean producing over 10,000 more issues of the newspaper! I thought of Brian Abbot, the political reporter, who had started on Evening Informer straight after school and would stay there until he retired or died. Would I become like him? Would I still be rotting away in my chair four decades from now, sending young trainees scurrying at the sight of my haggard face?

My glass was empty and my fingers were starting to prune, so I got out the bath without bothering to wash my hair and towelled myself dry.

My daydream had dampened my mood further and I tried unsuccessfully to snap out of it as I painted my toes and fingers, put on a little bit of make-up and slipped on a pair of jeans and a top.

The Red Lion pub was a ten minute walk from my house and I left home at 7.50pm, not anticipating a very enjoyable evening.

Chapter 3

The Red Lion pub had the bleak atmosphere of a hospice for the terminally ill. In many ways, I suppose that's exactly what it was: a communal place where bitter and bored old men sat alone at sticky tables muttering self-pityingly to themselves as they waited for cirrhosis to whisk them off to oblivion.

The weary barmaid would attempt to muster some banter as she sent each shuffling cadaver on his way with another pint of medication, but in reality her smile was as tired as the threadbare burgundy sofas and frayed beige curtains.

Every now and then some work-shy parasite would light the place up as he tipped his benefits into the gaudy, pinging fruit machine, but apart from that the place was nothing more than a stale-smelling purgatory between life and death.

Phil Crichton, Brian Abbot and Jenny Davis were sat around a table near the bar, a pint of Stella, a pint of Best and a slim-line tonic in front of each of them respectively. I wondered where the hell Simon was.

"Ah, our hospital correspondent is here," announced Phil, standing up to welcome me, or more probably to show off his Versace T-shirt. "What are you drinking?"

"I'll have a white wine spritzer with lemonade please."

"Coming right up."

My phone bleeped. It was Simon texting to say he was picking up one of the other reporters, Stuart, and would be there in ten minutes.

"I wouldn't get too close, Hannah," sniffed Jenny as I sat down. "I think I've got the flu coming."

"Oh dear, perhaps you'd better take tomorrow off."

"I can't. Everyone knows I'm down the pub. They'll think I'm skiving off with a hangover."

"Well, no editors have been invited, so I'm sure you'll be safe. How are you, Brian?"

"Huh?" Abbot blearily looked over at me with a foamy white moustache bubbling away on his top lip from the bitter.

"How was your day?" I repeated.

"Oh, the usual. Bloody development control committee up in arms, Malcolm going potty about that thing with the bypass…"

My attention wandered as his reply descended into a garbled mish-mash of words that may or may not have been connected.

Phil came back with my drink and caught the tail end of Abbot's description of his day.

"You want to get yourself up onto one of the nationals, mate," he said, jabbing his finger at the alcoholic. "All those bars around Westminster…I remember when I was at the Screws there was this guy…"

A cold blast hit my back as the door opened and Simon walked in with Stuart. They were both dressed in T-shirts, jeans and trainers and they sat either side of me, Stuart ignoring Jenny's protestations about her impending flu.

"Drinks?" asked Simon.

I asked for another spritzer, Stuart a Carling and Brian another pint of Best. The conversation went from work to films, back to work, a bit of what we all hoped to do eventually, a bit of football chat from the guys and then back to work talk. I was allowing myself to get a bit tipsy because I was working from 3pm to 11pm for the rest of the week and Simon must have realised this because he started flirting more than usual.

"You coming somewhere after the pub?" he asked me.

"No, an early night for me."

"But you're on lates this week, aren't you? You get a lie in."

"I just don't fancy it tonight."

He frowned. "What's up? You've been well grumpy lately."

"I'm fine, Simon. I just don't fancy it tonight, okay."

"How about a smoke? I got a nice bit of skunk earlier."

"Not tonight."

Simon pissed me off when he started pestering me. He finally took the hint and turned to Stuart. I looked at my watch and saw it was nearly 10pm, so I finished my drink and got up to leave."

"Right, I'm off," I said to the group.

"Want me to walk you home?" Simon still hadn't given up, several pints of lager fuelling his persistence.

"I can manage," I said.

"Okay, well let's meet up in here again for lunch tomorrow before you start your shift. Shall we say at about midday?"

"I'll call you in the morning," I said and left.

There was a paragraph in our employment contracts which clearly stated that consuming alcohol on the job was gross misconduct punishable by instant dismissal. The reality, however, was somewhat more liberal.

While none of us would waltz into the editor's office gargling gin, heavy drinking for most of us was just as much part of being a reporter as phoning councillors and fiddling expenses.

Good days on a local newspaper came along with comet-like irregularity and so getting pissed with your colleagues was a way of bitching and moaning about how shit life was. The boozing wasn't necessarily depressing though. We all knew the job was shit so we got drunk with each other to reassure ourselves that we weren't alone in having a shit life, and that helped you enjoy yourself a little bit more.

The Evening Informer was so poorly staffed that if you pulled the evening shift you knew that you would be alone in the office after about 7pm. It was therefore quite reasonable to turn up to work with a cheap bottle of red in your bag and sit at your desk getting drunk.

Most of the reporters still lived at home with their parents, so if you were working on "drag" – the late shift – on a Thursday or Friday it was quite common for the lads to come back to the office with a couple of slags they'd dragged away from the local club. I remember one evening trying to write up a family's tribute to their dead son while a colleague sat opposite me unashamedly fingering some vile blob that looked like Miss Piggy on ketamine.

Even if they had been unsuccessful in the clubs, reporters would still come back to the office, carry on drinking and curl up on the sofa in the interview room so they could be at their desks for 7am the following day.

Drinking during the day was fairly commonplace too and it almost became a challenge sometimes to see who could come up with the best excuse for spending all day in the pub. We'd often tell the newsdesk we were going out to milk our contacts for stories, then sit in the pub all day before returning at 4pm to write up a story we'd actually been emailed the day before.

Of course, all the drinking led to some truly excruciating hangovers, the worst of which would always come on the morning of a big breaking story. I arrived in the office one morning so hungover that I was convinced

I would lose my sight and had suffered irreparable brain damage. The news editor gleefully told me that a family of five had died in a house fire overnight and ordered me down to the scene. When I arrived at the smouldering remains of the semi-detached house, the street was alive with emergency personnel, other reporters and extremely hostile neighbours. I struggled as best as I could to get a better story than my rivals, but I just wasn't up to it. I got chased down the street by an old woman with a mop who was flapping her arms and calling me a vulture, then jumped into my car and was so eager to escape that I reversed into a bollard and knocked out a tail-light. Later that morning, I walked into the press conference at the local police station and threw up all over the floor in front of everyone. The story I filed at the end of the day was shit and I got a serious bollocking from the editor and a week of dull community news stories to write up as punishment.

The day after the Red Lion, I woke up at around 11am with a headache, but forced myself under a cold shower, pulled on my tracksuit bottoms and a sports top and drove to the gym. It was empty apart from a couple of male bimbos spotting each other on the bench press and a fat old woman going purple on the cross-trainer. I did an easy ten minutes on the rowing machine, a 20 minute run and some stomach exercises then sat in the sauna for ten minutes and showered again. In the lobby I drank a black coffee and ate a cereal bar as I watched a report on Sky News about a triple murder in a West London brothel. I looked at the elegant reporter enviously as she filled the screen with her expertly made up face, well cut suit and Gucci scarf. That's where I should be, I thought to myself.

I drove home to change into my work clothes and called Phil at the office to say I would be going straight to the police station in the afternoon.

I pulled up at Rockingsworth police station at 3.20pm and asked at reception for Detective Inspector King.

"Is he expecting you?" The stern-faced receptionist – the same bitch I had spoken to on the phone the day before – sneered at me.

"Tell him it's Hannah from the Informer."

The woman sighed and dialled his internal number.

"There's a girl from the paper to see you, Liam, are you busy? Oh, right." She hung up looking slightly put out. "Take a seat. He'll be down in a minute."

I sat on one of the hard plastic chairs and read the various Crimestoppers posters and Neighbourhood Watch pamphlets that I had read a hundred times before. The door opposite then clicked open and Liam King poked his head around it.

"Hannah, come on up." He smiled warmly.

I followed him up a flight of stairs and down a corridor flanked by deserted offices until we got to CID.

"Tea? Coffee?" he asked.

"Coffee please."

He walked to the kettle and put coffee in two mugs.

"So, what's been going on?" I asked, notebook already on the desk in front of me.

"Bugger all, to be honest. Got some little angel smashing up cars around Holland Square and a couple of minor assaults, but apart from that all the bad guys seem to be on holiday."

He passed over a coffee and sat down opposite me. I have to admit, I fancied him like mad. He was around 35, very well built with close-cropped black hair and no ring on the finger that matters. He always seemed to be dressed with carefully planned casualness and always kept things informal and relaxed between us by asking about my weekends or making gentle jokes about the Superintendent. I generally found most of the cops I dealt with fairly dull and self-important, but Liam was witty and down-to-earth and I decided it would be interesting to perhaps go out on a date with him at some point in the future.

"Did our witness appeal throw up any new info about those petrol station raids from last week?" I asked, trying to steer my mind away from inappropriate thoughts about him and keep to business.

"Couple of local curtain twitchers reckon they saw a white Transit van driving around looking suspicious just before the second robbery, but the CCTV from both garages is crap and the cashiers have given us next to nothing."

"God, what we need is a serial killer!" I said.

He gave me a strange look, then roared with laughter. "You might, but I'm quite happy with a bit of peace and quiet and the Superintendent loves nothing better than seeing the year-on-year crime figures falling."

He picked up the incident log which was on his desk and opened it.

"Let's see if there's anything here I can give you."

I got back to the office just before 4.50pm with a notebook full of minor burglaries, attempted burglaries and bogus callers. Jenny was the only reporter left in the office and she was on her way home with a handkerchief pushed against her face.

"God, I feel awful. Maybe see you tomorrow, Hannah."

"Night."

The editor was loitering about with the news editor and a couple of subs, so I dutifully phoned round the usual suspects and turned on the radio to listen to the 5 o'clock news bulletin.

"Hello, Hannah. Are you on lates this week?"

I turned round and Tina, the editor, was smiling at me.

"Um, yes. I've got a few things to be getting on with. How's tomorrow's paper looking?"

"Oh, we've got a couple of reasonable bits. There was quite a bad smash on the ring road this afternoon, a young woman's in hospital with pretty serious head injuries. That looks like our best bet for a splash tomorrow. Can you keep an eye on it tonight please and check her condition before you go. If she dies we might be able to get an ID before the morning."

"No problem."

She went back to her office and I checked my emails to see what crap stories the news editor had dreamt up for me tonight. There evidently wasn't much happening, so he had sent me the dreaded instructions to "have a look at what a few of the regular bloggers are putting out".

Whenever it was a quiet news day the editors would tell us to go online and trawl through some of the local blogs to see if there was anything newsworthy we could pick out.

I hated the bloggers and point blank refused to ever rehash any of the shit they spouted. I took it as an affront, to be quite honest, that I had trained and worked my arse off to become a journalist yet thanks to the internet any fool with a computer and enough fingers to type could now become a "virtual reporter".

Obviously I had nothing against the internet per se – it made my job and life a hell of a lot easier – but I felt that by giving a free platform to millions of bloggers across the planet to rant and rave about anything they wanted, completely unchecked and unedited, it was dramatically diluting the value of proper journalism and professional newspapers.

The blind masses were increasingly turning to blogs for their information and shunning the mainstream media, presumably oblivious to the fact that the bloggers can write just about anything they like, irrespective of fact, accuracy or balance, because they know that the internet is an infinite grey area when it comes to the normal laws of defamation, prejudice and malicious comment that police the press.

My loathing was also based on a sweeping stereotype I had of all bloggers, based on three I knew of who spoon-fed bile, rumour and conjecture to some of the reporters on the Informer as if it were stone-cold fact. None of them would ever dream of writing under their own name, they all used pseudonyms: jedi1974, Veteran_Ken and The Real Crusader. All three were unemployed and would never post anything before midday, apart from on Mondays when they got up a bit earlier to pollute the Post Office as they lined up to siphon off their benefits. I imagined them sitting in their squalid little flats with the filthy curtains pulled, slurping tea and chain-smoking spliffs, while a little mountain of chocolate bar wrappers accumulated at their stinking feet and 99p lasagnes rotated limply in bean-stained microwaves. They would be wearing three-day-old pants and t-shirts streaked with the grey-slime from chicken and mushroom slices, picking their noses and scratching boils as they flicked between porn sites that were borderline illegal and their own excruciating little blogs.

What I could never understand was what gave any of them the idea that anybody would ever be in the slightest bit interested in anything they had to say. These people were the lowest common denominator in society. The only subjects they could authoritatively comment on would be the benefits system, the long-term effects of weed and cheap alcohol, junk food, bitterness and masturbation. Yet, despite their vacuous lack of qualifications, experience, ability or wit, they saw nothing wrong in maligning every Government body, corporate entity, religious movement or individual personality they could think of. They would happily invent the salaries of civil servants, rewrite the corporate objectives of global conglomerates, decide upon the sexual preferences of celebrities and reinterpret the meaning of holy books.

They spent their entire days basically shitting on the society that handed them everything on a plate and nursed them through their sorry little lives. If you ever actually read a few of their blogs you would find that they contradicted themselves constantly and had so little understanding of the issues they were writing about that it was embarrassing.

By 7pm all the staff had gone home and the cleaners were going around emptying bins with nothing in them and rearranging the pens and papers on people's desks. I had called Naomi for a chat, texted Simon to apologise for last night, wasted some time on Facebook and was bored out of my mind.

Boredom, I had long ago realised, was the one thing that truly drove me to despair above anything else, and right now I was trapped in a maddening straitjacket of boredom that had no end in sight. I dragged myself out of bed at the crack of dawn, sat in a traffic jam listening to the same inane songs and DJs, then sat in a soulless office with a bunch of desperately average people pretending to be busy. At lunchtime I would force myself to eat a tasteless sandwich while listening to one of several people I had no interest in complaining about other people I had no interest in. The afternoons were spent counting seconds, sitting on the toilet and riding up and down in the lift until it was time to go home. I would sit in another traffic jam listening to more inane songs and DJs, get home and eat something from a tin or packet, wash myself, gaze at the morons flickering past me on the television screen for a couple of hours, and then go to bed.

That was the routine from Monday to Friday, and then at weekends I would get up a bit later, drink a bit more alcohol and join the rest of the credit-card zombies shuffling around the air-conditioned shopping malls looking at things I had no interest in buying in the same shops I went to every weekend.

And there it was: my existence was a life-threateningly stagnant routine of soporific mediocrity, punctuated by the infrequent and unreliable highs of trips abroad, nights of chemicals and sex. Nothing seemed able to motivate or excite me, and the disturbing thing was that I couldn't imagine a scenario, however fanciful, in which I would find true fulfilment and happiness. Fame and fortune might temporarily lift my spirits, but would it lift me permanently from the shackles of boredom, routine, frustration and malaise? I doubted it.

The rules of society, it seemed, had been fine-tuned over millennia to ensure that everyone walked pretty much the same path and was unlikely to question or bend the rules. A certain degree of errant behaviour was grudgingly tolerated in your early years, but as the years went by that tolerance from others diminished and the slightest deviation or indiscretion was frowned upon and admonished. Society called for responsibility, routine, certainty, obedience, rules, convention and followers. Thinkers, mavericks, disobedience, uncertainty, irresponsibility, originality and subversives were at best treated with suspicion.

Finding a cure for my boredom would not, therefore, be easy. But that didn't mean it was impossible.

Chapter 4

At a relatively young age I stopped believing in the concept of God and the idea of an afterlife.

At university I spent long periods alone, often drinking heavily, and it was during this time that I suffocated myself with a blanket of anxiety as I pondered the meaningless and sheer futility of my life. What the hell was the point of studying, developing myself, forming relationships and enduring hardships if my entire existence was going to come to an end in a matter of decades, if not sooner?

I became very withdrawn for a while and told myself that I had become an existentialist, unable to resume my life until I had adequately resolved what the meaning of it was.

Locked in my room for days on end, my impressionable young mind was seduced by the work of philosophers Friedrich Nietzsche and Albert Camus, who argued that because God is dead it is up to us as individuals to determine what the purpose of our life is.

Some people may become overwhelmed by the enormity of such a task and, without God, slip into chaos. The majority of people will simply avoid the issue by becoming sheep and following the herd. Keep up with your colleagues and neighbours, become a consumer of materialist trash, and avoid questions about your own life and impending death by following the lives of others – real or fictitious – in magazines and soap operas.

I, however, would be courageous. I would accept my own mortality and constantly strive to find meaning, excitement and adventure in my life. Boredom would be my sworn enemy and I would fight it with every weapon at my disposal.

At the moment however, with life at the Rockingsworth Evening Informer grinding my soul into dust, I was losing the war against boredom and there was very little meaning, excitement or adventure in my life.

Desperate for inspiration, I returned to Nietzsche and interpreted his thoughts about Godlessness as meaning that without God there can be no such things as good and evil, right and wrong. God is the definition of good, but without him good is merely a set of values determined by a particular society – by my fellow humans.

I have never considered anyone to be better or morally superior to me, so I would define my own right and wrong. It was my life and I wouldn't be governed by others or apologise for my actions. My freedom was a gift and on the day that I stared death in the face I wanted to be able to reflect on the path I had chosen and have no regrets.

I spent a lot of time plotting how best to liven up my life and found myself constantly frustrated by the fact that I didn't live in a consequence-free environment.

Although I would have dearly loved to live with the reckless abandon of someone who has less than 12 hours to live, I had to accept that in a world shackled by law enforcement it was simply not sensible to shoot up on heroin, attack my boss with a hammer then steal a car, strip naked and ram-raid a crowded department store. Equally, however, I realised that if all I was prepared to do was dye my hair and swear at people, I would be nothing more than a petulant teenager.

The trick would be to either seriously break convention without quite breaking the law, or else break the law without getting caught. As it turned out I ended up doing both.

I had already stopped caring about any sort of long term career at the Rockingsworth Evening Informer so I decided to use it as a playground for testing how far I could push the boundaries.

I told the editor I had been attacked by a gang of men on a weekend trip to Glasgow and only avoided being raped because two fire engines had come past and the crew saw us. Although this was completely untrue, she was predictably concerned and said she would do anything she could for me. I asked to be moved away from Phil Crichton, because he reminded me of one of the attackers, and asked if I could start going home an hour earlier so I wouldn't have to leave in the dark. She agreed to both. It was a promising start.

A couple of days later I turned up for work drunk after deciding to have tequila on my cornflakes at breakfast. Some time in the morning Jenny went to the toilet and I followed her, and when she went into one of the cubicles I barged in after her and locked the door behind us.

"Hannah? What the hell are you doing?" she asked, looking absolutely terrified.

"Pull down your knickers, Jenny. I want to eat your pussy."

Jenny's mouth fell open and she murmured something I didn't understand.

"You make me so wet, Jenny. For months now I've wanted to feel, smell and taste you. Let me inside you, Jenny."

"Ha-Ha-Hannah...I...I...don't want, don't know what...to say. You're not...I'm not...a....er, er...lesbian."

"Of course you are. Come on, show me your sweet pussy, I can almost smell it."

"Please, Hannah!" she pleaded. "I...I don't want to."

I sighed dramatically. "Don't play hard to get Jenny, I know you fancy me. I've seen the way you look at me."

"Hannah! No!" She looked petrified now. "Please get out, or I'll have to scream."

I looked at her for a few seconds, then calmly unbolted the door and walked back to my desk. Jenny remained in the toilet for ten minutes then came out and scurried into Tina's office. She obviously told her about my "attack" because Jenny came out with tears in her eyes and told me to return to the toilet with her.

"Hannah, I'm so sorry," she whimpered. "I had no idea. Look, I can't even begin to imagine how much you must hate men right now. Why don't you stay at mine for a couple of nights, we can have some wine, chat about girlie stuff. You can...um...sleep in the same bed as me if you like."

I stared at her like she was insane, said I had no idea what she was talking about, called her a cunt and told her to fuck off out of my face or I would decapitate her. I wandered calmly back to my desk leaving her sobbing.

She resigned the very next day, citing personal reasons.

Chapter 5

Everybody is born and everybody dies, but how many people really live in between?

By live, I don't simply mean breathing, drinking and eating enough to survive from one day to the next. I mean actually being aware of their existence and feeling alive, being happy and excited about life, and following their dreams and ambitions no matter what.

For me, ambition is the arch enemy of boredom. It is what makes life worth living and staves off the spectre of mediocrity. I had always pitied those who had no grand dreams, looking down at them with a patronising shake of the head as I struggled to comprehend how a human being could float along inexorably towards the grave without showing the slightest inclination to be something special.

Childhood is our most profitable period in terms of ambition, but the constant erosion caused by parents and teachers telling people to grow up, join the real world and set more realistic targets soon wears down all but a tiny few.

The little boy who was going to be a fighter pilot, marry a supermodel and live in California becomes a forklift truck operative at a logistics warehouse in Slough, who lives in a two-bedroom council flat in Bracknell and is married to an alcoholic hag he accidently impregnated after an ill-fated encounter at a Reading nightclub. The little girl who was going to move to Paris with her film star husband and launch an haute-couture fashion chain, winds up hanging clothes on the racks at a High Street retailer in Bolton and lives at home with her parents because her unemployed boyfriend left her for a supermarket checkout girl.

The details changed from person to person, but the story was essentially the same: phenomenal success proves elusive so that vivid ambition is muscled out by the acceptance of a normal life.

Perhaps Friedrich Nietzsche hit the nail on the head when he said that the two great European narcotics are alcohol and Christianity. While I had little enthusiasm for his abstinence from alcohol, I definitely agreed that Christianity had to shoulder the blame for much of the submissiveness in the world. All those messages in the bible about the meek inheriting the earth, of the meek being lifted up by God and of the poor being judged with righteousness give people the perfect excuse to sit back and give up. "Don't worry about being a loser on earth", they think, "because it's fine – honourable even – and I will be rewarded in heaven." I wonder if the pathetic Roman slaves who wrote the Bible really believed what they were writing.

I just don't buy into the fact that some people are simply born to be great. With the exception of those who have a profound disability, I believe we are born with an even chance of success. Certainly, success will be defined differently depending on a range of cultural, social and geographic factors, but if we can accept and conquer suffering, difficulty, hardship and doubt, and not be crushed by the suspicion, jealousy and humiliation of others then we can be whatever we want.

I, personally, thrived on derision and scepticism by people who told me to be more realistic, to get with the real world and to accept my fate. I welcomed it when somebody told me I wouldn't amount to anything and that I should be happy with my lot. That was all the encouragement I needed to throw their mockery back in their faces by proving them wrong.

The problem I was facing at the Rockingsworth Informer though was that I wasn't being pissed on and mocked. I was being congratulated for churning out reams of irrelevant drivel and my ambition was gradually being eaten away as I was reeled into the cosy bosom of nine-to-five simplicity, avid consumption of mass media and unblinking consumerism.

I couldn't let that happen. I had to stay strong and focussed. I am capable of anything, just like my peers, but the difference between them and me is that I know it and won't rest until it is done.

A few weeks after the incident with Jenny, I found myself back on the night shift (Tina had rescinded her decision to let me leave the office before dark, presumably because she suspected I had something to do with Jenny's sudden resignation).

It was a typically dull evening and my enthusiasm for life was being severely tested once more. While my games with Jenny had certainly contravened several socially acceptable codes of conduct, it did nothing to diminish my long-term boredom, or put Hannah Harker on the world map. Anarchy for anarchy's sake might well offer me amusing diversions from the norm, but there was little chance of it propelling me out of Rockingsworth and away from the local newspaper, unless of course I wound up in prison. Pouring party spirits on the breakfast cereal and feigning lesbianism with colleagues would therefore need to be abandoned in favour of more productive anarchy.

Sick of the sight of my desk, I decided to go out and get something to eat. I grabbed my car keys and ran out into the drizzle, swearing as I fumbled with the door lock and got wet. I did a little wheel spin as I swung out of the car park onto the main road and pushed the car to 65mph before braking hard as I reached a T-junction. As I turned right the steering pulled hard to the left. I took both hands off the wheel and the car ploughed straight towards the kerb. I had a bloody puncture.

I turned off the main road into a quiet street on a run-down industrial estate and pulled over under a flickering street lamp. The drizzle had eased off so I went to the boot, got the jack and the spare and changed the flat tyre in a few minutes.

As I was about to climb back in, I stopped to look at the building next to me. It was two storeys high, daubed with graffiti and every window was boarded up. It looked like it might have once been some kind of old showroom, but there were no signs to confirm this and the building was obviously derelict. The main doors were chained shut, but as I looked I saw there was a side door, which was only held shut by tape. Whether it was curiosity, boredom or something else, I don't know, but I suddenly found myself pulling a torch out of the glove compartment and walking towards the door.

The tape came away easily and the door creaked open. I stepped inside, sending a rat scuttling across the floor, and pointed my torch towards the centre of the building, but the dim beam barely cut through the gloom. There was a smell of chemicals, maybe paint, in the air and as my eyes adjusted to the darkness I could see more clearly. It was indeed some sort of old showroom with a spacious ground floor and stairs leading up to a second level. Most of the shop fittings had been removed, but there were still one or two shelves up and the aisles were still in place where the checkouts had been. In the middle of the ground floor was a tower of cardboard boxes, half empty tins of paint, bundles of plastic bubble wrapping, rags and paper. It looked like a giant bonfire.

A bonfire! Something happened in my head. A rush of adrenaline hit my stomach and set my heart hammering. I raced back out to my car, checked that my digital camera was in the glove compartment, then grabbed a lighter, scanned the street for any signs of activity and ran back into the building. I shone the torch at the ceiling and saw it was supported by several wooden rafters. I would have to get out quick once those went up.

Part of me was waiting for a signal from my brain telling me to take a reality check, get the fuck out and drive away, but no message came. Instead, my brain told my right thumb to flick the lighter on and hold the orange flame to the edge of a newspaper that was sticking out from the edge of the bonfire. As the fire took a big brown bite out of the paper, I noticed it was an old copy of the Informer, but it soon became a glowing pile of ash and the fire, its appetite whetted, greedily devoured the side of a cardboard box. I could feel the heat on my face and toxic smoke started drifting in my direction as the plastic wrapping bubbled and curled and disappeared in the fire. I watched as another rat scurried past me towards the door and when I turned back to the fire it had grown to four times my height and flames were licking the wooden beams on the ceiling. It was time to get out.

I walked, not ran, out of the building and as I got back to the car and took my mobile out the first flame shot through the roof and lit up the sky. I reversed my car to a safe distance and dialled 999.

Within moments of reporting the blaze I heard the sound of sirens approaching. The whole roof of the building was well alight now and I started taking pictures as two fire engines screamed round the corner.

The road was suddenly alive with activity and as men started running around, shouting and preparing equipment, a man in a white helmet began co-ordinating things, barking orders with measured authority.

"Call in Andy," he said, "and get both appliances from Harmeswood down here and the ALP from Battleford. Dean, Mike, Gary – kit up in BA and get a hose reel in on the ground, but watch that roof, it looks like it's ready to come down."

"Yes, Guv."

"Tom, tell control we've got an industrial unit, approximately 25m by 30m 80 per cent alight. When Harmeswood get here I want a hose reel wetting that roof down." He spoke into a radio on his chest. "Dean, what have you got in there?"

I heard a crackle of static and a voice, barely audible over the roar of the fire.

"Ground floor completely alight, Guv, most of the second floor has gone up and the roof needs to come down."

"Any people in there?"

"Doesn't look like it, Guv. There's a hell of a lot of smoke but the thermal imager isn't showing anything. Looks like it's an abandoned warehouse - kids, probably."

"Have you made sure there are no canisters or anything in there?"

"Yeah, it's just a load of cardboard and paper. The ceiling's looking pretty dodgy now; I reckon it's time we got everyone off the ground here."

"Okay, Dean. Harmeswood are here now. Do a final quick check for people and pull out."

"Guv."

Three more fire engines had arrived on the scene now, one with an Aerial Ladder Platform. Police cars had cordoned off the street, a paramedic rapid response car was parked up on a verge, and Alex Hammond, Rockingsworth's fire investigation officer, had just arrived in his brigade car.

Meanwhile, I was snapping everything: firefighters up ladders, arty shots of flashing blue lights, close-ups of tough-looking firefighters spraying the building with hoses, and the flames themselves, which were now twisting up into the air, almost taunting the men and women on the ground.

"You got here quick." The firefighter in the white hat was talking to me.

"I called it in," I said. "I saw it as I was driving out to McDonalds. Hannah Harker, from the Informer." I held out a hand.

"Station Officer Morgan." He shook my hand.

"Are you going to be able to save the building?" I asked.

"Doesn't look like it, the fire's taken quite a hold. Place should have been torn down months ago. These places are nothing more than death-traps once the kids figure out how to get in."

"So you're treating this as arson then?"

"It's far too early to say." We were joined by Hammond. "I'm sure we will be treating this one as suspicious though."

I was scribbling furiously in my notebook as Hammond cut in.

"You might want to write this down as well: the developer who owns the building lodged a planning application with the council nearly eight months ago and they keep rejecting it because of technicalities and sending the application back to be amended. There are nearly 20 sites like this in the district waiting to be developed, but the old fools – paraphrase that please – on the council's planning committee won't pass anything if there's so much as one objection to it. I'm meeting the chief executive and council leader about it tomorrow because someone is going to get killed soon if this situation isn't sorted out."

By the time I finished writing down what he'd said, both men had left me. The story was coming together nicely and the pictures were amazing.

My mobile rang. It was Vicky Gardner, one of the news editors.

"Have you picked up that fire on the Langley Estate? I've just had a call about it?"

"I'm down there now. It's huge and Alex Hammond, the fire investigation guy, is down here threatening to crucify the council over it."

"Is it one of those derelict sites the council won't give planning consent to?"

"Yeah."

"Excellent. Have you got pictures?"

"Yep, looks like they'll be really good ones," I said smugly.

"Brilliant. When you get back to the office send your copy to the news basket and email it to me as well, in case there's any problem. Download your pictures and leave the memory card on the picture desk, again just in case there's a problem."

"Okay, sure."

"Great. Sounds like you've done a good job, Hannah. See you tomorrow."

I put the phone back in my pocket, got some colour quotes from a couple of exhausted firefighters and headed back to the office to write up the story.

I was already starting to forget that it was me who started it.

Chapter 6

FIRE CHIEFS BLAST COUNCIL LEADERS OVER INFERNO
Heel-dragging on planning decisions will cost lives, investigators warn
By Hannah Harker

FURIOUS *fire officials were set for showdown talks with dithering council leaders today after an inferno gutted a derelict warehouse.*

Dozens of firefighters spent more than two hours tackling the blaze at an old furniture showroom on the Langley industrial estate in Bourne Road, Rockingsworth, at around 8pm last night.

Fire investigators revealed that a developer submitted a planning application to Rockingsworth District Council to renovate the building nearly eight months ago, but the council's planning committee has repeatedly refused it, despite amendments.

There are around 20 similar sites in the district, and although nobody was injured in last night's incident, fire investigator Alex Hammond said there was "a tragedy waiting to happen".

He added: "Councillors keep rejecting the application because of silly little technicalities and sending it back to be amended.

"The council's planning committee don't seem to want to pass anything if there's so much as one objection to it, but these sites urgently need to be developed and made safe.

"I'm meeting the chief executive and council leader about it because somebody is going to get killed soon."

Council leader Richard Bentley said last night: "The application submitted to us for the site in Bourne Road has repeatedly failed to address the concerns of councillors regarding traffic issues and the visual impact on the surrounding area.

"We will meet with Mr Hammond and look at ways of reducing the potential for incidents like this on brownfield sites."

The developer who owns the site was unavailable for comment last night.

An investigation into the cause of the fire has been launched and it is being treated as suspicious.

I proudly read every word of my story as I sat at my desk two hours earlier than I needed to. There were five pictures used with my by-line and a sidebar with some of the colour comments from the firefighters. I glanced up and saw the editor walking towards me.

"Hello, Hannah. How are you?"

"Fine thanks, Tina."

"Great job on the fire. We printed an extra 2,000 copies this morning and already newsagents are phoning in to get more. There's a lot of legs in this story, especially if we can get hold of the developer that owns that warehouse. Make sure you get hold of Hammond later as well, see how his meeting up at the town hall went; I reckon today's story will have fanned the flames even more, if you'll forgive the terrible pun."

Hard house music blasted into my ears through my iPod as I pounded the running machine at the gym early the next morning. I'd done nearly 6km without really noticing as hundreds of thoughts and ideas tumbled about inside my head and I tried to make sense of them.

The developer had phoned me back the night before to say that he didn't want to make any comment at the moment because he was seeking legal advice. Alex Hammond would only say that his meeting with the council leaders had been "productive", which wasn't a very strong angle. I'd written the follow up on the line that the developer was considering legal action, but it was unlikely to make tomorrow's splash because there was a story about a 15-year-old schoolgirl who had gone missing completely out of the blue over in Harmeswood, which Simon had written, and Abbot had some story about council proposals to implement Sunday parking charges around the town centre.

The one idea that kept coming back into my head as my feet hammered down on the treadmill was too insane to contemplate. But I was contemplating it, seriously. I was thinking about starting another fire.

I got off the running machine and wandered back to the changing room, so deep in thought that I walked straight into one of the instructors on the way. I stripped out of my wet clothes and had a cold shower, before going to sit in the sauna.

Starting the first fire hadn't troubled me, if anything it had given me a thrill I'd not experienced for a long time, and I'd not even had time to be bored over the last couple of days. But if I did it again would it mean I was crazy? I would be a serial arsonist! Obviously, if I got caught I would be fucked, national news possibly, but even if I didn't what would I become inside myself? As I sat there, the heat and tension causing sweat to roll down my body, I got excited by the thought of doing it again and I slowly talked myself into it. In a way, I would be helping the community because another fire would put pressure on the council to sort out the remaining derelict buildings once and for all.

The obvious target was Venna Mansions, a derelict block of flats a couple of miles outside of Rockingsworth. The ugly 1960s monolith had been an eyesore when people lived there, but since it closed two years ago after a health and safety inspection classified the whole building as a death trap, the vandals had got to work and it was officially the most hated building in the district, according to a recent Informer poll. The problem was that the only serious proposal put forward for the site was to demolish the flats and build a huge nightclub in their place, a plan which had nearby residents, councillors and the police pulling their hair out in frustration. If Venna Mansions was razed to the ground, I would be doing a public service.

The adrenaline coursed through me once more as I quickly showered again, got dressed, did my make-up and drove into town for a coffee so I could make plans to do it that very night before I came to my senses.

Chapter 7

I parked my car in a secluded area behind Venna Mansions at 8pm and tried to still my trembling hands. The 16-storey building loomed over me in the darkness as litter danced around its base in the strong breeze. Gaping holes in the filthy walls where windows had once been seemed to be trying to suck me in, daring me to come and destroy it.

Just a week ago Abbot had written a story about people complaining because there was no CCTV or police patrols in the area to catch the drug users and vandals who used the flats as a playground, but as I scanned the area there was no sign of life. I pulled my baseball cap low over my face and went to the boot of my car, taking out a can of petrol and two large cardboard boxes stuffed with newspaper and old bedsheets. I balanced them on top of each other and stumbled with them over to a rear door that was banging in the wind, the padlock used to secure it having been smashed off months ago. I put the boxes down and, using my torch, checked all the rooms on the ground floor to see if I could get in, but they were boarded up. I climbed the piss-soaked stairs to the first floor, and saw a door slightly ajar. Every muscle was taught as I pushed it open and shone the torch inside.

It was a tinderbox. The small room had been stripped of furniture, but wallpaper hung off the plywood walls and the ceiling looked like it was made out of cheap board. This place would go up like a roll of tissue paper.

I hurried down to collect the boxes and the petrol and took them back up to the room. A curtain rail was still up so I draped a bedsheet over it and soaked it with petrol. The fumes made me dizzy but I continued my task, pouring petrol in the cardboard boxes, over the walls and finally making a trail of it out the room and back down the stairs. My breathing was heavy and my head swimming from the smell of petrol, but I was almost done. I checked the route back to the entrance to make sure there were no obstacles, then took out my lighter and held it to the puddle of petrol at the foot of the stairs. It caught light with a little whoomph sound, and an orange flame was suddenly snaking up the stairs, following the route I had prepared for it, to the room above.

I knew I had to hurry, so I went back to my car, fumbled with the key in the ignition and took a deep breath as I slipped it into gear.

"God help you, Hannah," I muttered to myself, glancing at the building, which still looked calm, as I pulled away and raced back to the office.

I got back to the Informer building six minutes later, and was at my desk in the empty newsroom eight minutes after starting the fire. I tried to control my breathing as I carefully dialled the number for Rockingsworth fire station.

"Rockingsworth fire station, good evening," answered the cheerful voice of a firefighter.

"Hi, it's Hannah at the Informer. Anything much going on?"

"No, I'm afraid it's very quiet at the moment, Hannah."

What the fuck? Had it gone out? Had nobody reported it yet?

"Oh, hold on a minute," he interrupted my thoughts, "what's this coming through...?" I heard him mumbling as he read the details of the 999 call which had just been sent to the station. "Looks like I spoke too soon. There's something over at Venna Mansions; I've got to go."

"I might come out and have a look…" I started to say, but he had already hung up.

Exactly 19 minutes after I left Venna Mansions, I pulled up again and was physically paralysed by what I saw.

The entire building was illuminated by an orange glow and flames were waving at me from at least half of the empty windows as black smoke rolled skyward and blocked the moonlight. The first fire engines were already on the scene and I watched the usual commotion of firefighters getting kitted out in breathing apparatus, rolling out hose-reels and erecting spotlights as the sound of sirens and the flashing of blue lights signalled the arrival of more appliances, police cars and ambulances.

Heat and noise hit me like an explosion as I climbed out the car with my camera and notebook. Someone screamed at me to keep back as a real explosion threw a fireball out of the ninth floor and sent everyone running for cover as bits of burning debris peppered the ground.

People had gathered to watch and were kept at bay by a hastily erected police barrier, while I saw firefighters racing into the inferno through the door I had walked out of less than half hour earlier.

I couldn't get close enough to hear what was being said by the emergency crews and nobody would be able to talk to me yet anyway, so I wandered among the spectators and got some witness quotes.

Then there was another loud explosion and we suddenly heard screams.

"Jesus! Over there." One of the onlookers pointed towards the door.

I spun round and saw two firefighters dragging a third one out of the building, his protective suit smoking as two paramedics rushed over.

"The floor came down on him and he was trapped in the fire." One of the firefighters screamed, quite hysterical. "His mask caught fire, his face is burned. Fucking Jesus! His face was just burning!"

A colleague led the firefighter away as the paramedics put the injured man on a stretcher, gave him oxygen and put him into an ambulance. I saw the paramedics give each other a grim look as they saw the extent of the injuries.

Nausea welled inside me as the ambulance raced off to the hospital and the station officer in charge attempted to reorganise the crews.

My head was out of control; I couldn't focus or concentrate on anything. Roaring fire, screaming, shouting, water, heat, flashing lights, a female firefighter with a blackened face coming out of the building with a melted mobile phone in her hand and tears in her eyes, more shouting, a frenzied commotion.

Something else had happened.

The action unfolded around me as I stood there, silent and shaking. Something was being brought out of the building – some sort of blackened bundle - and I knew I had to work, take photographs. More paramedics dashed over, police were having to force the crowd back, people were crying everywhere, huddling in groups, talking on mobiles. Another bundle was brought out of the building, then another, and another. I didn't want to see, my eyes didn't want to let me, but I forced myself to look.

Nearby, someone was sick and another let out a blood-curdling shriek like an animal being slaughtered.

The police were struggling, radioing for back-up, the fire was out of control, but all I could do was stare through the throng of paramedics and firefighters.

Laid out in a neat row on the ground in front of me were the charred, smoking corpses of four children.

Chapter 8

Danny Storey, 14, reached out a badly burned hand to grab the bottom of my jacket as I ran screaming down another bleak corridor that seemed to narrow the further I invaded it. I turned my head and the boy grinned, his white blocks of teeth like a bright panel against his blackened and horribly deformed face. Behind Danny I saw Matty Storey, 16, Steven Francis, 16, and Tony Small, 15, also gaining ground on me, their own scarred features occasionally lit up as they passed underneath one of the dim light bulbs which swung violently at regular intervals along the corridor. I turned away from the faces, flickering lights and jumping shadows to concentrate on escape. The corridor had no doors and all I saw ahead of me was the weak yellow light from more swinging bulbs bouncing off filthy walls, which definitely now seemed to be closing in, trying to wedge me between them so the boys could catch up with me and…and what? What the hell would they do to me?

There was a cackle not more than two paces behind me and I shrieked as Danny caught hold of my jacket with what was left of his hands. Without breaking stride, I let both my arms slip out the sleeves, leaving Danny clutching the empty jacket with possibly a disappointed expression on his featureless face.

I realised my shirt was sodden with sweat and noticed for the first time that the corridor was like a sauna, and the walls were growling as if there was some kind of animal trapped inside them. The boys hadn't given up their chase though and I had to ignore my senses and the stabbing pain in my chest to continue sprinting away from them. Had my senses been slightly more focused I would have seen the three steps ahead which dropped the corridor to a lower level. I pushed my right leg down expecting to find ground, but instead finding only air. My body went down like a stone and as my right leg did eventually make contact with the floor, it landed with such force at such an unnatural angle that my shin simply snapped in two like a lolly-stick.

The jagged and bloodied edge of my lower tibia tore through my trousers, and as I went down my head hit the concrete floor…

Blood and tears blinded me as I rolled around on the hard, stinking ground and twisted my mouth in a silent scream.

When the stinging mist had cleared and I saw the four boys standing side by side at the top of the small flight of stairs, I begged the blindness to return. The hideously altered faces smiled down at me and I saw Matty Storey holding a straight razor between his thumb and the two remaining fingers of his right hand, which had been fused together by unimaginable heat. The other three boys stood and watched as Matty purposefully strode down the steps towards me and slashed the razor across my eyes. I screamed, and screamed, and screamed, and screamed…

…A half full glass of neat vodka went flying across the room as I knocked it off the bedside table in a fit of terror and sat bolt upright in bed, shaking so violently that my alarm clock followed the glass onto the floor. I used the corner of the duvet to dry my face, which was dripping with sweat and tears, but no blood.

By now my brain had registered that my ordeal had only happened in sleep, but my hands were still convulsing and when I tried to stand up I quickly had to sit back down on the corner of the bed.

The luminous dial of the alarm clock was facing up from the floor and told me it was 5.30am. I took a long swig from what was left of the litre bottle of Smirnoff on the floor, retched, then picked up my mobile and called the office.

"Hello?" Marc Sullivan, the early shift news editor that day, was clearly surprised to be getting a direct phone call at 5.30am.

"It's Hannah," I croaked.

"Jesus, Hannah, you sound bloody awful. I hope you're not coming in today?"

"Er, no. I'm sorry. Hopefully I'll feel a bit better tomorrow," I replied, pleased that I didn't have to invent another excuse for staying off work. This would be the third day in a row off.

"I'll let Phil know," said Marc.

"Thanks, I'm sorry…" I began, but Marc had already hung up.

I dragged myself to the bathroom and noticed my splitting headache for the first time as I stripped and stepped under a steaming hot shower and cried my heart out.

Since the fire which had killed brothers Danny and Matty Storey, Steven Francis and Tony Small and left firefighter John McGrath with no face, I had completely broken down.

On the actual night of the fire I had somehow managed to return to the office, download my pictures and write up the story, which was heavily edited before it appeared on pages one, three, four, five, seven, eight and nine the next morning. I was still sitting at my desk in a comatose state when Marc Sullivan had arrived at 5am that morning and he told me to go home immediately. Desperate as I was to do just that, part of my head told me I needed to stay and finish the job I had started, so I insisted that I was fine, grabbed a cup of coffee and switched my brain to autopilot so that I would just concentrate on being a journalist.

Several witnesses at Venna Mansions had told me the victims were "probably the Storey boys and those two kids they hang around with from Baker Road". Apparently they were often seen lurking near the derelict flats. The pea-brained duty sergeant at the police station I spoke to at 6am wouldn't confirm or deny anything and told me to call the press office at 9am.

I was very reluctant to call Rockingsworth fire station, but I eventually dialled the number at 6.45am.

"Station Officer Adams," a weak voice answered.

"Hello, it's Hannah Harker, from the Informer. I was at the fire last night."

There was a pause before he spoke. "Yes?"

"I just wondered if you'd heard any news about the firefighter that was injured last night. Is he going to be all right?"

"The surgeons have been working all night, but he's still critical. They reckon he'll probably pull through, but even if he does his injuries are... extreme. Most of his Watch are at the hospital now with his family. All we can do is pray."

"Christ, I'm so sorry." I hoped Adams didn't notice that I said this with such sincerity.

"Well, like I said, all we can do is pray." He adopted a more business-like tone, pushing his personal torment to one side. "And sift through every millimetre of that building to find out who started that fire."

I had felt sick at this, but forced myself to carry on. "You're definitely treating this as arson then?"

"Oh yes, and we'll find out who it was if it's the last thing this station does."

"Of course," I murmured. "Don't you think it was the boys themselves then? Perhaps they were messing about in there and got caught out."

"No way," Adams said vehemently. "The fire started three floors below where their bodies were found. We already know that an accelerant was used and the way that death-trap was built, the fire would've been on top of them before they knew what was happening. Judging by the injuries, it looks like they opened the door to a fireball."

I had wanted to drop the phone and drop dead. "Any idea who the victims were?" I managed.

"You'll need to speak to the police on that one. They'll also be investigating with us, of course. I suppose it will probably be a murder investigation."

"I suppose so." I put the phone down, ran to the bathroom and threw up.

I ignored the other reporters as they started arriving for work and asking me about the fire. Instead I called Detective Inspector Liam King on his mobile and asked him if he would be involved in the fire investigation. He told me he would be, and tipped me off that the police press office hoped to release the kids' identification at around midday.

"They were burnt beyond recognition, but their parents know it was them all right," he had told me. "The four of them had apparently been hanging out there for weeks, getting stoned and pissing about."

"Can you give me any names in advance?" I asked, already knowing the answer.

"No way."

"Am I likely to hear the name Storey later today?"

"Not from me, Hannah. Listen, if you come down and see me later we'll get a nice witness appeal together, I'll give you very strong police quotes and we'll talk about getting the victims' families together for a press conference. How's that?"

"You sound more like a press officer every day, Liam. Can't you give me anything to get me started?"

"Absolutely not, but if you were going to ring round the local schools to try and find where these kids went, you might perhaps start with Laura Strauss, the headteacher at St John's."

"Thanks, Liam. I'll see you at two, and I'll even buy the coffee."

I had only spoken to Laura a couple of times previously on pretty innocuous stories, but when I dialled the number for St John's High School at 8.05am and innocently asked if she had heard about the fire, she gave it to me on a plate. Fifteen minutes later I had the four boys' names, ages and glowing tributes to each of them, which I suspected didn't accurately reflect how they had been regarded by their teachers before the fire.

I walked into the editor's office without knocking after this call and told her what I had and that I could do a revised version of the story for the final edition of that day's paper. She was thrilled, and after I had knocked out a new splash and more background incorporating the tributes I ran down to the car park with my mobile and called John Townsend, a reporter for The Sun newspaper. His patch covered our news area and every now and then I would call him if I had a good story going in the Informer which I thought could be used nationally. It was usually something quirky, or a minor celebrity story, and if it went in The Sun I would get a cheque for anything between £20 and £500. There was nothing quirky about four kids dying in a fire, but I knew it was national news.

Townsend had already heard about the fire, but was interested in the stuff I had from the headteacher and the eyewitness quotes. He told me to email him everything I had and call if anything else came up.

When I returned to my desk I had called the police press office and was told the four bodies had now been formally identified. I of course already knew the names, but dutifully wrote down everything I was told and asked all the usual questions. Phil Crichton was hovering when I got off the phone and I told him what I'd just heard.

"Right, we can approach the families then," he said gleefully. "I've asked Simon to track down Steven Francis' family, Emma is doing Tony Small and I've just got an address for the Storey brothers off directory inquiries. Can you go round there and do the death knock please."

I nodded grimly, knowing that I was about to have a hellish experience.

Chapter 9

Virtually every journalist in the world, particularly those in the local media, will agree that doing a "death knock" is one of the least pleasant aspects of the job. It involves turning up uninvited at the home of someone who has very recently lost a loved one and asking them to describe their feelings, string together a poignant tribute and either provide or pose for pictures to go in the newspaper for everyone to see. Visiting the widow of an elderly councillor is hard, visiting the mother of a child taken by cancer is very hard, visiting the parents of a murder victim is harrowing and visiting the parents of two boys you murdered the night before is... well, I soon found out.

The curtains were drawn at the unremarkable terraced house in Vickery Crescent when I drove up at 12.35pm and I prayed that nobody would be home. When I saw a curtain twitch, I knew I was about to have the worst moment of my life.

A tall, thin man wearing tracksuit bottoms and a dirty T-shirt opened the door and stared right through me without uttering a word.

"Mr Storey?" I asked, repeating myself when the man didn't answer.

"Um, yes." He looked aimlessly at his front garden. "Police?"

"No, sir. My name is Hannah Harker; I'm a reporter at the Rockingsworth Evening Informer."

"Oh," he murmured, apparently unsure of what I could possibly want with him.

"It's about Danny and Matty," I said solemnly.

"Yes, of course." He still looked right through me and stood on the doorstep making no attempt to invite me in.

"We would really like to publish a tribute piece to the boys, and the police have asked us to run as much coverage as we can to help them catch whoever was responsible for the fire."

"Right, yeah," he said, finally resting his eyes on me. "Where are you from?"

"The Evening Informer," I repeated extremely patiently.

"Sure. Um, come in."

The next hour was indeed the worst of my life and when Geoff Storey and his partner, Janet Howard, brought out holiday snaps of Danny and Matty I couldn't help but let my tears flow with theirs.

I have no recollection of leaving the house in Vickery Crescent and driving to Rockingsworth police station to see Liam King. He asked me several times if I was all right during our meeting and I assured him unconvincingly that I was. In hindsight, I saw he had flirted with me more than usual, perhaps thinking he could get away with it as he had tipped me off about the school, but all I did was get the quotes I needed for my story and left in a hurry.

Back at the office I found Simon had sent me a gushing email about what a great job I'd done on the story, but I didn't bother replying and instead shut everything out and concentrated on writing the following day's splash on the parents' tributes and a two-page special edition spread, which would comprise photographs, various quotes from police and fire sources, more from teachers and relatives and a lengthy sidebar from Alex Hammond about his initial investigation into the fire and an extremely strong rebuke for the council.

I left the office at 9pm after getting a very big pat on the back from Tina Karageorghis and drove straight to the off-licence, where I bought a litre bottle of Smirnoff.

That night, the professional front I had imposed on myself collapsed and after the first glass of vodka I started to face up to what I had done. The more I drank, the worse it became and I found that I literally didn't know what to do with myself. I punched my thighs so hard they bruised. I actually pulled my hair out. I writhed on the sofa with muscles so tense they nearly burst. I screamed. I punched the wall increasingly hard until I felt my knuckles cracking. I tore my work clothes with my bare hands. I threw glasses of neat vodka down my throat and pressed my fists hard into my temples hoping to knock myself out. I half ran a lukewarm bath and tried to force my face under the water, but my brain wouldn't permit self destruction, so I curled up on the wet bathroom floor and hammered my swollen knuckles into my stomach and thighs. The vodka hit harder than I could and I threw up on the floor, then slipped in it as I tried to get up and smashed my chin on the edge of the toilet bowl. I couldn't hurt myself enough, but at the same time I hurt so much that every passing second

I was enduring emotional, mental and physical pain that I could never describe in words. When I did finally pass out, I was in such a desperate state that I didn't even notice my head shutting down and the merciful darkness swallowing my misery.

The following day I was due in work at 8am. When my mobile rang at 8.45am I was still laying on the bathroom floor in my own vomit.

It was Phil Crichton calling to find out where I was. Still barely conscious, I told him I was ill and asked for the day off. I didn't hear his reply, but assumed it was all right. Hauling myself up, I looked in the mirror and was shocked at what I saw. My hair was tangled with lumps of dried vomit, my eyes were badly bloodshot, my skin red and blotchy and on my chin was an ugly black bruise. I was only wearing knickers and I saw more dried vomit down the right side of my body and purple bruises on my thighs.

A hot shower repaired some of the damage and I lazily cleaned up some of the mess on the bathroom floor, but I soon had images of charred bodies forcing their way into my head and before long the unbearable guilt returned. Not willing to deal with it, I slipped out to the newsagent at the end of the road, bought two litre bottles of cheap vodka and ran home. I switched off my phone and drew the curtains in my bedroom, then climbed under my duvet and started on the first bottle of vodka. I pulled the wastepaper basket close to the bed for when I threw up again, but by midday I had cried and drunk myself into a deep sleep plagued by vile images.

I next awoke at 7pm screaming and sweating. I downed a shot of vodka and turned on my phone, ignoring text messages from Simon and Naomi, and dialled Phil Crichton's mobile number to tell him I was still feeling ill and wouldn't be in tomorrow either.

I tried to get back to sleep but I had been laying in bed so long my arms and legs were driving me mad and my body was starting to itch. I went down to the lounge and sat on the sofa to see if maybe I could now analyse my feelings and perhaps find a way of dealing with them, but my head was so intoxicated that I couldn't concentrate on anything. I started on the vodka again and having not eaten anything for as long as I could remember, the room was soon spinning and I passed out on the sofa.

The next day I didn't even wake until noon and it wasn't until 2pm that I eventually rolled off the sofa into a puddle of vodka. My head was really dizzy and my stomach tight with hunger, but I couldn't even consider eating anything. Walking upstairs to the bathroom was a massive struggle and when I looked in the mirror I hated myself. My eyes now had a hollow look, my cheeks seemed to have sunk in like a skeleton and my chin was covered in red spots. My teeth looked yellow and when I stripped naked my body looked grey and emaciated, with more red spots on my shoulders and back. I sat on the toilet but nothing came out and I noticed for the first time that I stank. Part of me wanted to sort all this out, but another part told me not to and it was this latter part which easily won the argument. I pulled a dressing gown on and went back down to the sofa and worked my way through the second bottle of vodka. During the day I picked at my spots, cried, punched the sofa, hit myself, tried to force my fists into my ears, threw cushions at the mantelpiece and broke various ornaments, buried my face into the sofa and screamed until my throat hurt. Some time when it had gone dark, I crawled up to bed and fell into a nightmare world where burnt children chased me with razor blades. This is when I had woken up in tears, knocked the vodka and alarm clock on the floor, called Marc Sullivan to take another day off and gone into the shower and cried my heart out.

As the tears flowed in the shower that morning, my head finally cleared and I decided that the time had come to sort myself out. I firstly scrubbed my body clean and washed my hair thoroughly, then shaved my legs and armpits and brushed my aching teeth for several minutes. I blow-dried my hair and brushed it, put some concealer over my spots and the bruise on my chin, used a bit of eyeliner and then pulled on clean underwear, a pair of clean jeans and a vest top. I opened my bedroom curtains and threw the windows open then took a deep breath and headed downstairs.

The smell in the lounge made me heave, but I managed to tidy some of the mess and I opened the windows here as well, before venturing out into the kitchen for the first time in days. I made myself a cup of sugary tea and two slices of toast, which scratched my throat as I painfully forced them down, and then I made myself think and make some decisions.

I began by admitting out loud that I had burnt down a block of flats and killed four children. I also admitted that no punishment on earth would ever be adequate for this, but as it had happened there was nothing I could do to change it so there was no point in making myself suffer for ever more because of it.

I was somehow able to draw consolation from the fact that I had never intended to hurt anyone and that the boys had no business being in the building anyway. The burnt fireman was gradually drifting out of the whole equation as I couldn't find a way of reconciling my actions with his injuries, although he would have known the risks when he took the job. I decided that my overall motivation for starting the fire was justified really because I wanted the council to tear down all the derelict death traps in the area. The deaths of the boys was a horrific and tragic consequence, but now the council would have to act and more tragedies, possibly several more, would be averted, thanks to me.

From what I had learned about the boys they were well known local trouble makers who had brought misery and terror to their community. Although they in no way deserved to die the way they did, this helped ease my guilt further and I started to think about occasions where far more innocent people had had to die for changes to be made and sacrificial decisions taken which had ultimately benefited countless more people.

These thoughts were on the surface of my mind and were a mixture of what I wanted to believe, what I really did believe to an extent and what I was trying desperately to make myself believe. Deeper down I was admitting to myself that I had done it partly for a thrill and partly in an attempt to make people on the newspaper sit up and take notice of me. In short, I hadn't done it for any greater good or desire to make the world a better place at all; I had done it for purely selfish reasons.

I tried to keep these feelings buried and concentrated on believing the surface thoughts, but the truth gradually pushed its way through and I was eventually forced to confront the fact that I had started a fire which killed four people in order to further my career and get a bit of excitement. There it was. If any good came of it, then that would be a welcome consequence, but to pretend that I had set out to do it for any altruistic reason was a lie.

Faced with this more chilling reality, I decided to see if I could deal with this version of events. I was surprised by how easily I could. My work on both fires had earned me a new level of respect in the office and I knew from the reactions of Tina and the news editors that I was now considered a very competent reporter and had proved I could cut it on the big stories. At the end of the day, the four victims were delinquent trouble makers who were trespassing in a building they had no right or reason to be in. I had never met them before and I had no reason to feel any emotion towards them. The pain I had caused their families was hard to justify, but who knew what misery the boys would have caused in years to come as they stole, took drugs, got involved in serious crime and spent their time either in prison, the court house or on probation.

I had not felt any guilt when I attacked Ruth Chapman in the park all those years ago because she was a nasty, spiteful bully who had deserved what she got. I wasn't saying that the four boys deserved what they got, but they were certainly no angels and as such I shouldn't let myself be crushed by guilt.

What was really concerning me was the realisation that however much my efforts impressed the powers that be on the Rockingsworth Evening Informer, other than a brief conversation with John Townsend on The Sun my work would have gone virtually unnoticed at a national level.

I decided to give my dad a call.

"Hello, Peter Harker," he answered, after several rings of his mobile.

"Hello, Dad, it's Hannah. How are you?"

"Hello, darling I'm fine. What's up?"

"Did you hear about the big fire up here the other night?"

"Yes, I read your stuff on the paper's website; excellent job, Hannah, excellent."

"Thanks. You know, though, I was thinking. I really like it on the Informer and everything, but stories like that only come along once in a blue moon. I want to be on a national, where the real action is all the time."

"Oh, you get just as many dull days on the nationals, darling, believe you me: standing in the rain waiting for some two-bit telly star to come home, sitting in tedious press conferences for hours on end, trying to hunt down people you know don't want to talk to you. Besides, as I've told you plenty of times, you need to cut your teeth first at a local level before you think about moving on. I can see you're doing really well at the Informer, but you've got to get more experience before you even consider shifting for the nationals. If you make a mistake up there they'll eat you alive and you'll never be given another chance."

"But what could I do that would really impress them?" I pressed.

"Well, it's hard. They have so many stories coming in from their own reporters, from news agencies, from the authorities and from the public that it's hard to get yourself noticed. I did see that The Sun carried a report of your fire with several of your witness quotes in it. Did you sell that to them?"

"Yeah."

"Well, that's a good place to start. Whenever you get a good story tout it around the nationals. It gets your name known and things can sometimes develop from there."

"What sort of stuff do they really want though? What's going to make them go wow?"

"If you want to impress the tabloids you need sex, scandal and celebrity – preferably a combination of the three. The broadsheets obviously want more political or international stuff, things you're going to struggle to come across at the Informer. I'm sure this is all stuff you know already though. Anyway, enough of this shop-talk, Hannah, when are you next going to come down to see your mother and I?"

"In a couple of weekends hopefully, I'll let you know."

"Okay darling. Well, don't forget about us."

"Of course I won't, silly. Love you loads, and love to mum."

"Love you too, speak to you soon."

As we said our goodbyes, the seeds of an idea were already forming in my head.

Chapter 10

The following morning I made it into work, looking like shit but feeling a hell of a lot better. Everyone seemed to be engrossed in their work and Simon seemed to be off with me for some reason, so I went to see Liam at the police station.

The detective was unshaven and he smelt strongly of coffee, but his drawn face lit up when I walked into his office.

"A friendly face!" He smiled as he rose to greet me. "I've not seen many of those lately."

"Problems?"

"The bloody Venna Mansions fire. We've got a full-scale investigation up and running with a dozen of us working on it full-time and not a damn thing has turned up."

"Really?" I said, relieved at hearing this. "Do you want me to do another witness appeal?"

"Phil Crichton did one for us yesterday and Tina Karageorghis promised me she'd get some posters printed up by the end of the week urging readers to help catch the killer."

"That's good," I lied. "The forensic people haven't turned up anything then?"

"The room where the fire was started was completely gutted. Even if the killer had left finger prints, strands of hair and fibres of clothing everywhere they would have been destroyed. Door-to-door inquiries have given us nothing and the only messages on the special hotline we set up have been from people congratulating the fire-starter for ridding the estate of troublemakers, some mad old bastard who said his dead mother started it and a woman phoning to report that her garden has been vandalised. Jesus, our family liaison guys are copping it from the parents, the force will soon be copping it from you lot and the bloody television, and then I'll be copping it from the Superintendent!"

"Sounds like a complete dead end. I reckon you'll have to hold your hands up on this one and chalk it up in the unsolved crimes statistics."

"I can't really see that happening, Hannah! When four kids get murdered it doesn't matter if you investigate for two hours, two days, two years or 20 years – at the end of the day you've got to find someone. We'll get a break sooner or later."

He must have noticed the pained expression on my face because he suddenly changed the subject.

"What have you been up to the past couple of days?" he asked.

"I wasn't feeling well. I guess everything at work must've been getting to me."

"I'm not surprised," he said sympathetically. "I guess you saw those bodies when they pulled them out?"

"Um, yeah."

"Shit, that must've been awful."

He looked at me for a while as if trying to decipher my expression and then finally asked me what I was doing that evening.

"No plans," I answered.

"Well, look, do you want to go and get a drink somewhere. It sounds like we could both use one."

A drink was the last thing I could use, but I decided I did want to see him that evening so I said okay. We agreed to meet in a High Street bar at 8.30pm and we gave each other friendly smiles as I left.

When I got back to the office I had an email from Simon asking if he could have a word. I went to the canteen with him and asked him what he wanted.

"Are you all right with me?" he asked as we sat down at a bean-stained plastic table with plastic cups of warm water.

"Of course I am, why?"

"Well, you've not replied to any of my emails or texts the last few days and you haven't spoken a word to me."

"Oh, Simon, I've been up to my neck in this fire stuff and the last few days I've been dying in bed. I've not spoken to anyone or returned their messages."

"So we're okay then?"

"We're fine, Simon," I assured him.

"Cool. What are you doing tonight? Do you fancy a drink?"

"Sorry, I've got plans tonight."

"Oh, um, maybe tomorrow night then? It doesn't have to be a big one."

"I'm not sure what I'm doing yet, but I'll let you know in the morning."

"Okay," he said, and his sulky expression returned.

"I've got to get back," I said, getting up.

He didn't reply and I left him sitting alone at the table, rolling the plastic cup between his hands.

The pretentious Pacific Lounge bar was noisy and packed with wankers when I squeezed in at 8.45pm. I had dressed to impress, my hair was down and I had taken extra time on my make-up to camouflage the scars of the days I had spent trying to kill myself at home.

Several male heads turned in my direction as I headed to the bar, where Liam was sitting on a stall chatting to one of the barmen, who was pulling him another pint of Stella.

"Good evening, Liam," I said, creeping up behind him.

"Hey." He spun round and an approving look appeared on his face as he looked me up and down. "Wow, you look pretty damn fantastic. I didn't realise I was taking you to Paris Fashion Week."

"Very funny." I blushed, thinking he also looked good in a black shirt, smart jeans and black shoes.

"What can I get you to drink?"

"Just a coke please," I said, glancing at the spirits behind the bar and feeling queasy.

"Coke! We're supposed to be ridding ourselves of stress. What are you really having?"

I turned to the waiting barman with a "what am I going to do with him?" look and asked for a white wine spritzer with lots of lemonade.

"Of course," he said.

"Make it a large one, Kev," Liam winked at the barman.

"I'm not going to get drunk," I warned him.

"Of course not, you'll probably have to rush off to another fire in a minute anyway if your recent adventures are anything to go by."

What the hell did he mean by that? Surely he can't be on to me. It's an innocent comment, Hannah, don't be paranoid, girl. I hope he's not looking at my face.

"No," I replied eventually, "I've got a feeling tonight is going to be nice and quiet."

"How boring, aren't we at least going to go dancing later?"

"You're too old to go dancing; the bouncers won't let you in."

"I'll show my warrant card."

"Then they'll definitely not let you in!"

"Well, if I'm that much of an embarrassment perhaps we shouldn't go out in public again," he said, pretending to be hurt.

I put my hand on his shoulder and said: "Oh, detective, don't be like that. We can still go out – just nowhere somebody might see me!"

"I'm the one who should be worried," he chuckled, "sitting around getting drunk with a journalist."

"You can trust me, Liam. I promise I won't take advantage of you." I patted his shoulder again.

"I was rather hoping you would." He grinned and I smiled back.

I finished my second drink at just after 10pm and I said I had to go. He asked if I wanted to go on somewhere but I declined and also refused to let him pay for my taxi.

"Well," he said as we parted at the door, "thanks for coming out. It's been nice."

"My pleasure, thanks for inviting me."

"Perhaps we can do it again next week sometime when we're both a little less stressed; maybe on Friday night or something?"

"That would be nice." I smiled at him, looking into his blue eyes.

A taxi pulled up and we went through the clichéd awkward parting routine, which ended with him leaning forward to give me a kiss goodbye just as I turned to get in the taxi. He got a mouthful of hair just above my ear and I bumped my head on the door as I turned back to smile at him.

Sinking back into the rear seat at the taxi pulled away I grinned to myself. We had chatted easily and there was none of the awkward silences you get so often when two people who know each other through work meet socially. There was enough eye contact and body contact for us both to know we wanted each other, but I think he realised quite early on that he wasn't going to get lucky on the first night. He seemed to relax after that and we both had a much-needed laugh.

As the taxi crawled along West Street into the late night traffic I looked out of the window. West Street was Rockingsworth's main bar and club area and even though it was a Wednesday night, crowds of people were milling around as the midweek clubbers poured out of the pubs to join the queues for Galaxy, Club 90 and The Den. Once inside, shaven-headed morons in pink T-shirts tops or fake Burberry would get carried away by the two-for-one Budweiser offers, all try and pull the same tart with the fake Louis Vuitton bag and then start a big fight.

As we passed Tony's Kebab Shack I saw a brawl was already well underway. A fat girl in what looked like a size six top, a mini skirt and slag boots was screaming at two skinheads in lurid Ben Sherman shirts and school shoes who were rolling about on the pavement while a crowd of identical people stood around enjoying the free show, shouting comments which may or may not have been in English. Eventually a meat wagon screeched up and six coppers jumped out, dragged the bleeding skinheads apart and started shouting at everyone.

The taxi driver said something I didn't hear, so I grunted and smiled at him in the rear-view mirror.

So long as Naomi didn't change her mind, this time on Saturday I would be at a club called Network in London with a man called Jason Brady who was going to help me break into the big time and escape from all this shit.

Chapter 11

Jason Brady was an ugly, spotty 20-year-old from a sink estate in Sunderland who was so detestable that, according to press interviews, even his parents turned their noses up in disgust at him. He had achieved nothing at school, was bullied by virtually every other kid he met and was widely expected to be a complete failure in life.

Luckily for Jason, though, he turned out to be an exceptionally gifted footballer and was signed by a struggling lower league team in the north east upon leaving school. He scored 30 goals in his first season and was poached by one of London's top Premiership clubs. He took the league by storm, netting 23 goals and helping his club lift the FA Cup, and was currently the toast of the nation after scoring a hat-trick on his international debut as England came from two goals down to beat Germany in a crucial World Cup qualifier.

I had read an interview with him in a lads' magazine that was laying around at work a couple of weeks previously and learnt that he loved clubbing at Network and his favourite DJ was Unknown Artist, who was playing at Network on Saturday.

When my dad had told me on the phone that if I wanted to get something in the nationals I should go for celebrity, sex and scandal, I immediately thought of Jason Brady. Stuart at work told me that Jason had badly injured his wrist in a game last week and wouldn't be travelling to the north west for his club's match against Manchester City on Sunday. I took a gamble that he would use the opportunity to go to Network to see Unknown Artist and began devising my plan.

Naomi had moved to Crouch End in north London when we returned from travelling and she got her job in public relations. After work on Friday night I took the train from Rockingsworth into London and got a bus to her flat, where we spent the evening discussing my scheme and ironing out the details.

After breakfast on Saturday morning we went to Camden, where I had paid a small fortune to book a suite at the new Diamond Regency Hotel, which was just a short walk from Network. After checking in we got a cab to an anonymous looking flat in Kilburn, where one of the guys from Naomi's work, who I gather she was sleeping with, supplied us with a gram of cocaine and let us drop off a bag of clothes.

Naomi told me so many outrageous stories about the things she got up to with colleagues from her work that I wondered if she ever had any time left for promoting the needy causes she was paid to promote.

At university, she was always popular, but very much her own person. In many ways she was like me and we soon started sitting together in lectures and hanging out in the student union bar a lot. When my brothers died I did my best to shut everybody out, but Naomi was always there for me if I did need to talk to someone and she helped me catch up with work when I fell behind with my studies around this time.

After the first year she started to lead me astray and we spent more time in the bar than we did in lectures, and she also got me into the club and drugs scene. Together we tried just about every drug under the sun, from ecstasy and cocaine to ketamine and salvia. We actually smoked salvia before an exam one afternoon and sat next to each other at the back of the hall convinced we were dice. It was a two hour exam and we spent the entire time rocking back and forth trying to roll a double six! After the exam we thought all the other students were pieces of rail track and we did our best to make them line up into a railway line.

Naomi was also very sexually active and was willing to try anything with anyone, male or female. I was a lot more reserved and slept with just two guys the whole time I was at university. I did very briefly kiss a girl in a club, but at the time I was paralysed by ketamine and don't really recall much about it.

The adventures continued after university when we went on our incredible two-year trip around the world and our friendship developed into a bond that we knew would last forever. All of my favourite memories involved Naomi and she had always been there for the highs and the lows. I had even considered telling her about the fire and the boys, but decided against it. That was too much. That was a secret that couldn't be shared because it would change everything between us.

After we came back from travelling, Naomi walked straight into her public relations job, where it seemed that all of her colleagues had the same hedonistic mind-set as her. She was happy and having fun, and I knew she'd be the perfect person to help me with the Jason Brady plan.

We dropped the coke back at the hotel and strolled up to Camden Market, where we spent three hours choosing the sluttiest clubbing outfits we could find.

After a couple of drinks at a pub by Camden Lock we went back to the hotel, cracked open a bottle of wine and got ready to go out. Naomi insisted on getting ready in private in the bathroom so she could surprise me, and when she stepped out at just gone 11pm I could only gawp at her with my mouth wide open, unwittingly feeling a little stir between my legs.

Nearly 6ft tall, slim with dark brown hair, almond eyes, a long thin nose and full lips, Naomi was beautiful at the best of times. Standing in the bathroom doorway wearing a black bikini top, thigh-high black leather boots and blue latex hot-pants she looked incredible. Her hair was shining and combed back off her forehead into a high ponytail and her make-up was dark and severe. On the wrong girl the outfit would have looked downright ridiculous or horrible, but on Naomi it made me question my sexuality.

"So, what do you think?" she asked. "Do you reckon he'll fancy me?"

"I think I fucking fancy you! Jesus, you look amazing."

"Thanks, babe." She pranced across the room and gave me a kiss on the cheek. "You look rather fit yourself, Mistress Harker."

I was dressed in black mini skirt, black knee-high boots and stockings, and a tight black shirt, which was only done up by two buttons halfway down, and no bra. I had my belly button ring in, a leather collar was wrapped around my neck and my make-up was dark and severe like Naomi's.

We finished our wine and Naomi asked if I wanted "a line for the road".

"It's supposed to be for Jason," I said.

"There'll be plenty for him," she replied, already sitting down and tipping a mound of white powder onto the table. "Can you find some dance tunes on the telly and turn it up a bit."

I found a music channel and turned it up loud as Naomi chopped out two fat lines of cocaine, rolled up a £20 note and passed it to me.

"A bit of Colombian Courage to make sure things go smoothly tonight," she said.

I snorted half the line up my left nostril and the other half up my right then gave the £20 to Naomi, who scooped up her line in one go. We both licked the table clean as I felt a satisfying lump in the back of my throat and asked Naomi to chop out two more small lines.

We left the hotel at nearly midnight, both buzzing from nerves, excitement, two bottles of wine and a generous helping of coke. We had phoned the club the day before and put our names on the guest list, and were pleased we had when we got there and saw the queue of people snaking round the block. With our long coats pulled tightly around ourselves, we joined the much shorter guest list queue and after just a few minutes we were walking down a long flight of stairs towards the increasingly loud boom that was escaping from the doors at the bottom.

We got an approving nod from the guy in the cloakroom when we took our coats off and as we walked through the doors into the main room of Network I came up on a massive rush of cocaine.

I grabbed Naomi's hand and grinned at her as we stood there in our outfits staring at 2,000 or so bending, twisting, writhing bodies, which seemed to be moving in unison to the thumping drums, bass and electronic squelches that were being manipulated by the warm-up DJ, who presided over proceedings from a booth on a platform to the right of the stage at the opposite end of the club to us. A communal cheer went up as a huge green laser fanned out over the crowd, flickered a few times and sunk down onto the heads of the euphoric dancers. The green light showed me a few individual faces – sweating, beaming, twitching, chewing faces looking for another face to smile at and share the incredible moment with – and I realised that even so early on in the night nearly everyone was off their heads. It was going to be very messy in here by the time Unknown Artist came on at around 3am.

"I'm going to score some pills," said Naomi, stopping me from being absorbed by the club.

"We can't get too fucked," I warned her.

"Half each, that'll be fine."

"All right."

"I'll get a couple just in case."

While Naomi disappeared into the crowd, followed by a mass of groping hands and leering eyes, I went to the bar, bought two bottles of water and scanned the club for any sign of Jason Brady. There was a chill-out room to the left of the stage, but it was unlikely he would be in there. If he had arrived yet he would almost certainly be upstairs in the small VIP room, which overlooked the main room. If Jason didn't spot me and Naomi and come down to say hello, we would have to try and blag our way in there to get to him.

Naomi returned with a shifty looking man, whose name I didn't catch when she introduced him. We tried to exchange small talk over the din of the club for a couple of minutes, then Naomi slipped him a tenner and he passed her two pills. Naomi kissed him on the cheek, gave him a hug and he walked off.

"Down the hatch then, my darling," she said as she popped one of the pills onto my tongue and I swallowed it with a mouthful of water. She took hers and asked if Jason was around yet, and when I said he wasn't she suggested we go and dance.

We held hands and pushed towards the stage. The music was getting harder now and the beats thumping out of the giant speakers were pretty ferocious. The green laser was still demanding everyone's attention, but as Naomi and I pushed through the mass of sweaty bodies, many topless, several male and some female eyes followed us. I saw hands reaching out to grab Naomi's arse and felt a couple brush not too innocently against mine. A small space opened up for us just below the DJ booth and Naomi turned to face me, smiled and we danced together.

Already high on cocaine, I wondered if I'd get a big rush off the E, but when my heart started to tremor some time later and my limbs went as light as paper I knew it was going to be a powerful one. A burst of serotonin and adrenaline surged through my brain and chest to my arms and legs and I felt scared, excited, strangely sad, confident, sexy, hot and deliriously happy all at the same time. Naomi was grinning at me like a fool and I loved her so much I grabbed her by the shoulders and kissed her hard on the mouth four times.

"Thank you so much for coming," I screamed at her. "This is fucking brilliant. Really, really brilliant. Are you all right?"

"Yeah, I've just come up. I'm fucked, absolutely fucked, Han'. This is fucking amazing. How are you? Are you all right?"

"Yeah, I'm brilliant. I'm fucked. This is amazing, absolutely fucking amazing. Oh God, Nay, I love you so much."

"Ah baby, I love you too. Give me a hug."

We embraced like long lost sisters, our hips unable to stop moving to the music and we kissed each other on the head, ear, cheek and mouth over and over again with huge smiles and tears of uncontrollable joy in our eyes.

I felt someone rubbing themselves against me from behind and I turned round to see a really lovely, beautiful girl in a pink fluffy top looking longingly at me.

"Hi, what's your name?" I asked.

"Sam," the girl shouted back. "You look amazing, you're beautiful."

"Thanks Sam, you look really lovely too. I love your hair. Do you want some water?"

"Yeah, thanks." She took a swig from my bottle. "Is this your girlfriend?" She nodded at Naomi.

"This is my friend, Naomi. We're not together though. I've got a boyfriend," I lied, sensing that Sam wanted more than just my water.

"Oh, okay." Sam was really wide-eyed. "It's a really nice place in here, everyone seems really friendly. I've done quite a lot of MDMA. I feel really incredible. Like, really nice inside, you know."

"Yeah, me too," I beamed at her, "I'm buzzing like a Rampant Rabbit!"

"I feel really nice as well," Naomi chipped in.

We were interrupted by a boy of about 17, who was topless and clearly off his brains.

"All right girls. Ha ha! I really like your outfits," he slurred.

"Thanks mate," I replied unenthusiastically.

"Sweet. You are proper fit, can I have a kiss?"

"No."

"Go on, just a little one. I don't, like, love you, but I really like you and I just want to give you a quick kiss."

"No, go away." I turned my back.

"What about you, darling?" He turned to Sam.

"Okay then," she said.

He leant in and kissed her quickly on the mouth.

"Ha ha, your mouth feels hard. So does mine actually. Do you want to go and get some water?"

"Yeah, okay."

The two of them walked off hand in hand leaving me and Naomi to carry on dancing together.

We suddenly realised the music had gone quiet, the green laser had been replaced by a slowly flickering strobe light and a deep, low rumble of bass was creeping across the floor and up our legs. Unknown Artist had arrived.

Whistles and cheers grew frantic around us as the long, growling bass got louder and hands and feet itched to throw themselves around. The strobe switched off and the room went dark. There were more screams and whistles, but still the DJ wouldn't give us the explosion we so desperately craved. The bass looped again, louder and longer and we were all shrieking at Unknown Artist to let us have it. Another bass loop. We were going out of our minds. Another bass loop, only this time it was followed by the sound of a distant explosion. As this faded out there was complete silence until…

BANG! 2,000 people had a synchronised fit as the drums, bass, effects and strobes kicked in at once and we all seemed to get a second rush of whatever cocktail of drugs we had taken. Naomi and I didn't say a word to each other for the next 90 minutes, but just danced alone, danced together, cheered, screamed, whistled, drank water, shared water and absorbed all the energy, love and emotion around us into our bodies.

When he was suddenly standing in front of us with a smile on his face, I didn't even recognise Jason Brady or recall anything about why we had come to Network.

"Hey, girls," he said smarmily. "I've been watching you from the VIP room upstairs. Your dancing is something else."

"Thank you," we replied together.

"Listen, my name's Jason Brady and I wondered if you'd like to join me upstairs for some champagne?"

My brain started working again and I remembered what was going on.

"Shit, you're that England footballer aren't you?"

He nodded and smiled, brushing his chin with a heavily bandaged hand. Naomi and I fixed extremely impressed expressions on our faces, eagerly accepted his offer and followed him up a set of metal stairs to the VIP room.

A suited bouncer waved us in and we walked into a fairly small room, with expensively-dressed people, who all looked familiar, sipping champagne on very stylish armchairs while a DJ stood unnoticed in the corner playing rather tame funky house. There was none of the buzz of the main room downstairs and I suddenly felt my body go cold and my legs become really heavy.

Jason, who was dressed in a disgusting purple shirt, black trousers and a black blazer, hurriedly introduced us to four men sitting round a table, then waved them away and invited us to sit down.

"So," he said, "can I get you some champagne?"

We both nodded and moments later a barman appeared with a bottle of Bollinger in an ice bucket. He filled three glasses and left without a word.

"What are your names?" Jason asked, raising his glass.

We told him and he proposed a toast to us. We chinked glasses and were soon chatting away with one of the most obnoxious little pricks we had ever come across. He was all over us and even though that's what I wanted, it repulsed us.

After a while, Naomi and I went to the bathroom together to form a plan.

"I'm so not fucking him," Naomi said firmly as she touched up her lipstick in the mirror.

"You don't have to," I said, doing the same. "We just have to let him think we will so we can get him back to the hotel. He's absolutely wasted anyway, so it won't be a problem."

We squirted ourselves with perfume from a tray and returned to the VIP room, where Jason quickly put down his mobile phone when he saw us coming. I guessed he was probably bragging to someone.

"Listen, Jason," I said as we sat back down, "me and Naomi have just about had enough here. What do you reckon about making a move? We've got a really nice suite at the Diamond Regency. Just the three of us; could be fun."

"I have to be careful," he said, a rather small erection poking through his trousers. "I'm supposed to be injured so I can't really be seen going off with a couple of birds from a club. There's fucking paps crawling all over the place outside."

"Aw, we'll look after you," I said, taking Naomi completely by surprise when I slowly ran two fingers down the length of her chest and kissed the corner of her mouth.

"Yeah," Naomi got into character again, "we'll give you any help you need." We both tried not to laugh as she slid a hand under my arse and gave it a little squeeze.

"Oh shit, what the hell." Jason looked ready to burst. "I'll call my driver and get him to bring the car round to the back entrance. I'll have a word with the bouncers on the front door and get them to tell the paps that someone big is on the way out – that'll keep the fuckers busy."

We collected our coats and were soon all sitting in the back of a very smart black Jaguar cruising through deserted London streets. Although it was only a short ride, Jason got very frisky and we had to keep him at bay by groping and stroking each other and telling him to just watch.

At the hotel he told his driver to leave, then ran past the front counter shielding his face as we followed in his wake.

By the time we got the door to the suite open he was virtually beside himself with excitement and we had to guide him to the sofa to stop him making a beeline straight to the bedroom. I got three miniature bacardis from the minibar and switched on the tape recorder in my handbag.

"Hey, can we put some music on?" Jason asked.

"No, it's late," I said. "Besides, we've got other things in mind."

"Like what?" he drooled

"Naomi, give this gentleman some of your finest Class A narcotics."

"Hey, I can't," he said. "They have random drugs tests all the time."

"Coke passes through your blood stream in just a few hours," I said, "they'll never find a trace."

"Besides," Naomi added, "it makes us so fucking horny." She groaned and started chopping out a line on the table in front of him.

I snuck into the bedroom and picked up my digital camera. I would have to be bloody subtle but I needed video of Jason doing the cocaine.

Naomi had just done a line and passed the £20 note to him as I walked behind the sofa and stood over him.

"There's a good boy," Naomi coaxed him, putting a hand on his knee.

As he put the note in his nose and started running it up the line I turned off the flash and took a couple of still pictures. They were good and clearly showed his face, but I wanted a video clip too so I told Naomi to fix him another line. He had fallen back onto the sofa with his eyes closed so I went and sat on the floor directly opposite him with the camera hidden behind my back.

"Take your cock out," I said to him.

"Huh!" He opened his eyes and blinked as Naomi finished chopping the line.

"Take your trousers and pants down if you want another line. If your wrist hurts too much, Naomi can help you."

Naomi glared at me.

"I can manage," he said. "The wrist isn't really that bad at all, I just couldn't go up to fucking Manchester because of the abuse I'll get for breaking Giovanni's leg last season."

He unzipped his trousers with his bandaged hand and dropped them and his pants round his ankles. Naomi and I nearly pissed ourselves laughing when we saw his tiny, spotty dick, which looked for all the world like it was actually tapered at the end.

"Good boy," I said, stifling a snigger. "Now, close your eyes again, hold your big cock with your bandaged hand, put that bank note up your nose and Naomi will slide it down that lovely line of cocaine for you."

He grunted and did as he was told, and as Naomi very slowly helped him snort the coke, I made a perfect video clip of the whole scene. I hid the camera again just as he finished snorting and opened his eyes.

"Christ, I'm fucked," he croaked.

"You will be," Naomi muttered.

"Now," I said, "we want you to go into the bedroom and lie on your back with your eyes closed and your cock in your hand. For the next ten minutes, Nay and I are going to sit out here and make each other wet; then we're going to come in there and fuck your brains out."

"Oh my God! I want to watch you two fuck," he pleaded.

"No way, we do our thing in private. You'll see quite enough of us in ten minutes."

"Please, let me help you!"

"Jason, do you want us to go home and leave you here with nothing? Go and do as you're told and in ten minutes you will have the two hottest and wettest girls in London crawling all over you. Now go."

His eyes bulged, he swallowed hard and staggered off to the bedroom with his pants still down around his ankles.

"That's a good boy," I called after him.

"You're about to have the best night of your life," Naomi promised.

He turned to look at us pleadingly again as he sat on the bed, so I planted both my hands on Naomi's arse and kissed her on the lips while I kicked the door shut. As soon as it was closed, we looked at each other and grinned, making grunting and panting noises and screaming "use more fingers" as we gathered our things, put our coats on and very quietly left the room.

We had paid for the suite in advance in cash, so the receptionist didn't mind us walking out of the hotel at 5.30am in fits of laughter. We got a taxi back to Naomi's place, polished off the coke and cried with laughter until we both passed out next to each other on the sofa.

Chapter 12

Sunday was a write off and we didn't get up until 5pm. We showered and changed into slightly more sensible and respectable clothes then went to the pub for a hair-of-the-dog bottle of wine and a bite to eat.

Later that evening Naomi asked me who I was going to sell the story to. The obvious choice was the News of the World or one of the other "red tops", but the paper I really wanted to work for was the International Morning Post, a hugely respected broadsheet that focussed primarily on serious international news. This had been my goal since I was young, and my dad made no secret of the fact that he too would be delighted if I could get a job there. Football, sex and drugs weren't the usual sort of things the newspaper went for, but I figured that it was a big enough story and if I offered it to them as an exclusive they would go for it. Besides, the quality of my video was excellent and the tape recorder in my handbag had picked up everything Jason said, so the paper should hopefully have no great difficulty in circumventing any injunctions or super injunctions that Brady and his publicists may try to arrange. If the worst came to the worst and the Morning Post declined, I could always flog the story to one of the tabloids and net myself a tidy little windfall.

I had to get back to Rockingsworth that night and at the station Naomi wished me luck. I gave her a big hug and thanked her for everything over the weekend.

"My pleasure, darling," she said. "I can't remember the last time I had such a brilliant night."

On the train home I checked my text messages and saw I had one from Liam, asking me if I was having a good weekend and if I wanted to go out next Friday. I smiled and sent a message back saying I was having an excellent weekend and said Friday would be fine. I didn't put any kisses, but when he replied immediately to say he would talk to me in the week to make plans, he added a kiss.

I went to sleep that night happier and more excited than I had been in ages.

The next day at work, however, I was tired, miserable and filled with trepidation about calling the International Morning Post. I think Simon sensed that I was on a downer after a weekend of drug abuse and he wisely kept his distance, as did everyone else.

There had been no more serious fires over the weekend – unsurprisingly, given my trip to London – so I frittered away a couple of hours writing a story about house prices in the district then took my mobile down to the car park and sat nervously in my car.

I was hoping to speak to the editor of the Post, Charles Courtney, but if not him then William Laing, the news editor. Finally conquering my nerves, I dialled the central London number and waited.

"Good morning, this is the International Morning Post, how may I direct your call?" a female receptionist answered.

"May I speak to Charles Courtney please," I said confidently.

"I'll put you through to his PA, one moment please."

The line was transferred and the butterflies returned to my stomach. A woman picked up the phone, her voice was stern and terse. She was clearly the editor's personal assistant.

"This is Rebecca Carmody."

"Good morning, may I speak to Mr Courtney please?" My voice was timid and polite in comparison.

"I'm afraid he's in meetings all day today. May I ask who is calling?"

"My name is Hannah Harker; I'm a reporter with the Rockingsworth Evening Informer." I cringed as I said it.

"Would you like to leave a message, Miss Harker?"

"Well, um, I have a very good story which I was hoping to speak to Mr Courtney about directly."

The secretary audibly sighed.

"I'll transfer you to the newsroom," she said. "I'm sure one of the reporters can help you."

She had gone before I could reply.

"Newsdesk," another voice said almost immediately.

"Hello, can I speak to William Laing please?"

"Who's calling?"

"Hannah Harker."

"Just a moment." The male reporter cupped the phone and asked Laing if he was expecting a call from a Hannah Harker. Obviously not. "Can I ask what it's about?"

"I have an extremely good story which I need to speak to him about urgently."

"Well, he's very busy at the moment. Email your story over to the newsdesk, put your number at the bottom and if it's any use to us we'll call you back."

"It's a bit better than that," I said haughtily, my confidence triggered by his patronising manner.

"Just a minute." He too sighed, but transferred me.

"Bill Laing," said a harried voice after several rings.

"Yes, sorry to bother you, but my name is Hannah Harker and I wondered if you'd like a story with pictures, audio and video of Jason Brady doing cocaine with two prostitutes on Saturday night?" Why not just cut to the chase.

There was a pause as Laing took this information in.

"Who are you?" he asked.

"I'm a reporter on the Rockingsworth Evening Informer. I have the pictures, tape and video with me now, if I can come and see you."

"Have you offered this to anyone else?"

"Not yet. I wanted to offer it to the Post first as an exclusive."

"Where is this story from? Are you certain there are no agencies or other papers on it? Your source may already have gone to the tabloids."

"Trust me," I assured him. "I've got this all to myself."

"Okay," he sounded keener now. "It's 11am now, what time can you get up here?"

"By one," I said, without thinking.

"Okay, ask for me at reception and I'll send someone down to meet you."

He hung up and I sat there shaking with excitement. I ran back to my desk and saw Phil was on the phone. Perfect. I scribbled on a Post-It note that I was going to meet a council contact and would be back later in the afternoon.

I checked I had my camera and tape recorder then drove to the station, where I got a train into London and then took the Tube to Farringdon.

The International Morning Post was based in a modern glass tower block on Clerkenwell Road, not all that far from the Guardian and Observer offices. It was currently the best-selling broadsheet in Britain with a circulation of just over two million and was the paper that I had decided many years ago I most wanted to write for.

It had been set up after World War Two by a consortium of London-based businessmen closely aligned to Clement Attlee's Labour Government. In fact, much of the funding for the Post in the early years came indirectly from the Treasury.

The newspaper in those days was little more than a mouth-piece for the British Government to let people know what a grand job British troops were doing around the world and to publish stories designed to encourage investment and rebuild the economy. Its patriotic reporting, however, appealed to post-War Britain and it soon made a modest, but wholly unexpected impact on Fleet Street.

Several highly-respected journalists were signed up and advertising revenues soared as the British and global economies got back on track, people started spending money again and international companies redis-covered the power of advertising. Much of this profit found its way back to the Treasury.

Controversy erupted following the 1951 General Election when Attlee's Labour Government fell to Churchill's rejuvenated Tories. Not wanting to lose their cash cow, Labour came clean about their financing of the Post and argued that they owned it and that it was Party property. A bitter row ensued between the political parties, with the Tories countering that it was a public company and so its ownership should transfer to them with the handover of political power.

The Conservatives eventually won the battle, but by the mid-1950s the British public had lost their appetite for political propaganda and post-War back-slapping. The circulation dropped as readers, keen to put the War behind them, switched back to the Times and the Telegraph and the advertising soon followed suit.

With the Post now losing money, redundancies were inevitable, and when high-profile journalists started defecting to other newspapers the Tories decided the time had come to privatise the International Morning Post. Several bids came in from abroad, but the Government was wise enough to realise that even though the Post's popularity was on the wane, the British public would still not be too impressed to see the patriotic, Union Jack-waving Blighty broadsheet being handed over to Johnny Foreigner.

In the end, it was agreed to sell to two Oxford-educated brothers with impressive war records who had made a fortune in property development and were looking to move into publishing. Robert and Graham Holland took control of the Post in early 1955 and immediately set about reviving its ailing fortunes. They began by running a front page editorial renouncing any political affiliations and vowed to bring readers "the best, most truthful, most exciting and most exotic news coverage from Britain and around the world". A hugely experienced editor was poached from Fleet Street and big name journalists posted to major cities around the world. There are rumours that Ian Fleming was approached for a senior position, but his James Bond novels had started to take off so he declined the offer.

To offset the increasing costs, scores of staff who were little more than civil servants were made redundant, amid much protestation from Downing Street and the unions.

The paper started paying good money for good, colour photographs and pushed out the existing staff photographers, who were better suited to weddings and the local press.

As exciting, unusual and fascinating tales started appearing in the Post from the plains of Africa, the bustling east coast of America and mysterious Russia and China, sales began creeping up again. People rediscovered international travel and a sense of adventure, advertisers dusted off their cheque books and by the end of the 1950s the Post was making serious money again.

Over the following decades it kept up with the times and the Holland brothers made sure it was always ahead of the pack. While their rivals were slashing investment costs, the brothers pumped millions into printing presses, computers, an unrivalled library and, latterly, digital technologies and an excellent website. While their rivals were culling staff in every department, the Post not only retained its best people and its foreign bureaus, but it paid and treated them well.

This meant that staff turnover was low and job vacancies were few and far between. If I wanted to get a contracted job at the International Morning Post, therefore, I would have to be damn impressive.

Heart-in-mouth and stomach in knots, I walked through the revolving door at the entrance of the newspaper's headquarters into an imposing reception area that would shame the lobbies of many five-star hotels. A continuous mist of water from an extravagant fountain in the centre of the marbled reception area obscured the faces of the three immaculate staff waiting attentively behind a thick glass desk at the far end of the room. There was an unnerving hush as I strode purposefully around the fountain, taking in the expensive-looking oil paintings that adorned the walls, the neat rows of that day's paper laid out on a long oak shelf and the bronze busts of Robert and Graham Holland. The two female and one male receptionist all watched my approach like hawks and by the time I stopped in front of them my hands were trembling.

"Good afternoon," asked one of the pretty young women with the insincere smile and dead eyes of a second-rate air stewardess. "How may I help you?"

"My name is Hannah Harker, I'm here to see William Laing. He's expecting me."

"One moment please."

The girl picked up a phone, punched in an extension number and looked me up and down with rather bored expression as she waited for an answer.

"Hello, it's front desk. I've got a Hannah Harker here to see William Laing...Okay, fine, good bye." She replaced the phone. "Someone will be down in a minute, please have a seat."

She gestured towards six black leather chairs arranged around a huge glass coffee table. I perched on the edge of one and flicked through a copy of the newspaper, counting every one of the next 14 minutes until there was a loud ping to my left and a lift door slid open.

An attractive brunette girl, probably about my age, dressed in a designer skirt and silk shirt walked towards me with a friendly smile and her hand extended.

"Hannah? Hi, my name's Pandora Male, I'm the newsdesk assistant."

"Good to meet you," I said, shaking her hand.

"Do you want to come up, I gather you've got something rather important to discuss. Even the lunchtime conference has been postponed for you."

"Well, that's a good sign, I guess."

We walked into the mirrored lift and after she pushed the number eight, the door eased shut and we travelled in silence up to the eighth floor.

When the doors opened again I stood rooted to the spot for a good few seconds as I took in the apparent chaos of the International Morning Post's newsroom.

"Get hold of that fucking arsehole now!" were the first words I heard as a young man in his shirt sleeves raced across the floor to grab a ringing phone and another reporter slammed down her phone with the words:

"Fucking wanker!" I hoped first impressions didn't count too much.

Everywhere people were walking, jogging or running around the random clusters of computers, scanners, photocopiers, television sets, recycling bins and other office paraphernalia. Jackets were slung carelessly over chairs and people hurled polystyrene coffee cups at non-existent bins while they sat on the phone with fingers in their ears to try and hear the caller over the din. My own ears were bombarded with snippets of bizarre conversations:

"...just stay down there until he fucking talks to you, or hits you..."

"...even by Japanese standards an eight-year-old serial killer is extreme..."

"...get him to call me the second he finishes with the Dalai Lama..."

"...Beijing are saying there's only 12 dead but Phil Greenways is at the station now and he's saying there are hundreds of casualties..."

Pandora noticed my expression and gave me a friendly smile.

"It's always dead like this at lunchtime; you should see them five minutes before deadline!"

"I'm not sure I do," I replied, following her through the madness to an office at the back of the newsroom.

She knocked once on the large wooden door and walked straight in.

"Becca, this is Hannah Harker. Are they ready in there?" She pointed towards another door at the rear of this office.

"Yes, of course." The slim, dark-haired woman smiled at me from behind her desk. "My name's Rebecca Carmody, we spoke on the phone."

"That's right, nice to meet you."

We didn't shake hands and she picked up her phone without dialling any numbers.

"Hannah Harker is here...Right away." She put the phone down. "They're waiting; in you go."

The two women seemed to shrink into the background, leaving me facing the imposing wooden door alone. With as much confidence as I could muster, I twisted the brass knob and pushed the door open to step into the office.

"Hannah? Please come in, sit yourself down." A tall man in an exquisite suit rose from his leather chair at the far end of a long conference table to greet me. He was well over six feet tall, broad shouldered and had a full head of silver grey hair. His face was tanned and lean, but with visible signs of stress, and his eyes made an instant judgement of what sort of person he thought I was. I instantly recognised him as Charles Courtney, editor of the International Morning Post.

"Thank you, Mr Courtney. May I say it's an honour to meet you sir."

"Jesus!" he roared with laughter and looked at the others around the table. "There's no need to bow and curtsey around here; I'm really just a hack like you at heart. Now, sit, I'll get some coffee brought in." As I sat he ordered four coffees over the intercom on the desk: one for him, one for me and one for each of the other two men in the room, who were eyeing me somewhat suspiciously. Courtney took care of the introductions.

"Right," he began, "Hannah, this is Bill Laing, our senior news editor here at the Morning Post."

I rose slightly from my chair to shake hands with the middle-aged man opposite me. Laing, dressed in a smart white shirt and navy tie, managed to fix a weary smile on his pale and haggard face. I couldn't tell if it had been a hard day or a hard life, probably both, but his jaded eyes and tousled hair suggested that this was a man to whom the expressions "nine-to-five" and "social life" meant absolutely nothing.

"Hi," he said simply.

"Nice to meet you, Mr Laing," I beamed at him.

"And this," said Courtney, pointing to a much younger man in a pinstripe suit, "is the guy who makes us spike all our best stories and hand lying politicians six-figure out-of-court settlements. Mr Clinton Cohen-Reed, the International Morning Post's senior legal adviser."

The lawyer didn't bother to offer a hand, but gave me a pleasant smile and quick hello.

Rebecca came in with the coffee and handed it out. She asked if anything else was needed, and when she was told there wasn't she left the room and Charles Courtney got down to business.

"So, Hannah, tell us what you've got."

"I have England footballer Jason Brady snorting cocaine with his pants around his ankles, begging for sex with two girls and bragging about faking an injury because he doesn't want to play a game up in Manchester."

I passed a pile of photographs, which I had printed from my digital camera, to Courtney and pressed play on the camera so they could see the video clip. As the video played, Courtney passed the photographs to the lawyer and Laing, whispering something in Cohen-Reed's ear and nodding slightly at his whispered answer.

After a short while the clip came to an end and Courtney looked up at Laing.

"Bill?"

The news editor looked at me, glanced once more at the photographs in front of him and spoke.

"When and where were these taken?"

"Saturday just gone at the Diamond Regency Hotel in Camden."

"Okay, I'm not going to fuck around. I take it the girls on the video and in these pictures are you and a sidekick and you've deliberately stitched this kid up to make some money."

Bang. My stomach rose, heart sank and I felt sick. The three men were all looking at me and I had to say something.

"Well, um, it's not quite as, like, bad as that. A friend of mine knows him from school, keeps in touch with him, and mentioned that he was a bit of a livewire, so I just did a bit of investigative journalism to see how true it was." The lies tumbled easily off my tongue once I got into the flow. "I watched him at a club a couple of weeks ago and he was acting up, groping girls, throwing champagne about, that sort of thing, so I put together a little, um, scenario, to see just how far he would go. The pictures, the video and the tape recording I have here are 100 per cent genuine. They haven't been doctored in any way, he wasn't drugged, apart from his own doing, and I have not been to any other newspaper, magazine, radio station or television network with this. If you want it, it's yours."

Courtney was smiling slightly as he turned to Cohen-Reed.

"Well, what do you reckon, Clinton?"

The lawyer, who had been making copious notes since I started speaking, put down his pen and looked up.

"Well, to cut through the legal jargon, which I know you so hate, I'd say this kid hasn't got a leg to stand on and we should be fine. I don't know his agent, but he'll have a good one, and a good lawyer, and they'll probably threaten us with everything from super injunctions to seven-figure lawsuits. They will argue that the boy has been a victim of entrapment, which he clearly is, but the evidence quite clearly shows that nobody forced him into any of this. We've got public interest on our side, the cocaine means he's broken the law, and he first approached these girls in a public place rather than a private residence. However the circumstances came about, we have video, audio and photographic evidence of one of the country's brightest young footballers, a role model to millions, snorting cocaine, waving his genitals around with a hand that's supposed to be injured and begging for kinky sex. Go to him for a comment of course, just so he's had a chance to defend himself, and get something from his club and the FA, but let them know that we've got so much evidence that we're not afraid to go to court. The kid's people will know we've got him and that legal action will be a big, expensive waste of time."

"Thank you, Clinton," said Courtney, looking satisfied. "Any comments, Bill?"

"Well, it's not really our sort of thing – I'd prefer to leave this lurid smut to the tabloids – but it's clearly something that's going to sell papers. The fact that there's cocaine involved and he's an England international make it stronger than the usual kiss-and-tell crap. I'll get some people putting in the calls now. I assume we'll be splashing with this tomorrow?"

"Unless Elvis and Marilyn turn up at Buckingham Palace in a flying saucer," Courtney said with a smile. "Get Hannah here to write the story and we'll look over it afterwards. Are you okay to stick around this afternoon, Hannah?" Courtney looked at me and I was almost wetting myself with excitement.

"That's fine; I'll stay as long as it takes."

"Great, well then, if that's all…" Courtney put his pen in his pocket and got ready to leave, but there was one very big issue outstanding.

"Um, Mr Courtney," I said, stopping him.

"Yes?"

"I was hoping I wouldn't have to ask, but surely for such a big, exclusive story there will be some sort of remuneration. I don't actually work for the Post, after all."

He smiled, nodded and sat back down, looking at the other two men.

"Well, perhaps we should get you on a contract one of these days, eh." He winked at Laing. "How much did you have in mind?"

"£50,000." I had no idea how much it was worth and just plucked a number out of the air.

He raised an eyebrow, glanced at his watch and said: "Way off target. £10,000."

"Come on, circulation was up three per cent last month, which means advertising revenue is up. It's worth at least £40,000."

"And perhaps in that same Press Gazette article you read that the

National Union of Journalists is planning to push for four per cent annual pay rises next month. £20,000, that's the absolute final offer. Take it or leave it." His eyes bored into mine and I tried to look reluctant about accepting £20,000 for a night's work.

"Okay, Mr Courtney. It's a deal."

"Great. Give your details to Rebecca on the way out and the paperwork can be sorted out. Now, I've got work to be getting on with and I want to see a draft of the Brady story in one hour so we can start laying the pages out. Bill, get as much reaction as you can and liaise with sport because it's going to be their back page tomorrow too. We'll splash on this and the Beijing train crash can go page one anchor and turn to two with pictures. Brady can run across four and five with pictures and sport can take out three or four of their pages with reaction and comment. Okay?"

"No problem. Come on, Hannah," Bill Laing looked at me.

I stopped in Rebecca's office on the way and clearly printed my details on a piece of note paper for her and made sure she knew we had agreed on £20,000.

"Not bad for a night's work," she commented, but in a friendly way. "Here," she passed me a tissue and I realised my brow was wet with sweat. "You can stop worrying now; you've done the hard bit."

"Thanks, I think that's probably the most nervous I've ever been."

"Well you must have had something pretty impressive to tell them because Mr Courtney cancelled a meeting with the Education Secretary to be here when you arrived."

"Really?" I couldn't suppress a big grin.

"Absolutely. Maybe if you play your cards right we'll be seeing you again."

"I really, really hope so."

In the newsroom my head was still swirling and I didn't really take in any of the other reporters Laing introduced me to. I sat at a computer and wrote out a very tabloid version of the sordid tale, which was swiftly and brutally edited by Laing to make it more suitable for the International Morning Post. Quotes were added which other reporters had got and the sports editor, an obese bald man called Dave something, kept wobbling over and arguing with Laing about what was going in news and what was going in sport.

At one point my mobile rang and I had to sprint to the toilet because it was Phil Crichton calling to find out where the hell I was. A major story was breaking and everyone was being called into the office. Just my typical fucking luck!

"I'm in court covering that big fraud trial," I lied through my teeth. "I can't leave now we're expecting a verdict. What's going on?"

"What fraud trial…never mind, do you remember that teenage girl who went missing a little while ago? Well she's been found raped and strangled in a skip just off the bloody High Street here in Rockingsworth."

"Jesus," I said shocked. This was massive news for Rockingsworth. It was also news, I realised guiltily, which would divert police resources away from the Venna Mansions investigation.

"I need you in here, Hannah," Phil persisted.

"Look Phil, I really need to get this court verdict. Let Simon have a crack at this one, I've had all the juicy stories lately."

Phil eventually relented when I promised that I'd spend all the next day working on the murder story, and I was able to hurry back to the Jason Brady story.

Sometime in the early evening Charles Courtney appeared and read through the story on my screen.

"Good," he said. "Let's start laying this out on the page."

I watched over a sub editor's shoulder as the front page of the following day's paper was pieced together and it nearly broke my heart when I had to ask that my name was not put on the story. I could have had a front page by-line on the International Morning Post, but if Tina Karageorghis, Phil Crichton or anyone else senior at the Informer saw it, I would probably lose my job there. With no job at the Morning Post in the immediate offing, I had to look on with a tear in my eye as the names of two other reporters were typed just under the banner headline: WORLD EXCLUSIVE: ENGLAND HERO'S DRUGS AND VICE SHAME.

It was gone 9pm by the time everyone was happy with the story and its layout and people started drifting off home. Bill Laing took the opportunity to sit at his desk with a coffee and I took the opportunity to collar him for a chat.

"Blimey, is it always that busy here?" I asked, falling dramatically into a chair next to him.

"Today's been fairly quiet," he replied, I'm not sure whether sarcastically or not.

"I guess it must be one hell of a tough job working here."

"Tougher than you could ever know," the seasoned journalist answered.

"I'd like to find out."

"Then maybe one day you will."

"I'd like to find out now, Bill. Do you think there might be a place for me here?"

Bill Laing put his coffee down and looked at me hard for several seconds, choosing his words very carefully, as he always did.

"Listen, Hannah, I'll be honest with you. Tomorrow we've got a good front page story thanks to you, but pretty girls pull this shit week in, week out for the tabloids. Okay, you hooked a bigger fish, maybe used a bit more panache, and you didn't have to fuck the guy, but it's not what journalism is about here.

"The tabloids, yes, they'll take that shit and pay you for it, but personally I'd spike the fucking lot of it. A kid with more money than sense wants to take drugs and get laid – so fucking what! Who wouldn't? Call me old-fashioned, out-of-touch, naïve, whatever, but I think journalists should be weeding out real bad guys and corrupt politicians, exposing injustice and poverty, fighting for the people and all the rest of it. That might sound like crap to you, but I've been reporting in one place or another for nearly 30 years and I've never changed that opinion, even when I was writing about pop stars taking drugs to impress the editor on my first national tabloid.

"I know I'm a dying breed, but it sickens me sometimes to see the way our news is being diluted into materialistic, showbiz bilge. Two hundred kids can get massacred in Africa but it will end up on page 12 because the first 11 pages are about a soap star getting pissed or a fucking game show contestant getting ditched by her boyfriend. Christ! The editors and programmers say they only put out what the people want, but that's bullshit. People love soap stars because they're told to; it's all they're given. And the media put that crap out because it's spoon fed to them by the PR machines and therefore cheaper, quicker and easier to get hold of than proper news.

"Most of the national papers employ little more than a skeleton staff of reporters these days because the bulk of their copy is neatly packaged and served up to them by the PR agencies, Government press offices, corporate marketing teams and the Press Association.

"The quality of these papers naturally suffers as a result, readership drops, advertising revenues drop, more staff are laid off, the quality suffers further, and so it goes on. I think the press as we traditionally know it is on the verge of extinction unless there is a radical change, but sadly I can't see that change happening because newspapers are simply commercial enterprises now and quality journalism falls well behind lower costs in the list of priorities."

Laing sighed wistfully at the end of his lament, and looked at me.

"You seem like a nice girl, Hannah, so I'll give you the benefit of the doubt. You've pulled this stunt with Brady to get a foot in the door of the big media circus, and you've done just that, so well done. Now though, forget that shit. Start going after stories and people that matter. I know you're after a contract here but I can't offer you one just like that; you need to come up here and do some shifts and we'll see how you get on. You've got brains, motivation and balls, so put them to good use. You'll have to put up with the shit jobs like everyone else that shifts, but stick at it and you never know - an opening might appear for you one day. Come up here on Saturday at 10am, ask for me, and we'll see if you can do this. If not, it's up to you. Enjoy the 20 grand, nail another footballer when it runs out and you can have a fun few years, until you lose your looks."

He paused for a moment, catching his breath, and looked at me for an answer. "Well," he said, "what's it to be?"

"I'll see you on Saturday."

Chapter 13

A final salmon slash of cloud bisected the gunmetal sky as a dark blanket dropped over central London to signal the shift from day to night. A sharp gust of wind sent a heap of litter and dried leaves scuttling along a quiet stretch of the south bank of the Thames and gave Liam King an excuse to put an arm around me.

"Are you warm enough?" he asked, gently pulling me closer to him.

"I'm fine," I replied, turning and smiling at him.

"There's a bench up ahead," he said, "let's sit for a while."

We sat on the wooden bench with the names of a hundred other couples scratched onto it and he put an arm around me as we looked across the Thames at the twinkles and flashes of light and fading outlines of the buildings lining the north bank of the river.

"I love it here," I said. "There's so much shit and everything going on across the rest of the city, but here it's just so peaceful and romantic."

"How does it compare with all the other places you've visited on your travels? You must have seen incredible things."

"Sure, I've seen bigger rivers, better views, certainly smarter benches, but this is home so I guess it automatically wins."

"And how does the company compare?"

"I've been with better…" I looked at him and laughed, pushing my shoulder against his and feeling a tingle as his fingers gently brushed the back of my neck. "I'm joking, Liam; there's nobody I'd rather be with more right now and I'm happier than I have been in months."

I leant in and kissed him once on the mouth, keeping my eyes open so I could watch his expression. He smiled and returned the kiss, so I let his tongue dart briefly into my mouth. Instinctively I pushed him away slightly and thought about making him wait a bit longer, but I decided that I didn't want to wait myself so I pulled him close and kissed him properly.

Seconds later an elderly couple walked past, their attempts at a disapproving look betrayed by smiles as they watched us passionately attacking each other on the bench. We needed a room, and quickly.

One week earlier I had woken up at 6am with the feverish anticipation of a young child on Christmas morning and dashed to the newsagent to buy up several copies of the International Morning Post.

As I entered the shop, I spotted a neat stack of papers on the counter and immediately recognised the headline and pictures on the front page. I grabbed half a dozen copies, threw a £5 note on the counter and ran home, the top paper creasing and flapping in the wind as I tried to read it on the go.

I had already skim-read the article by the time I got home and by the time I sat at the kitchen table with a cup of coffee I knew every word of it off by heart. It was perfect. Brilliant. The only thing missing was my name – and how I wished it wasn't.

I called Naomi, who was less than delighted to hear from me so early on her day off, and she promised to go out and buy the paper straight away. I desperately wanted to call my dad and tell him, but I knew I couldn't without also telling him how I'd got the story. Had he come from a tabloid background I might have risked it, but he was a true broadsheet man with deeply entrenched values and beliefs like Bill Laing so I knew he would be angry and, more importantly, disappointed if he knew the truth. I would have to wait for another time, another story, before I could tell him about my progress.

I had barely slept during the night and was having trouble keeping my eyes open, but I breezed into work with such alacrity that everyone must have thought I'd had an evening of mind-blowing sex. Phil was reading the Jason Brady story over Simon's shoulder and I was bursting to tell them that it was all me, but no one at the Informer could know, not while I was employed there at least.

After the buzz and excitement of being at the International Morning Post life at the Informer brought me back down to earth with a tedious bump and by the Wednesday I was tearing my hair out with boredom. I nearly went mad listening to the dismal soundtrack of scribbling pens, clattering keyboards and hushed telephone conversations. I looked around the office at the vacant faces and wondered if they were as agonisingly bored as me. Surely they must have been, but perhaps they were such empty people they didn't even realise it.

In fact, the only thing of any interest at the Informer was the arrival of Hugh Pennington, an 18-year-old who had just been recruited as a trainee reporter after finishing his A-levels.

Hugh was a short, red-haired boy with oily skin and a superiority complex that would make Genghis Khan seem shy. He strolled around the office as if surveying his empire and seemed to think he had a God-given right to speak to anyone he wanted however he liked. In less than a fortnight the editor had already received four complaints about him from outraged contacts.

Unfortunately, Hugh was a fairly typical local newspaper trainee reporter. Maybe it was because Hollywood portrays all journalists as aggressive, cynical, sneering bastards who only have to open their note-pads for Governments to topple, that the new reporters coming in to the paper thought that was the way to succeed.

In the past I'd heard 16-year-olds on work experience who could barely spell their own names, on the phone to the Chief Superintendent demanding that he reveal the details of undercover operations. The same kids would get all high and mighty with the Tesco press office, threatening that the multi-billion pound supermarket giant would make an enemy of the Rockingsworth Evening Informer if they didn't immediately supply a quote in response to a story about a trolley being dumped in the local pond.

The problem was that the kids coming through lacked any real guidance from seasoned professionals. The pay and conditions on a local news-paper are similar to those of an Asian sweat shop. You would join a local paper straight from school, college or possibly university and after two or three years of writing about school fetes and road accidents for £12,000 a year, anyone with any real talent would recognise the futility of it all and fuck off into public relations. The only ones who remained were the middle-aged alcoholics who knew they would be unemployable anywhere else, or the completely incompetent ones who also knew they would be unemployable anywhere else.

So, the bulk of the stories you find in the local newspaper are written by children, alcoholics or fuckwits. All of them are expected to write expertly and authoritatively about everything from the intricacies of NHS funding and development control policy to complex financial fraud trials and company reports. Often, they will be writing several stories about each of these things on the same day and will be expected to come at them from the strongest angle, regardless of what the facts or truth might be.

When a reporter finishes a story he files it - in other words emails it to an inbox of all the unedited stories. In the past, the news editor would go through and delete all of the crap stuff so that only the best stories were left. With so few reporters now and so much pressure to fill the paper, you would have to write something spectacularly libellous or brazenly false for it to get deleted. To be honest, if you wrote a story about Elvis Presley being spotted in a High Street café sitting on a giraffe wearing a rubber gimp suit, the news editor would most probably tell you to give the local councillor a call to try and corroborate it.

One of the first things you learn as a hack is that the local councillors will say absolutely anything you ask them to, and pose for absolutely any photograph you want, if it means them getting their name and face in the paper. The Rockingsworth traffic wardens were once issued with new uniforms that consisted of little black caps, black ties and long black trench coats with epaulets on the shoulders for wet weather. One of our local councillors was of Polish descent and the news editor suggested I contact him to see if he thought the new uniforms reminded him of Nazis and brought back the horrors of the Holocaust. I phoned the councillor and he whole-heartedly agreed, slamming the "heartless town hall bureaucrats" who sanctioned the "sickening and frankly anti-semitic" uniforms and calling for them to be changed immediately. He even posed outside his house clutching my Schindler's List DVD and shaking his fist at the camera. I sold the story to a national tabloid for £200 and the council withdrew the uniforms at great expense to the taxpayer.

You couldn't make it up, although we often did!

Anyway, poor Hugh Pennington was fired less than a month into his new job. Having grown up in a Daily Mail-reading household, his racial views were a little bit 18th Century. When we were on a job together one afternoon I told him that the deputy editor, Colin Anderson, was secretly an old-school racist who would often make inappropriate comments after a few beers, and that the way to get in with him was to subtly let him know that you were of the same mindset.

A few days later the whole office was out in the pub to celebrate a big scoop about a human trafficking gang operating in the district. Hugh, who had been quaffing brandies and was steaming drunk, leaned across the table to Anderson and, in full earshot of everyone, announced: "If it's apparently so easy to traffic people into this country, how hard could it be to start trafficking the blacks out?"

My earlier comments to Hugh about Anderson being a racist were completely untrue. In fact, he was actually married to a very nice Nigerian woman. As silence fell at the table and tumble-weed started rolling across the floor of the pub, Anderson very calmly looked at Hugh and said to him: "Finish your brandy, put your office swipe card on the table and leave. Your employment is terminated with immediate effect and if I ever see you again I will beat you into a fucking coma."

Thursday dragged interminably and after several hours of staring at the second hand creeping agonisingly around the office clock, I called Rockingsworth police station and asked Liam out for a drink that night.

Within minutes of meeting each other after work that night in a West Street bar we knew there would be no sex this time. A day spent compiling community news for an absent trainee had sapped my energy and enthusiasm and Liam was still pre-occupied with the deaths of the four boys in the Venna Mansions fire, and now the murdered schoolgirl as well. Each time he mentioned the fire my heart gripped tight and I wanted to run away from him, but this evening he spoke about it with exasperation and I realised he wasn't getting anywhere with the investigation. As I'd hoped as well, the death of the schoolgirl – 15-year-old Claire Dutton – had become the number one priority for the force and as a result less time was being spent probing the fire.

My nightmares about the fire were less frequent now and the demons with no faces didn't chase me in my sleep as often. My conscious self had fully put the incident behind me and hopefully it wouldn't be long now until my unconscious inner self was able to do the same and file it away deep in Hannah Harker's historical archives.

Liam and I only had a couple of drinks that night but our parting wasn't awkward because we both admitted that we weren't feeling up to it and would meet up again after the weekend.

On Friday Simon took me out for a long lunch, which was really nice, and I admitted to him that I had a shift on the Morning Post the next day.

"Oh wow, how did you get that?" he asked with sincere excitement for me.

"I just sent in my CV on spec and got a call last night asking me to come in. I'm really nervous."

"Jesus, you must have the most incredible CV known to man! Anyway, they'll probably be expecting you to be nervous, so just go up there and enjoy it, do what they tell you and who knows where it could lead."

"I'm not really expecting it to lead anywhere," I lied, "but it's a bit of extra money if nothing else."

"Come off it, Hannah. Everyone knows you're wasted here on the Informer. It was only a matter of time before you moved on."

"Well, we'll see. Getting one shift isn't the same as being offered a contract, but I appreciate your support and confidence in me, Si."

"Hey, I'm just keeping you sweet so you offer me something up there when you're a hotshot news editor in a couple of months."

We both laughed and I gave him the receipt from our meal so he could pretend I had been a contact and claim it back on expenses.

I stayed in by myself watching television on the Friday night and cracked open a bottle of wine to make sure I'd definitely get to sleep. It didn't work and I was still tossing and turning in bed at gone 3am, but I must have dozed off for a while after that because my alarm clock spitefully hauled me out of a deep slumber at 7am on Saturday morning.

I showered, put on my best suit and enough make-up to mask the black rings under my eyes and had some tea and toast.

I had already decided to drive into London in case I needed my car during the day so I set off at just before 8am to give me plenty of time to get to Clerkenwell. Inevitably, the central London traffic was a bitch, despite it being a Saturday, and as I swung my car into a space in the Morning Post's underground car park my watch read 9.50am. The ordeal of waiting in reception for someone to collect me was far less daunting the second time around and when a pleasant-looking young reporter called Adrian arrived to take me up to the newsroom I was eager to get started.

The Post didn't have a Sunday edition and I soon learned that Saturdays were therefore very quiet, with only a handful of people milling around and not looking particularly busy. I was pleased to see Bill Laing sitting at his desk, dressed again in a white shirt and navy tie, and as Adrian had simply left me by the lifts I decided to make a beeline towards him.

"Hello, Bill," I said warmly.

"Oh, hello, Hannah," he replied, looking surprised to see me. "Is it Saturday already? Shit, I really should go and see the wife, for all the good it will do."

I sat down at an empty desk near him and smiled, not sure what I should say to this, so I decided to say nothing.

"I take it you saw the paper the other morning?" He broke the silence. "The Jason Brady stuff went down very well with readers. One of the guys from the sports desk was telling me Brady's been suspended by his club pending an investigation. Word from the FA is that his England career has come to an early end as well and the police are considering charges over the cocaine."

"Well, he's only got himself to blame," I said, without the slightest twinge of guilt.

"Hmm," mumbled Laing, firing me a look to say "that's not really true, is it Hannah?"

"Anyway, what would you like me to do today?" I asked, quite keen to change the subject.

"Well, to be honest Saturdays are a bit dead round here and there's not a lot to do, unless something really big breaks that we need to work on for Monday. At noon Diane Petani, the weekend news editor, should be coming in so I suggest you keep an eye on the Press Association feed and the television and have a summary of what's going on ready for her when she gets in.

"Between you and me, and everyone else in the office," he added quietly, "Diane's a bit of a Dragon Lady and is known for lashing her tongue at the shifters, but I'll email her now and tell her to be nice to you."

"Thanks Bill," I grinned at him. "Will Mr Courtney be in today?"

"He might pop in for an hour after his golf, but don't expect him to stick around." He waved an arm at the few staff in the office. "This lot only come in on a Saturday so the editor sees them here, but once he's gone they'll be straight down the pub."

Five minutes later Laing left, telling me he was off to try and salvage his marriage. I asked about coming back for more shifts and he said to call on Monday.

I suddenly found myself alone at a big desk with no real idea of what to do. I hoped to Christ nothing big blew up before Diane Petani arrived. Across the wide office I spotted a tea-making area so I crept over to it, feeling like a trespasser as I tip-toed past sport, features and the foreign desk and filled a polystyrene cup with coffee.

I switched on the television nearest my desk and saw that BBC News was leading on the Prime Minister's visit to Washington for a thinly-disguised jolly-up with the President. They followed it with a short piece about a car bomb in the Saudi city of Jeddah killing six people, a plane crash in India which had just happened and a tribute to British film director Douglas Greenslade, who had died that morning aged 92 after a long battle with cancer. The sports segment previewed the afternoon's Premiership football fixtures – mentioning that Jason Brady would be absent from his team's squad – but I didn't bother noting any of this.

I turned my attention to the continuous feed of stories which came in on the news wire from the Press Association, but the only things of interest were more tributes to Douglas Greenslade and regular updates on the plane crash, which had apparently come down shortly after take-off from Delhi's Indira Gandhi Airport bound for Hong Kong with more than 250 people on board. I fell into a nostalgic daydream about the time I was at the same airport at 4am unable to find my ticket to Hong Kong because I had been blind drunk with Naomi when I packed my rucksack the night before. After a row with the guy on the Cathay Pacific desk, I ended up having to fork out more than £300 for a new ticket and blagged my way into the executive lounge to drown my sorrows on complimentary brandy and croissants.

My daydream ended as the lift doors at the end of the newsroom opened and I looked up to see an absolutely hideous woman wobbling towards me with alarming speed. She was about 40-years-old and I guessed that her weight in stone wasn't far off this figure either. Her hair was a tangled mousy mop which hung just above thick black eyebrows, which in turn hung above toad-like eyes. Her nose was pitted and red and thick black hairs covered the space between this and her twisted mouth, the lips caked in awful pink lipstick that did nothing to disguise the cracks and chewed skin. A gold scarf was tied around what I imagined to be a very thick neck and she was dressed in a white blouse, dark green jacket and long pleated skirt.

This was, I assumed, Diane Petani. She fell into a chair at the same desk as me, glanced at me with a frown and then rummaged about in her handbag. I returned to PA.

"What's the latest on the plane crash?" she suddenly asked.

I was engrossed in PA and assumed she was speaking to someone else as she hadn't yet acknowledged my presence.

"Hello? What's the latest on the plane crash?" she repeated, her voice laced with exasperation.

I looked up and saw she was staring at me.

"Oh, um, it was a 737 Cathay Pacific flight to Hong Kong coming out of Indira Gandhi in Delhi with more than 250 passengers on board. It looks like it has come down on a slum on the outskirts of the city. No idea of casualties yet and nobody is speculating about what happened or whether it might be terrorists. Eye witness quotes are just starting to come across on PA."

"Good," said the woman cryptically. She looked at something on her computer screen and smiled. "So, Hannah Harker is it?"

"Yes, nice to meet you."

"The girl behind Jason Brady's downfall, I gather."

"I did the investigation, yes."

"Investigation!" she scoffed. "What else is going on in the world today?"

I read out the list I had made earlier and offered to write Douglas Greenslade's obituary.

"No, I'll get one of the reporters to do it."

I shot her a nasty glare at this remark, but she wasn't even looking at me. Fucking bitch.

The phone rang next to me and Petani showed no interest in answering it, so I picked it up.

"Good afternoon, newsdesk."

"Who's that?" asked a male voice.

"Hannah Harker. Who is this please?"

"Harker? Harker…oh yes, Hannah Harker. The Jason Brady story. Good work, Hannah, we sold a lot of papers with that." Still, the man didn't identify himself, although the voice was familiar.

"Thank you, Mr…?"

"It's Charles Courtney, Hannah. Sorry, didn't I say so already?"

Oh shit. "No, sir, sorry. I didn't recognise your voice over the phone."

"Never mind. Is the Dragon Lady there?"

I sniggered. "Yes she is. I'll just transfer you sir." I looked at Diane Petani. "It's Mr Courtney for you, what's your extension please?"

"2017."

I transferred the call and went back to PA, listening as Dragon Lady said "yes" eight times and hung up with a sigh.

"Have you got a car?" she asked me finally.

"Yes, downstairs."

"Good. The Chief reckons the News of the World is splashing tomorrow on the Chancellor having an affair with a 25-year-old Treasury assistant. Nobody's having any luck tracking down his wife at home, but Charles has heard that her parents live down in Southend. Get down there and see what you can get. Maybe we'll turn up something fresh for Monday's paper."

"No problem, what's the address?"

She told me and asked me to leave my mobile number with her and keep in touch. I was in my car in less than two minutes.

The drive down to Southend along the A12 and then the A127 took nearly an hour and a half in the Saturday afternoon traffic and once I reached the seaside town I had no A-Z or sat-nav so it took me another 25 minutes of stopping and asking people before I found the address in the Thorpe Bay area. The address I had been given was of a large, white detached house with a long balcony and an even longer driveway, both of which were empty. I walked to the front door and pressed the bell, not in the slightest bit surprised when nobody answered. I took out my mobile and called Dragon Lady's direct line.

"Newsdesk!" she snarled down the phone.

"It's Hannah. I'm in Southend, but there's no one home at the address you gave me."

She tutted. "Are there any dogs?"

"I'm sorry?"

"Dogs. Did any dogs bark when you rang the bell? If there are dogs in the house, someone will need to turn up eventually to feed them and clean their shit up."

"There are no dogs," I assured her. "Shall I wait?"

"Yes." She hung up.

I went back to my car and waited, unable to even call any mates because my phone was low on battery. The minutes passed: half hour, 45 minutes, an hour, an hour and a half. Nothing. Fuck this, I thought, and called Dragon Lady back.

"There's still nobody been to the house," I told her. "What do you want me to do?"

"Keep waiting." She hung up again.

Darkness started to fall and lights came on in the houses around me, but still there was no sign of life at the address where the Chanceller of the Exchequer's wife's parents supposedly lived. A drizzle of rain dotted my windscreen and my stomach growled, reminding me that I'd not eaten since a couple of slices of toast at 7.30am. It was now approaching 6pm and I was starving, bored, pissed off and a very long way from Rockingsworth.

Once again I dialled Dragon Lady's number and this time it rang and rang before going through to voicemail. I called the main switchboard number of the Post and asked to be put through to Diane Petani.

"She went home an hour ago, madam," said the receptionist politely.

Fucking bitch!

I slammed my fist against the steering wheel and raced off for home, cursing and snarling so much I didn't see the speed camera on Southend seafront until it flashed in my rearview mirror. Fuck it!

After leaving the wooden bench by the Thames three days after this inauspicious start to my career at the Post, Liam and I ran hand in hand towards London Bridge station and waved down a taxi.

"You know any hotels, B&Bs or anything round here, mate?" Liam asked the driver.

"You've got The Summerfield a little way down Borough High Street. Apparently it's nothing fancy, but it's gentle on the wallet."

"Sounds perfect. Let's go."

When we got to The Summerfield moments later, Liam almost yanked me out of the taxi and into the nondescript hotel. We couldn't fill out the registration form quickly enough and we ran up to our room on the first floor pulling at each others clothes. It took Liam an age to unlock the door and when we eventually got in we slammed the door shut and I had my top off before it had even closed.

I was wearing a skirt and he pushed me back onto the bed and hitched it up around my waist. He rolled down my tights and I was already wet as he slipped my knickers off over my boots and pushed my legs apart. I could see him bulging through his trousers and was desperate to feel him inside me, but he knelt down, rested his hands on my knees and started licking furiously between my legs.

I mumbled that I needed a shower, but he ignored me and I groaned as he pushed his tongue inside me and I started fingering my clit with one hand, while pulling his head harder between my legs with the other, squeezing his face between my thighs. Writhing on the bed as an orgasm started to boil up inside me, I arched my back in readiness, but then he stopped.

"What the fuck are you stopping for?" I gasped.

He grinned, his mouth glistening with my juices, and took his trousers and boxer shorts down.

I held myself open and closed my eyes as he pushed himself inside me, then let out a little scream as he buried himself to the hilt and started pumping. I squeezed my tits and rubbed my clit as he built up a rhythm, then, just as I was about to come, he pulled out.

I moaned and reached for him and he slid back inside, then he leant forward and we squeezed each other so tightly that every inch of our bodies seemed to be touching. He used his hips to fuck me faster and harder and our panting became out-of-control as we urgently grabbed each other's flesh and kissed so hard it was like we were two animals trying to eat each other's faces. He pulled at my hair and I dug my finger nails into his arse as our sweating bodies bucked and jerked and I felt myself flooding with his come.

We laid there grunting and purring with his cock still throbbing inside me until our hearts and breathing returned to normal and he rolled off me. I could feel the sweat rolling off my body and I could feel his warm come inside me, and I laid there with my eyes closed enjoying every second of it.

After a while we peeled ourselves off the bed and washed each other in the shower. I made a mental note to stop at a pharmacy in the morning and then we climbed back into bed and made love again, this time much more slowly and gently.

Chapter 14

It was a rather bleak Friday morning three weeks later when two letters dropped onto my doormat as I got ready for work at the Informer. Seeing that they weren't the usual bills or credit card applications, I took them to the breakfast table and opened them over a cup of tea.

The first envelope contained a cheque for £150 from The Sun for the copy I had emailed John Townsend on the Venna Mansions fire. I was hit with a wave of guilt as I remembered how that money had been earned, and I decided I'd give it to charity! I ripped open the second envelope and a burst of excitement rocked me as I saw the mast-head of the International Morning Post at the top of the piece of paper inside, and I screamed out loud and jumped around the kitchen pumping my fists in the air when I opened up the cheque for £20,000! This one would definitely not be going to charity!

I paid both cheques into the bank on the way to work, not giving a damn about the strange look from the teller or the fact that I eventually got to the office 40 minutes late. At my desk I called Naomi to tell her I was taking her out that night, explaining that I didn't have another shift at the Morning Post until Monday night. Since the first wasted Saturday shift in Southend I had worked at the Post for each of the last three Saturdays and done some evening shifts during the week. It was bloody tiring and I was desperate for a good Friday night out, especially with 20 grand burning a hole in my bank account!

I treated Simon to a pub lunch and told him I'd got a cheque that morning for the shifts I had been doing at the Post.

"They seem to be really keen on you," he said.

"I've been a bit pushy to be honest, but the news editor, Bill Laing, seems to like me so I'm just trying to keep him sweet."

"What sort of things do you do up there?"

"Well, I told you the first shift was a complete waste of time doing that thing in Southend, but since then I've been going in during the week too, so it's been a lot busier…"

"Ah, so that's why you've had so many days off sick lately," he interrupted with a smile.

"Yeah," I admitted. "I've still had to do a lot of watching television news bulletins and sitting outside people's houses, but I've had a couple of little picture stories published and worked on a couple of page leads with senior reporters. A lot of them know me now and the editor always says hello, so I figure I must be doing something right."

"Definitely. It's a pity you can't break a really big story, then surely they'd offer you something permanent and you could hand in your notice here, not that I want to see you go, of course."

"Hmm." I smiled at him without really seeing him. His last comment had planted a little seed in my mind.

After work I drove home, packed a bag quickly and got the train up to Naomi's. I kept quiet about the £20,000 until she had changed out of her work clothes and we had got the tube into Covent Garden and found a bar packed with people full of the joys of Friday night.

"Okay, Hannah, I can't take the suspense any more," she said as I came back from the bar to our table with a bottle of champagne and two glasses. "What are we celebrating?"

I pulled an envelope from the pocket of my jeans and passed it to my best friend.

"Thank you for all your help," I said.

"What's this?" she asked, frowning at me as she opened the envelope.

She took out the cheque and stared at me in amazement.

"£5,000! What the fuck, Hannah!"

"I got a cheque from the Post this morning for that Jason Brady story. Twenty fucking grand, babe!"

"You're joking! Christ, I can't take all this money though, Han'. You did all the work."

"Oh shut up, you daft cow. You earned it and you're going to keep it."

She screamed and threw her arms around me in a big hug, squeezing me so hard she nearly cracked my ribs.

"Nay, you're crushing me to death," I gasped, laughing when she relaxed a bit. "Quick, let's neck this bottle and get some more."

We drank the first bottle in a little under 20 minutes and then we went into a toilet cubicle together and hoovered up a load of coke that Naomi had brought along. Back in the bar we were buzzing and I spent an obscene amount of money on cocktails while we took the piss out of two spotty City boys who had come in really drunk and were trying to pull us by telling us how much money they earned. They got £50,000 a year, apparently, and still wore ill-fitting suits and shoes with big buckles like schoolboys.

We ditched the geeks and went to a nearby, over-priced Italian restaurant where we pissed everyone off by swearing loudly, talking about drugs and generally being thoroughly obnoxious as we polished off another bottle of champagne, two big pizzas and a basket of garlic bread with cheese. We flirted outrageously with the camp Italian waiters, but they were more interested in giving us our bill than seeing our knickers, as Naomi kindly offered.

We paid up at the restaurant and went to a terrible Irish theme pub, where we thought we might be more welcome.

"It's shit in here," shouted Naomi very loudly at the bar as she unsubtly tipped half a gram of cocaine into her Guinness. "Let's go clubbing."

"We can't, we've got to go shopping tomorrow," I told her, taking a big gulp of the Guinness she had just thrust in my face.

"We don't have to stay all night. We could just go somewhere banging for a couple of hours."

"Yeah, I can just see you wanting to leave when some fit dealer is offering you free pills."

She grinned, knowing I was right.

"Okay then, how about a strip club?" she suggested.

"What? Why?"

"Why not? One of the girls from work dances at a place in Mayfair. Come on, it'll be a laugh, especially as we're loaded."

I took one look at the ruddy-faced drunk in a crumpled suit striding towards us and agreed.

A cab took us to Dover Street and the driver gave us a broad grin as we asked him to drop us outside The Mayfair Rooms. A single doorman dressed in the obligatory tuxedo didn't bat an eyelid as we staggered unsteadily towards the door and Naomi asked if we could go in.

"It's £50 each, first two drinks are free tonight, doesn't include champagne. The main show is free but tips are appreciated and if you want any private stuff you agree a price with the girls first."

"Brilliant."

Naomi took out five £20 notes and handed them to the receptionist as we walked through the main doors. Neither of us had coats so we walked straight down the tacky velvet stairs to the main room.

The last strip club I had been to was the accurately named Banana Bar in Amsterdam, where a short-lived boyfriend had taken me while we were at university. The Mayfair Rooms, by contrast, seemed a lot less sleazy and we were greeted at the bottom of the stairs by a stunning brunette girl in a black cocktail dress who introduced herself as Helena, led us to a dark table close to the stage and gave us a drinks menu with no prices on it. We both ordered vodka and cokes and when the hostess went off to fetch them, I took in the scene.

There were maybe 20 other tables all arranged around a long catwalk where a young black girl had just unclipped her bra and was crawling on all fours towards a table of 30-something Asian men dressed in very expensive suits. At the other tables were mostly middle-aged men also in suits, although there was one group of drunk lads, three tables with couples and one table right up against the catwalk where three women in their early forties sat clutching cocktails.

The girl on the catwalk was gyrating to cheesy dance music and one of the Asian guys leant in and said something to her. She stood up and smiled, dropped her thong to her ankles then kicked it playfully into the man's face, put her right hand between her legs and started masturbating unconvincingly. The man nodded, got up and walked towards the rear of the club and the girl hopped off the stage and followed him. As our drinks arrived I noticed that two of the women on the table near the stage were kissing.

"What do you think?" asked Naomi as a blonde girl swaggered onto the catwalk.

"Well, it's different, I suppose."

Naomi laughed.

"You need to get yourself back up to London; you're becoming a prude stuck down there in the sticks."

"I certainly am not," I countered defensively.

"Oh sorry, of course, there's the lovely Liam, isn't there. And how is it going with your friendly neighbourhood policeman?"

"Things are fucking great!" I said.

Since our night at the hotel in London we had seen a lot of each other and things seemed to be going fairly well, although I didn't for one minute think that he was "the one".

"What do you think he'd say if he knew you were in here?" she asked me.

"I don't know; it's not like I'm shagging anyone behind his back, is it."

Naomi didn't say anything, she just smiled as the blonde dancer disappeared backstage with one of the couples and a beautiful Chinese girl took her place wearing a rubber nurse's outfit.

She was gorgeous and I couldn't help but watch her as she slowly stripped down to her underwear, and then she caught Naomi's eye and came towards us.

"What are you doing?" I hissed at Naomi.

"Trust me, I know her."

"Hey, babe, how are things?" the stripper asked Naomi as she knelt in front of us.

"All good, Mei. You look smoking hot tonight; how about a dance backstage?"

The stripper was still gyrating in front of us and I felt a twinge between my legs as I had the other night when I was dancing with Naomi at Network. The girl was slim and had milky white skin, which was shining with oil. Her long, black hair fell straight down either side of a delicate face, and the pretty black lingerie set she was wearing left very little to the imagination. She had dark make up around her eyes, deep red lipstick and matching paint on her finger and toe nails.

"Sure," said Mei, "come with me."

I tried not to catch anyone's eye as I got up and followed Mei and Naomi across the club, through a curtain and into a private room, furnished with nothing but a small bar, sink and a futon.

Naomi and I sat next to each other on the futon as Mei poured us both fresh vodkas, handed them to us and then started performing a really, really sexy dance. She pouted at me coquettishly, walked to my side of the sofa, turned round on her heel and very slowly bent over to touch her toes. I was hot and had butterflies going crazy in my stomach, but my eyes were glued to the girl's firm white arse as it bobbed and jiggled just centimetres from my face, the thin black ribbon of her g-string wedged deeply between her cheeks and revealing a lot more than I was comfortable with.

Mei then knelt down in front of Naomi and although I knew that she had slept with girls before, I found myself gawping with amazement as she leant forward, unclipped Mei's bra and starting sucking her nipples.

The Chinese girl licked her lips and looked over at me with a wicked twinkle in her eyes.

"Take off your jeans," she said.

"Excuse me?" I swallowed hard.

"Take down your jeans."

Naomi was watching me, a smile creeping across her face, and I hesitated. I'd never done anything like this before and I wondered if I should, but the dilemma didn't last long though. Because of the combination of drink, drugs and my ongoing mission to try different things, anything really out of character to cure my boredom, I obeyed. I unbuttoned my jeans, slipped them off and tossed them on the floor.

Mei crawled over to me on all-fours, knelt between my legs then slipped her thumbs under the elastic of my knickers and peeled them off.

Her soft hands gently pushed my thighs apart and I closed my eyes as her lips excruciatingly slowly crept up the inside of my legs.

By the time she reached my crotch I was already sopping wet, and I pushed my hips towards her as she rolled her tongue up and down the length of the slit before poking it inside me.

Any inhibitions evaporated as she expertly used her mouth to bring me to orgasm and I watched through misty eyes as Naomi crawled behind Mei, pulled her thong to one side and started to finger her.

"I don't want you to do anything to me," I murmured to Naomi, conscious of our friendship despite my incredible horniness.

"Fine," she said. "Lay on your back and Mei will 69 you."

Trembling with excitement, trepidation and nerves I uneasily did as I was told, then watched Mei pull off her underwear and lower herself inch by inch onto my face. The smell and feel was incredible as she straddled me, her sticky, oiled thighs warm against my face and her pussy wet and slightly prickly on my nose and around my mouth. An orgasm tore through me even before she leant forward over my body and started fingering and licking me. I let myself go and dug my fingers into her delicious buttocks and pulled her towards me, grinding my nose and mouth deep inside her as she did the same to me.

My head was spinning and I became so lost in the moment that I didn't even fight when I felt another pair of hands – presumably Naomi's – running over my thighs and arse and lips kissing my body. I moaned loudly and starting squirming uncontrollably as the fingers and tongues sent me over the edge and I came over and over again. I then collapsed, exhausted, and lay there purring while Naomi played with my hair and Mei planted tender kisses on my legs and stroked my shaking body.

Chapter 15

Naomi and I woke up in the same bed quite early the next morning, my head in a considerably worse state than hers. Naomi was just wearing knickers, but I had pyjamas on and I was almost certain nothing further had gone on between us once we'd got home.

"We're cool," Naomi croaked, reading my thoughts.

"Sure?" I twisted my head on the pillow to look at her.

"Quite sure. Now get your ugly butt out of my bed and get showered; I'm going to put on some tea and make bacon sarnies."

"Bitch!" I grinned at her, pecked her on the cheek and rolled out of bed, a little bit too quickly for my poor head.

In the shower I replayed the events of the night before with Naomi and Mei.

Initially I felt extremely uneasy about the whole thing and my stomach tightened when I thought about exactly when I had done. Aside from the stupid little game with Jenny at work and briefly kissing a girl in a club when I was at university, I'd never entertained the idea of having sex with another girl before, much less my best friend and a stripper. The feel, taste and smell of Mei were vivid in my mind and I was trembling a little in the shower.

Then I thought about what I'd promised myself about ignoring convention and doing new things which would push the boundaries and rekindle the fire and passion in my life. Quickly the uneasiness faded and I found myself becoming horny again. I twisted the shower head so it was blasting a strong warm jet up between my legs and closed my eyes. I was suddenly back in the club, Mei straddling my face while fingers and tongues probed me. The jet of water was getting me excited and I toyed with my clit as the memories took shape in my mind. My breathing was getting heavier and I felt a bit dizzy, so I squatted down in the shower and eased two fingers into myself, quickly bringing myself to the verge of orgasm. I desperately tried to concentrate on Mei, but it was Naomi's face which kept replacing it and I guiltily let it remain, coming hard as I held an image of her running her tongue over my inner thighs.

I had to steady myself as I climbed out of the shower and stood in front of the mirror. My face was flushed and there was a sparkle in my eyes. I smiled at myself, towelled dry and went to join Naomi in the lounge, purposely avoiding eye contact with her for a while.

After the shower and food I started to recover and by 11am the Saturday morning television was annoying us both so we went out and caught the tube down to Bond Street. Neither of us had ever gone shopping with serious money to blow before, so when we walked into Selfridges it took me quite a while to pay £340 for a gorgeous black Karen Millen jacket. Naomi's first purchase of the day was a pair of £850 leather boots from Gucci, and after that the floodgates opened. We bought each other matching diamond pendants from Tiffany's at £1,800 a go then I treated her to a more modest £400 skirt from Vivienne Westwood and she bought me a nice pair of Armani jeans for a couple of hundred pounds.

Feeling giddy with excitement, we skipped to Oxford Street and blew a load of money in HMV then walked to Piccadilly and had tea followed by cocktails at The Ritz.

I wasn't really up for clubbing in the evening so we bought a couple of bottles of Bollinger and took them back to Naomi's, where we called out for a Chinese (food, not Mei), tried on our new things and sat through a couple of girlie films.

It was the next morning as I was reading the Sunday Times in Naomi's lounge that a plan started to take shape in my mind. It was a plan, I hoped, that would cement my position at the International Morning Post.

Firstly, I read a short story in the foreign section about a Malaysian guy called Mazlan Azmil. Mazlan, it said, ran a company which supplied low-tech military equipment – bullet-proof vests, helmets, gas masks and goggles etc – to legitimate armies across South East Asia from his headquarters in Kuala Lumpur. The story said, however, that anti-terrorist police had just raided a confirmed Jemaah Islamiyah training camp 100km south of the Indonesian capital Jakarta and seized a huge amount of automatic weapons, grenade launchers, ammunition and two medium-range surface-to-air missiles. A badly concealed paper trail allowed police to trace the weapons back to a warehouse in Singapore owned by Mazlan. He had already been questioned by police in Kuala Lumpur, but it was unlikely that anything firm could be pinned on him yet, so investigations were continuing.

The story concluded by briefly explaining that Jemaah Islamiyah (JI) was believed to be the South East Asian arm of Al Qaeda. Among the group's many atrocities was the Bali bombing in October 2002, which killed 202 people, the Australian embassy bombing in Jakarta in September 2004 which killed nine and injured many more, and the bombing of the JW Marriot and Ritz Carlton hotels in Jakarta in July 2009, which also killed nine and injured scores more.

The second story I read which got me thinking was about the British Secretary of State for Defence, Gerald Maybank. Maybank was only 37 but he was a close personal friend of the Prime Minister and after winning a previously safe Opposition seat in the north east at the age of just 33, he had shot up through the political ranks and was quickly handed a Cabinet post. During the last reshuffle it had been tipped that the Prime Minister might give him the coveted Foreign Secretary's position, but although that didn't happen, it was still a great coup for a man of his age to be entrusted with the defence role and many people within and outside the party believed that he had the potential to be a future Prime Minister. I'd never met the man, but from seeing him on television I found him smug and smarmy with a single-minded obsession for work that meant he didn't even have time for a wife or long-term girlfriend. His only diversion from politics that I knew of was that he was the patron of Children Orphaned by War, the humanitarian charity which Naomi worked for as a press officer, but I suspected that was merely to give him a more voter-friendly image.

The Sunday Times article explained that he was due to announce who had been chosen to supply the British Army with body armour for the next five years - a contract worth hundreds of millions of pounds and a lot of prestige – when he returned from a conference in Bangkok the week after next.

I closed the paper thoughtfully as Naomi came in with two cups of tea.

"Fancy going down the pub for a roast in a bit?" she asked.

"Mmm, sounds good. I'd like to pick your brains about something anyway."

We drank our tea then strolled down to the pub in pleasant sunshine. Neither of us fancied drinking, so we both ordered orange juices with our roast beef.

"So, what did you want to pick my brains about?" asked Naomi as we sat down in a quiet corner.

"What do you know about Gerald Maybank?"

"The defence guy? Our patron? Not much really. Met him a couple of times and just thought he was a bit of a creepy bastard; not pervy, just something kind of nasty about him. Why?"

"I've got an idea to properly nail him and get an amazing exclusive story for the International Morning Post."

I told her about the two stories I'd read that morning, but she just looked at me with a puzzled expression as our dinners arrived as we started to eat.

"So what's the connection between the British Secretary of State for Defence and a Malaysian arms dealer?" she asked.

"I'm going to get pictures of Maybank accepting a brown paper bag full of bank notes from Mazlan just before he announces who's got the army body armour contract."

"Oh right. Of course." Naomi shook her head in disbelief. "How exactly do you plan to do that, Hannah?"

"Well, I figure it won't be too hard from the Mazlan point of view. I call his office in KL and pretend to be one of Maybank's aides. I tell him that if he gets himself up to Bangkok and makes a very, very discreet £500,000 cash donation to Children Orphaned by War, he may well land the British Army contract."

"Jesus, Hannah," Naomi interrupted. "Don't you think you're going a bit over the top with all this? You're really planning to start knocking terrorists out of money? And what the hell has Maybank ever done to you to warrant this?"

"Oh, don't be so melodramatic. You said yourself that Maybank is a creepy bastard, and if he's stupid enough to fall for whatever ruse I come up with then he's only got himself to blame. What I can't figure out yet is how I'm going to get him to take the money. If I'm going to get the right sort of pictures to make this story work then I really do need him to take a wad of cash from Mazlan and pocket it."

Naomi sighed: "Well, I guess I can ask a few discreet questions at work tomorrow. There may be something that somebody knows about the guy which will give you a bit of inspiration."

"Great. I've got a shift at the Post on Tuesday so I'll do some subtle probing myself. I'm sure the political correspondents there must have some juicy gossip about him that they would love to print if they had enough evidence to prove it. I just can't believe that this guy is as saintly as everybody seems to think he is. Everyone has skeletons in their closest somewhere."

"Are you going to try and get them to send you to Thailand to cover this conference in Bangkok then?"

"No, I'm going to go to Thailand off my own back and cover the conference as a freelance job. That way I can offer the story to the Post in return for a contract. If for some reason they say no, I can sell it to another paper and pick up another hefty cheque."

"Christ, it still sounds fucking crazy and dangerous, babe."

"I'm not going to jump in without careful planning."

"But this is serious stuff; you don't know what these type of people are capable of doing."

"Trust me." I winked at her.

We finished dinner and went back to Naomi's, where I packed my case and got the train home.

I had work to do.

Chapter 16

My Monday morning idleness at the Rockingsworth Informer plunged to new depths the next day as I managed to go the whole day without writing a single word of copy.

Although nothing was said, people must have been baffled by my lack of productivity because I spent the whole day scribbling in my notebook and making hush-hush phone calls.

Before I booked flights or anything I wanted to make sure that Mazlan was at least interested and prepared to travel to Bangkok. I got the phone number for his company from the internet and nervously went to the public payphone near the office armed with a pocketful of pound coins.

Malaysia was eight hours ahead of Britain so it would be early evening in Kuala Lumpur, but I figured that Mazlan would still be in the office dealing with the fallout from the investigation into his company.

The first time I dialled the number it didn't work, but I tried again and there was a long pause, then a crackle and then the phone started ringing. My heart beat quickened.

"Asia Military Supply Corporation, good evening," said a thickly-accented receptionist in English.

"Hello, may I speak to Mazlan Azmil please."

"Not here."

"It's very important that I speak to him."

"He's not here."

"It involves a lot of money," I persisted.

There was a pause on the end of the phone and then a different male voice said: "Who is calling?"

"I'm not going to say on an unsecure line, but I am calling from London." Pause. "One moment."

I heard footsteps, then people speaking hurriedly in Malay. Someone eventually picked up the phone again.

"Write down this number and call back in exactly three minutes." The man reeled off a long number, which sounded like a mobile number.

I jotted it down, waited exactly three minutes, and dialled.

"This is Mazlan Azmil, who is this?" answered a deep, suspicious voice.

Earlier I had called the Ministry of Defence press office and got the name of a girl there in case Mazlan decided to check me out later. The girl whose name I chose was just starting a three week holiday.

"Hello Mr Mazlan, my name is Gemma Barnes and I work for Gerald Maybank, the British..."

"I know who he is," Mazlan interrupted impatiently. "What do you want?"

"Are you aware that he will soon decide who is to supply the British Army with body armour for the next five years?"

"I had heard, but what of it? I don't suppose he's going to offer it to someone with suspected links to Jemaah Islamiyah, or haven't you seen the news?"

"We are aware of the story, but it's not very big news in Britain, Mr Mazlan. What we do know is that giving the contract to an Asian firm will be a lot cheaper than paying a European or American supplier, and that will be very favourable to British taxpayers in this age of austerity. Because of this, so long as there are no further revelations about a connection with JI in the next few weeks and you are able to make the story go away, Mr Maybank is willing to overlook the recent negative media reports, especially if your company were to perhaps make a very discreet contribution to his favourite charity."

"And how do you propose I make the story go away?"

"Make a public statement to categorically deny any involvement with JI. Make a claim that you have been set up by a rival company to try and put you out of business. Say that your managers at the Singapore warehouse have gone rogue and were acting in cahoots with this rival company. You figure it out, Mr Mazlan, and if you're convincing enough then there's no reason for you not to be awarded the contract."

"So long as I make a 'discreet contribution' to Maybank, is that it?"

"You scratch his back and he'll scratch yours."

"I don't trust telephones," he said, cautiously but not dismissively.

"We can meet," I said. "Just you and I. We will be coming to Bangkok the week after next for the military conference."

"I'm not convinced by you, Miss Barnes. Why me? There are other military suppliers in Asia."

"Of course, and if you decide this isn't for you then we won't hesitate to make contact with them. It was felt by Mr Maybank, however, that given your no doubt undeserved link to JI you may be more willing to make a generous contribution to his charity and enhance your chances of winning the contract. The support of the British Government and the award of an extremely prestigious defence contract would surely go a long way towards quashing all of this unfortunate speculation and rumour."

"And how do I know you are who you say you are?" he replied. "An unannounced phone call and a very suspicious proposition make me extremely uneasy, particularly with most of the security services from across the region looking through my keyhole at the moment."

"Check me out; but I'm sure I need not tell you that discretion is rather important in this matter. Mr Maybank and I have a very close working relationship and this proposal is not something we have been shouting about, as I'm sure you understand."

Mazlan laughed sharply. "Okay, so say I was interested. When and where in Bangkok would we meet?"

I gripped the receiver tightly. The greedy fish had swallowed the hook.

"Nine days from today, the 18th, at 4pm local time in the Authors' Lounge at the Mandarin Oriental Hotel."

"And how much of a 'contribution' is Defence Secretary Maybank expecting for his charity?"

"£500,000. Cash."

"And how would the payment be made, assuming I'm even taking you seriously."

"We will discuss the details at the Oriental. How will you let me know if you are going to be there or not?"

"I won't. You won't know if I am going to show up or not until 4pm on the 18th. That's your risk."

"That won't leave us very much time to contact other suppliers before the announcement of the contract award is due. I need some advance warning." I felt I had to be firm.

"To hell with you!" he snapped, taking me by surprise. "You expect me to take a huge risk on the back of one unannounced phone call from a complete stranger? If I am there, I am there, if not, that's your problem. If you think that is unsatisfactory then we can end this matter right now."

"Okay, fine," I said with a defeatist tone, letting him think he had won the upper hand, and with it some security. "I will be there regardless and I – we – hope you will be too. Thank you very much for your time, Mr Mazlan. I look forward to meeting you."

I put the phone down without waiting to hear if he replied or not. I was sweating inside the phone box and my legs were shaking, but I was also buzzing.

On my way back up to the office Naomi called me on my mobile.

"I don't know if this will be any use to you," she said, "but I've done a bit of gentle probing about Maybank and apparently he likes a drink if he thinks nobody important is watching. He's also quite partial to a game of cards, again depending on the company. Apart from that though, he's squeaky clean."

"Who did you get that from?" I asked her, my mind already putting the information to work.

"One of the directors here is quite pally with him. But we've not had this conversation, Hannah, okay?"

"Okay. Thank you, sweetheart, I'll give you a bell a bit later."

Back at my desk I booked myself on a British Airways flight to Bangkok on the 17th and reserved a suite at the luxurious Oriental Hotel for four nights. Even if Mazlan didn't show up and this all turned out to be a massive waste of time, at least I could live it up for a few days in the Thai capital.

After work that night I stayed at Liam's place and learnt some disturbing news. The Venna Mansions fire still wouldn't go away and now an anonymous caller had rung the police to say they had seen a young woman loitering suspiciously near the flats just before the blaze. Liam had called the paper while I was away from my desk and asked Phil to put a story in asking for this witness to come forward to help put together an e-fit of the woman. He was even thinking of approaching the BBC to see if they would put out an appeal on fucking Crimewatch! He told me this just as we got into bed, and then obviously didn't understand why I suddenly lost my appetite for sex.

"I've got a headache," I whined. "Today was shit at work."

"You don't have to do anything; just lie on your back and I'll do all the work."

"Really, Liam, not tonight. Let's just sleep."

"How about a massage then?"

I stormed off to the bathroom in a huff and didn't go back until I was certain he had got the message, which seemed to always take quite a while with him. Naomi was always teasing me about him, asking how the "village bobby" was, and as I sat on his toilet waiting for him to fall asleep I found myself admitting that the thrill of our relationship had already worn off and my big, strong cop was actually quite a bore.

Chapter 17

The Boeing 747 shuddered and rocked as it dropped through a dense bank of storm clouds on its descent into Bangkok's international airport, Suvarnabhumi.

There were a few gasps around the cabin and fingers dug into armrests, while a sudden calm washed over me and a smile stretched the corners of my mouth.

I'd always had this morbid fascination with being killed in a plane crash, to the point where I almost hoped this would be the way I'd die. I liked the idea of going out spectacularly in a way that wasn't my fault. If I smashed my car into a wall my final moments would be filled with seething anger at myself for being stupid and careless. But nearly seven miles above the ground, sitting in a pressurized metal tube that was being controlled by someone I'd never seen and whose name I'd not even been able to catch during the pre-flight announcements, I couldn't possibly be to blame if something went wrong. I would be free to savour all those feelings, sensations and emotions of death that nobody has ever really been able to accurately describe to us.

Many people say they want their death to be instantaneous, or they want to slip away peacefully in their sleep. Why the fuck would you want that? These are the last moments of your fleeting and largely inconsequential existence; surely you want to cherish them, even in excruciating pain?

The older we get the less opportunity there is for new experiences, but this was the ultimate experience, the summit of our life. Surely nobody will ever feel more alive than at the precise moment they realise they are staring death in the face. What the hell was there to be scared of? I couldn't wait for it.

There was always something so inviting about the fluffy, bouncy-looking clouds outside the little oval window of an aeroplane. The pure white ones were the most appealing, but even when they were smudged with black the sky just looked like a giant wastepaper basket that had been filled with cotton wool balls by some glamorous Goddess in the heavens as she wiped away her mascara.

I was confident of being able to block out the terrified shrieking and gurgling of my fellow passengers as the fuselage fractured at 35,000ft and we found ourselves trying to suck up air that had a temperature of -55°c and just 20% of the oxygen it would at sea level.

I imagined a great rushing noise as I pulled my safety belt tighter and window seat 36F, along with passenger Harker, began tumbling through the frozen azure sky, deftly dodging shards of debris, flapping suitcases and blue-faced sun-seekers.

The clouds would probably be a damp and misty disappointment as I plopped through them, focussing to retain consciousness as hypoxia set in, but when I emerged from the bottom layer the twinkling, shimmering surface of some exotic ocean would be rolled out before me like an expansive welcome mat.

After my terminal splash and more leisurely peregrination to the seabed – where I would provide nourishment to countless mammals, fish and plankton for several weeks – my memory would forever be enshrined as one of the 428 people who lost their lives somewhere between the Bay of Bengal and the Andaman Sea in the British Airways 747 disaster.

Following the international shock as grim-faced correspondents related the final moments of the aircraft and its occupants on the BBC, CNN and other channels, there would be the more poignant personal tributes. My father and former colleagues would recite tearful eulogies to sit alongside my black and white by-line photo in the Rockingsworth Evening Informer and, hopefully, Charles Courtney would dictate a few sentences to his PA about how the tragedy had robbed journalism of my youthful verve and precocious talent. This, I thought, would sit nicely as a sidebar on the cover of the International Morning Post next to the main article detailing the crash itself.

My draft obituaries were rudely curtailed as the captain ordered the cabin crew to prepare for landing and as the runway came into view below me I set the daydream to one side. I would no doubt return to it on my next flight.

There was no delay on the ground as I eased through customs and my case was one of the first to appear on the carousel. As I stepped into the chaos of the arrivals hall I panicked for a moment when I couldn't see the name "Hannah Harker" on any of the placards being held up by hotel drivers, touts and tour reps, but then I remembered I was looking for "Gemma Barnes", the name of the MoD press officer whose identity I was borrowing for the next few days. I cursed myself for being so forgetful, even after such a long flight. I would have to be a damn sight sharper in future if I had any hope of pulling this off.

I spotted a uniformed Thai holding up the name "Gemma Barnes" on an Oriental Hotel placard so I went to him and let him take my case and guide us through the deafening, stinking, dazzling mass of stereotypical airport predators to the car park.

Within seconds of being outside I remembered what it was that I hated about this part of Asia: the heat. It was a relentless, energy-sapping humid heat that hugged you every moment you were outside, and every moment inside if you were not fortunate enough to have air-conditioning. I suddenly had a vivid flashback of laying awake all night in a box-like dorm, the mattress of the dirty bed wet with my sweat as a tiny wall fan lazily stirred up the stale hot air and forced it against my body like a duffel coat.

By the time we reached the driver's BMW my face, back and front were rolling in sweat, yet within moments of being shut in the car the air-conditioning was blasting me and I was soon so cold I wondered if perhaps I was deliberately being cryogenically frozen for the half hour journey to the Oriental.

My sense of adventure soon returned though as I was whisked along the seemingly rule-free roads in my refrigerated chariot, smiling at the thousands of things that had made me smile on my first visit to Thailand. Green and yellow taxis blasted their horns at the noisy tuk-tuks and mopeds that weaved suicidally through the gridlocked streets, while pedestrians walked calmly into the road and waltzed through ten lanes of traffic like they were strolling through an empty field. Gem stores, restaurants and gleaming glass tower blocks flashed by while the less fortunate sat eagerly on the pavement with a handful of pathetic trinkets by their feet, which they hoped might appeal to the thousands of farang – Westerners – who trawled the streets. The golden cones of historic temples sat incongruously among the ever-proliferating department stores and impoverished children with their hands out lived alongside wealthy expatriates, transsexuals, businessmen, drug dealers, backpackers, touts, illegal immigrants, police, tradesmen and just about every other person you might expect to come across, not to mention the countless people who wouldn't look out of place in a circus.

Although I couldn't experience it yet with the windows rolled up in the Mercedes, I knew the smells outside would be equally intoxicating. I think each country has its own unique smell, usually a wild blend of indigenous and foreign elements that form part of its identity, and Thailand was no exception: Tuk-tuk fumes, spicy food at roadside stalls, jasmine, sweat, incense, construction work, festering drains and a million other urban perfumes all contributed to the overpowering "Eau de Bangkok".

By the time we turned off Thanon Charoen Krung and approached the Oriental Hotel on the banks of the Mae Nam Chao Praya river, I was bubbling with excitement.

When I last visited Bangkok with Naomi we stayed in a 100 baht a night dorm on Khao San Road with a heroin addict from Edinburgh and a Thai man who was halfway to becoming a Thai girl. We wore grubby T-shirts and flip-flops and we'd taken it in turns to go out to Burger King because we were terrified that one of our suspect room mates would steal all our gear.

This time, however, I strode into the tall, opulent lobby of the Mandarin Oriental wearing a smart designer shirt and skirt and approached the reception desk with more self confidence than a French supermodel.

"Good afternoon, my name is Gemma Barnes; you have a reservation for me."

The receptionist gave me a warm smile and confirmed that I was indeed expected. After inquiring about my journey he ordered my private butler to carry my case to the Noel Coward Suite in the Authors' Wing – the only part of the original 19th Century hotel that still remained - along with a bottle of Bollinger, fresh fruit and flowers.

My spectacular suite actually took my breath away – I would have to choose which of the two four-poster beds to sleep in – and after texting a photo to Naomi I showered away all traces of my journey from London, slipped on a thin cotton dress and went down to the hotel's Riverside Terrace to soak up the atmosphere. I resisted the urge to ask the waiter for a Screaming Orgasm and instead ordered a vodka and tonic as I sunk into a chair overlooking the river and fixed a broad grin on my face.

The Mandarin Oriental Hotel is, very probably, Thailand's top hotel. Singapore has Raffles, Hong Kong has the Peninsula and Bangkok has the

Oriental. As a writer myself it pleased me to think that the likes of Graham Greene, Joseph Conrad, Noel Coward and W. Somerset Maugham had stayed at this famous old place as they explored Asia, finding inspiration for novels like Heart of Darkness, The Quiet American and countless other classics which I had eagerly devoured as I made my own way through this incredible continent.

I picked up the English language Bangkok Post and found a small piece on the forthcoming conference, which said that Gerald Maybank was due to arrive tomorrow, the 18th, and would spend a day as the guest of the Thai Prime Minister before the conference got underway on the 19th.

Three days earlier I had called Mazlan again in Kuala Lumpur and told him that if he was planning to make our appointment in Bangkok it was vital that he managed to book himself a place at this conference. He seemed surprised to hear from me and mentioned that he had run a few checks on me. Even though he was on the other side of the world at the time I had frozen with fear, until he revealed all he had done was call the Ministry of Defence and ask for Gemma Barnes. He was put through to the press office where a colleague told him that Gemma was on holiday for three weeks, so he had hung up, apparently satisfied.

He had been sceptical about getting a place at the conference at such short notice, particularly with the tight security arrangements and his current predicament regarding Jemaah Islamiyah, but he cleverly hinted to organisers that he wished to make a sizeable contribution to one of the leading landmine clearance charities and when I called him back again the next day he told me places had been allocated to him and "two associates", whoever the hell they were going to be.

Everything seemed to be falling into place as far as Mazlan was concerned. As for Maybank, he was out of my hands, but I hoped Mazlan would be able to take care of that for me.

My vodka and tonic arrived and as I sipped it in my comfortable armchair in this fabulous hotel I reflected on how excited and happy I was, and how things finally seemed to be looking up for me. I sunk another four vodkas and watched the river scene of noisy longtail boats bouncing on the wake of Chao Phraya River Express passenger boats as the sun set and painted a stunning red and orange masterpiece in the sky, then went up to my room and had a fitful night's sleep as I battled with jetlag and a billion thoughts bouncing around my head.

The following morning I went downstairs for breakfast and almost collided with a small group of balding men looking thoroughly miserable and uncomfortable in thick suits. At the centre of the group was Gerald Maybank, tall and arrogant looking, with narrow eyes focused ahead of him and a pugnacious jaw jutting forward. I ducked behind a pillar, even though he had no idea who I was.

It had never occurred to me that he would be staying at the same hotel, but if Mazlan saw him there that afternoon – assuming he even showed up – it would add credence to the fact that the two of us were together. I was planning to strongly hint to Mazlan that Maybank and I were an item and together we had cooked up this scam with the body armour contract. I was going to tell him that I had not been able to come to Bangkok in an official status so I had taken three weeks leave and come unofficially. I couldn't be seen publicly in Bangkok with Maybank because it would give away the fact we were having an affair, I would tell him, but I would instead be manipulating the strings in the shadows, and no doubt sneaking into the Secretary of State's room once his entourage had retired for the night. This would hopefully explain to Mazlan why I wasn't at the conference and why he would never see me and Maybank together.

I planned to spend the day shopping and sightseeing, but was constantly distracted by my impending meeting with Mazlan that afternoon so after a short walk I returned to the hotel, had a light lunch in my room and got ready. I assumed as Mazlan was Malaysian he would be a Muslim, so I made sure my shoulders and legs were covered in deference to his religious beliefs, but put on a bit of make-up in deference to the fact that he was still, I supposed, a red-blooded man.

At 3.45pm I sat down in a white wicker chair among the trees and colonial opulence of the wonderfully light and airy Authors' Lounge, ordered an orange juice and waited.

Four o' clock came and went and as 4.15pm ticked by I found myself looking more often at my watch. 4.20pm. 4.25pm. 4.30pm…

A horrible sense of failure was creeping up on me, when suddenly a giant appeared. There had been no picture of Mazlan in the Sunday Times article and I had been surprised not to find any pictures of him on the internet, but I was even more surprised when I did actually see him. He had to be almost 7ft fall, but he had such a huge frame that his height didn't look awkward. His dark brown head was completely bald and his eyes were shielded behind dark designer sunglasses, but his nose was almost Roman in appearance and beneath it was a thick black moustache that sat above a wide mouth. Despite the heat he was wearing a tight black shirt buttoned to the neck, a black jacket, black trousers and black shoes. He wore a gold Rolex on his left wrist and his fingers were heavy with gold rings. Adding to his impressive appearance were the two men who flanked him – bodyguards of some sort – who were not much shorter than he was and had ominous, gun-shaped bulges under their navy blazers.

I rose to meet my guest.

"Mr Mazlan?"

"That is correct. You are Miss Barnes?"

I nodded and he seemed to be studying me from behind his glasses before he squeezed my fingers with a jewel encrusted handshake.

He sat down opposite me and ordered a tomato juice as the bodyguards disappeared into the shadows and I surreptitiously nursed my wounded fingers.

"It's good of you to come," I said. "I take it this means you are interested in our proposal?"

"Just who exactly is 'we'?" he asked, removing the sunglasses to reveal piercing, almond eyes, which bored into mine.

"Ah," I smiled. "Mr Maybank and I have made the arrangements. Nobody else needed to be involved, we felt."

"I thought you were an aide, but then I found out you work in the public relations department of the ministry. Do you really have that much contact with him that you both feel safe entering into such a delicate situation together?"

"I don't recall mentioning that it was a solely professional relationship, Mr Mazlan..." I let the sentence trail off so that he could read between the lines.

He smiled at this, then started chuckling, then laughing out loud, which drew a few looks from other guests and a couple of waiters. He slapped a huge hand on the table and leaned in towards me conspiratorially.

"So, you and the British defence secretary are having a secret affair. He can't openly buy you gifts and treats because the finger-wagging British press will disapprove, so you make a plan to get your hands on a nice little cash, um, nest egg is it you say? How very ingenious."

He was looking at me and I had to act well. What he had just said was exactly what I wanted him to think, but I had to pretend I was surprised and unnerved.

"I don't really see that's any of your business, Mr Mazlan," I hissed. "All you need to care about is that for a relatively modest investment you are being virtually guaranteed a return of significant tangible and intangible profit. You're a businessman and this is a simple business deal."

"Of course," he laughed again, ignoring my feigned anger. "And as this is a simple business deal, I fully intend to negotiate the price with you. I will pay £150,000, not a single penny more."

"The price is £500,000 Mr Mazlan," I glared at him. "If you don't want to pay it, the contract will go elsewhere and you can go back to Kuala Lumpur and carry on selling guns to terrorists. By the way, I'm sure that the British secret service would be able to provide their Asian counterparts with all sorts of interesting information to link you to Jemaah Islamiyah. Tell me, what are the jails like in this part of the world? Treat their prisoners well do they?"

Mazlan's face darkened and he leant in close to me again.

"If you want to play a game of blackmail, Miss Barnes, you may like to know that I am recording this conversation. How much money do you think the British press will pay me for evidence that the defence minister is having an affair with a junior staff member and taking bribes to award key contracts?"

"You're lying." I held his stare.

He undid the top three buttons of his shirt, showed me the wires and small black recorder taped to his chest that had been hidden by his jacket then re-buttoned his shirt.

"I will pay £150,000, and for that I expect the defence contract, or this recording goes public."

I sighed and smiled at him. The bastard would make a good undercover reporter.

"Okay," I said, "it seems like we have a deal then."

"So when and where do you want me to hand you the briefcase of cash?"

"It's not that simple. I can't carry the case back to England because I'm here as a tourist and if Thai or British Customs find I'm carrying that much cash I'm likely to get locked up for being involved with drugs or something. Mr Maybank, however, can carry the money safely in a diplomatic bag."

"I can wire you the money, if that would be easier," he half joked.

"Oh, sure. £150,000 suddenly appears in the British defence secretary's personal bank account from a dodgy Malaysian arms dealer with terror links!"

Mazlan seemed to look hurt by this.

"It's all rumour and allegations," he protested half-heartedly.

"Whatever," I sighed. "Anyway, you have to give the money directly to Mr Maybank, but there has to be some kind of excuse for him if this goes wrong and it gets leaked that he has this money."

"What do you suggest?"

"He likes to play cards. While you are at the conference, befriend him, obviously not using your real name as there will be other people around him most of the time. He'll act like he doesn't know who you are so you just pretend you're another bored delegate and suggest a game of cards at the hotel later. He may try to decline if he is with people he knows, but be insistent in a friendly way. Tell him there aren't going to be any reporters hanging about after the conference finishes for the day so suggest a few drinks before the game. Your two 'associates' could turn up as well, posing as other bored delegates you've talked into the game. Blackjack is what he likes and once he gets going he'll play for hours. Win a bit, lose a bit, just keep it realistic because he may have an aide with him. When everyone's a bit merry you make your move. Wait until he's got the bank then get one of your guys to slip you a couple of aces, which you switch with the cards that Mr Maybank deals you. Act drunk but triumphant and claim you're splitting the aces and putting £75,000 on each. Mr Maybank will freak out and start screaming that you can't bet that much, but you insist and when he tries to leave you pull out a gun…"

"What the hell is this," Mazlan interrupted. "Are you crazy? I have absolutely no skill as a card cheat, and I really don't want to threaten the British defence minister with a gun, even if he is in on this! I can't go ahead with this, there has to be a simpler way of getting the money to him."

Mazlan actually looked nervous for the first time.

"It's all worked out between us," I assured him. "Pull out your gun, tell one of your associates to guard the door and order Mr Maybank to deal you cards for the aces. He will seem terrified and he'll protest and beg you to stop, but it will all be an act."

"And suppose he deals me two kings and I win? What then?"

"He won't. During the commotion with the gun, your other accomplice slips a handful of sixes and sevens onto the top of the deck. Mr Maybank will deal, you naturally won't get your 21 so you keep asking for more cards until you bust on both hands. You will owe £150,000 to the banker, Mr Maybank. He will act absolutely relieved and will probably try to refuse the money, but just insist and tell him that he must accept your money or you will lose face in front of the other players and that would be unacceptable. Tell him you don't care if he keeps it, burns it or gives it away, but you have to give it to him. Then tell him that you don't have that kind of money on you and ask him to be your guest at the Thai boxing the following night, where you will give it to him."

"Which stadium?"

"Sanam Muay Ratchadamnoen on Thanon Ratchadamnoen Nok. Sit ringside and bring the money in a briefcase. Let him check inside the case for a moment, just to be certain that everything is correct, and then you can leave and we will take care of everything else."

"I don't really want the whole world to see I have a case of money on my lap."

"And he will want to be there even less than you, rest assured. He will just want to check it's real money, see that it's all there and then he'll no doubt get the hell out of there as well. Okay?"

"Not really. This all sounds unnecessarily complicated. You're asking me to start pulling card switches and making violent threats in public. Surely we can do a simple drop somewhere?"

"Absolutely not. You obviously don't appreciate the delicacy of our position. Mr Maybank has aides, i.e. bodyguards, with him at all times and he may not be able to shake them. He can't just sneak off in the middle of the night to collect the money, and if one of his guards gets wind of a bribe there could very well be trouble. The British press pay a lot better than the Government when it comes to this sort of thing and someone might decide to sell the story. It has to be the card game and it has to be believable. Mr Maybank will be putting on the act of his life, and we expect you to do the same."

"And what assurance do I have that I will get the contract? I am going to a lot of trouble and a lot of expense, with very few guarantees."

"You will get it. Questions may be asked, but we can weather it. Just keep your nose clean for a while."

"I'll do my best. Where would you like us to play the game?"

"It doesn't matter, but the conference is here at the Oriental and Mr Maybank is staying here too. Where are you staying?"

"The Royal Orchid Sheraton, not far from here."

"Well, perhaps it's best to play here. Any guards with him will be much happier to have things on their own territory."

"As you wish. Do you demand anything else of me?" he asked churlishly.

"Don't be like that, Mr Mazlan, this is worth a lot of money to you."

"So be it. I suggest I should go now, Miss Barnes, as I have a rather busy day ahead tomorrow and I must instruct my associates how to handle a deck of cards before tomorrow night."

He got up to leave and the bodyguards were instantly by his side. We shook hands like reluctant business partners and he left.

I collapsed back in my chair, exhausted from tension and concentration. As a plan it was flaky at best, and very little of it would be within my control once it got underway. Even if Mazlan pulled off his end of the bargain, there was no way I could predict how Maybank would react and there was no way I could be sure that he would turn up at the Thai boxing to collect the cash. I had to just hope that the card game went according to plan and then Maybank's greed got the better of him so that he went to pick up the money.

With nothing left to do from my point of view until after the card game, I downed two large vodkas in quick succession then ordered a bottle of champagne and spent the afternoon getting drunk.

Chapter 18

I woke early the next morning, ran straight to the toilet and threw up a combination of hangover and nerves.

I skipped breakfast and got a tuk-tuk to Khao San Road, where I felt more at home with the backpackers than I did loitering around the Oriental or doing a temple tour with a load of overfed tourists.

To be honest, Khao San Road is probably one of the least pleasant streets in the whole of Thailand, with its stinking sewers, overpriced bars, questionable street food, jaded locals and hordes of pissed up travellers. But whether you love it or loathe it, there's no denying the energy and vibrancy of the place as backpackers from every corner of the globe use it as a convenient base for a couple of days before heading north to Chiang Mai or south to the islands.

After a bottle of Singha beer for old times' sake in the gloomy Gulliver's bar at the end of the road, I started picking my way through the stalls and bought a couple of tops, second-hand copies of Luke Rhinehart's The Dice Man and Alex Garland's The Beach, and a stack of pirate CDs and DVDs, haggling furiously with the stall owners over the equivalent of about 30p. I looked wistfully at the adverts in the windows of the countless travel agents offering hillside treks in the north, visits to the islands of Ko Samui and Ko Phi-Phi, guided excursions around the Weekend Market and klongs, and "luxury bus" trips across the Cambodian border to Angkor Wat and Phnom Penh. A wave of melancholy nostalgia washed over me and I made a vow to return to South East Asia one day soon and travel again.

I found an internet café and sent Naomi a long email. I was missing her a lot and wished she was with me. I thought that it was just her friendship that I was missing, but deep down I sensed that I was actually longing for her more intimate company.

I pushed the thought out of my head. I needed to concentrate on the task in hand and not allow myself to get distracted.

Feeling a bit sleepy in the heat after the beer, I went for a brutal Thai massage before heading back to the Oriental. The hotel was deserted, with most of the guests stuck in the conference that was by now well underway in the Royal Ballroom, so I had a delicious green curry for lunch then went up to my room for a nap.

I got up at 4pm and sat in the lobby to wait for Mazlan so I could hopefully ask him how things were going with Maybank. I took the The Dice Man down with me and soon became intrigued by the way the main character, a psychiatrist, starts making vital life decisions based solely on the roll of a dice. He remains committed to obeying the wishes of the dice, even when it involves raping his neighbour and other crimes, and I thought it was a strategy that I may find useful myself if I ever started sliding into boredom again. I tucked the idea away at the back of my mind to give more thought to at a later date.

It was gone 6pm by the time I heard voices approaching as the conference finally finished for the day and the delegates filed out, desperate for some traditional Thai excitement and hospitality. From the snippets of conversation I caught from the suited men who walked by, I gathered that most would be spending the night trawling the go-go bars and sex shows around Patpong, Soi 4 and Soi Cowboy – excited little boys several thousand miles away from prying wives.

I couldn't miss the towering Mazlan as he came striding towards me, looking thoroughly bored and fed up. He walked outside and I followed him as his two bodyguards took their positions at his side.

"Well? How did it go?" I asked anxiously, not really wanting to be seen talking to him.

"We're on. Tonight at 8pm in his suite. Me, Maybank and my two associates."

"Brilliant! He was keen on a game of cards then?"

"I think he and his advisors thought it would be wiser to stay in the hotel than get photographed at Dancing Queens with a couple of lady-boys and a bottle of rum."

"I quite agree. Good luck."

I walked back into the hotel with a sigh of relief, although I knew the hardest part was yet to come.

That night in my room I couldn't stay still, such was my anxiety. I ordered dinner but couldn't eat it, tried to watch television but couldn't concentrate on it and thought about getting drunk but knew I couldn't stomach alcohol. Instead I just waited and wondered what was happening upstairs in Maybank's suite.

There was suddenly a loud rap on the door, which woke me from a sleep I didn't remember falling into. The lights were on and I rolled off the sofa confused. There was another impatient knock on the door as I looked at my watch and saw it was 3am. Who the hell was it?

I nervously crept across the room to the door.

"Who is it?" I asked.

"Mazlan. Open up."

Shit, something must have gone wrong. Urgency hauled my consciousness into sharp focus and I whispered the name Gemma Barnes to myself, grateful for my foresight in checking in as her in case Mazlan should try and find my room.

"What happened?" I asked, before I'd even opened the door properly.

"It's done. The guy went fucking crazy, but it's done. I thought you'd want to know."

Mazlan looked exhausted and his light blue shirt had dark sweat patches all over it. He was alone.

"Good work. Was he alone?"

"No, he had an aide sit in with us, but neither of them saw what was going on with the card switches. I guess the aide was a bodyguard but he nearly had a heart attack when I pulled my gun. I have to say, Maybank is quite an actor too. It really was like he had no idea what was going on."

"He's a clever man," I smiled. "He's agreed to meet you at the Thai boxing tomorrow to collect the money?"

"Sure. Once he saw I'd 'lost' his eyes lit up like stars. He didn't even think about refusing the money."

"I guess he got a bit carried away. What time are you meeting tomorrow?"

"At 9pm. That's when the main fight starts and everyone's attention will be on the ring."

I wanted to give him a kiss I was so relieved and excited, but instead I gave him a handshake and a smile, which he returned. He said goodnight and I went to bed and slept like a log.

I was much less tense the following morning but knew that I still had the tricky job of getting good pictures of the handover at the boxing. The case of money would only be open for a couple of seconds so I would need to try and film Mazlan with the case, Mazlan opening it for Maybank, Maybank looking inside and then Maybank taking the case.

I spent the day in my room practicing with the video recorder on the expensive camera I had bought for the job, then in the early evening I dressed in dark clothes and a baseball cap and got a taxi to Thanon Ratchadamnoen Nok. I had a cheeseburger at a café near the stadium and composed myself for the evening ahead.

The Muay Thai Stadium Ratchadamnoen, one of the two main stadiums in Bangkok, is actually smaller than many first time visitors expect. Tickets are obviously most expensive for ringside, less for the middle circle and cheapest for a spot in the outer circle, but even here there is a clear view of the action.

I bought a ticket for the middle circle and entered the stadium, where I was ushered into the section set aside for farang. I sat on a big concrete step against the fence that separated the middle circle from the outer one and ordered a coke from one of the men who walked around selling crisps and peanuts, or who would go and fetch a beer for you. A few people had already arrived, including a lot of foreigners, so I checked the light levels on my camera and waited.

The evening would consist of 12 fights of five three-minute rounds and as 7.30pm arrived the announcer asked in Thai and English for everyone to rise for the national anthem. The command was obeyed by all and as the band to my right played the tune, an electric charge seemed to surge through the hot stadium.

The national anthem finished and two men – boys really – one in red and one in blue entered the stadium and bounced into the ring. The stadium suddenly seemed to be fill up and the smell of beer and sweat was thick in the muggy air as a slow, eerie sound started coming from the band. As the noise from the band and the crowd grew, the two fighters began their ram muay, a ritual boxing dance which is unique to each boxer and shows respect to their guru and the guardian spirit of Thai boxing. The slow, mesmerising dances drew to an end and the fighters took off their sacred head bands, checked their gloves and taped feet and waited to start. The sense of anticipation in the stadium was palpable.

It felt like a bomb had torn through the stadium as the referee set them off and the crowd erupted. The sound of the Thai oboe and percussion rose up again, giving the boxers a tune to dance to as they skipped around the ring, darting a fist here, swinging a leg there. The boxer in red caught his opponent with a lightning series of blows, drawing blood on his face, and the locals in the fenced off outer circle behind me went ballistic. All around me, men were shouting and waving fingers, hands and arms as they placed and took bets. I clenched my fists and leaned closer to the action as the fighter in blue retaliated with a powerful punch to his opponent's eye, which sent him crashing into the ropes.

The round came to an end and the second and third rounds were much more cautious, but as the fourth round got underway the boxer in red seemed to discover fresh reserves of energy and guile. The sound of the band reached a crescendo and the locals were gripping and rattling the fence behind me like crazed monkeys as blow after blow rained down on the boy in blue and he started rocking. Everywhere there were sweating, snarling, violent faces screaming towards the ring and I found myself getting caught up in it all, baying with the rest of the crowd and even getting aroused by the sight of the fighters hammering the shit out of each other. My shirt was sticking to my body and I undid a button as the boxer in red launched another assault, thundering blow after blow into his opponent until a great roar went up around the arena and the bloodied fighter in blue crashed to the canvas and didn't get up.

Before long the next two fighters, slightly older and bigger, came on and as they started their ram muay I spotted Mazlan walk in with a very large briefcase. I didn't see his two guards, which I thought was slightly odd, but he sat down in a perfect position ringside for me to be able to record my video.

I pulled my cap down to cover my face and took a couple of digital stills of him with the briefcase on his lap, then let the video run to record some film.

The second fight lacked the urgency and feral aggression of the first, both men seeming wary of one another. All five rounds were fought and at the end the guy in blue was declared the winner on points.

By the time the third bout got underway the stadium was so packed I nearly didn't see Maybank arrive. He was wearing a casual white shirt and dark trousers and he looked extremely nervous. I lifted my camera just in time to film him sitting down next to Mazlan.

As if on cue, the band started up again and two new fighters started prowling round the ring, eyeing each other like two tigers who had bumped into each other by chance, each daring the other to strike first if he felt brave enough. Both men pounced together and the crowd exploded in unison as the kicks and punches started flying. This time I didn't watch the fight, but concentrated on Mazlan and Maybank through the view-finder of the video camera. I got clear film of them talking together and then Mazlan nodded his head towards the briefcase.

An excited and drunk Australian guy nearly knocked the camera from my hand as he bounced up and hurled a torrent of abuse at the fighter in blue, who had just dropped to his knees with two red streams trickling from his nostrils. I angrily raised the camera again and saw Mazlan flipping the catches on the case. From my position I could see inside the case and zoomed in even closer so the money and their faces were clear. I then zoomed out slightly and couldn't believe my eyes when Maybank actually reached in and touched the bank notes then turned to Mazlan with a big grin on his stupid face. Absolutely fucking perfect! Mazlan shut the case and slid it over onto Maybank's lap, then, as if he could read my mind, the stupid fucker reached out and shook Mazlan's hand! They sat there like two grinning presidents posing for the press corps and I filmed it all. Maybank deserved everything he got, I thought to myself. What a stupid, greedy bastard.

The temperature in the stadium seemed to hit boiling point and the band was beating out its violent soundtrack as both fighters spat blood onto the canvas.

I was carefully putting my camera away and getting ready to leave when I saw that two men in incongruous dark suits were pushing through the crowds in my direction. I didn't recognise them as Mazlan's goons so I assumed they were here with Maybank, but I didn't plan to stick around and find out.

I stuffed the camera back in its case and threw the strap over my shoulder before getting up and walking quickly towards the exit.

Glancing back, I saw the men in suits had broken into a run, and they were fast. I swore and broke into a run myself, hurtling into a refreshments seller and sending him crashing to the ground in a shower of peanuts, beer and Thai profanities.

The area around the stadium entrance had cleared of the crowds which were gathered earlier, and I bolted out into the street and straight into the path of an oncoming tuk-tuk. Someone screamed as the machine skidded and clipped my left shoulder, sending me spinning into the air. There was a moment of dizziness as I landed on the road, then sharp pain in my shoulder and I felt blood on my face.

The tuk-tuk driver was running towards me, but so were the men in suits so I hauled myself up, pushed the driver aside and swung myself into the driver's seat. I had once driven a tuk-tuk on one of the islands on my last visit to Thailand, so I revved the little engine noisily a couple of times and screeched out onto Ratchadamnoen Nok, straight into the path of a taxi, which braked hard, went into a skid and ploughed through a fruit stall into another parked car. I looked in the rear-view mirror and saw the men chasing me pull the bloodied taxi driver out of his vehicle and dump him unceremoniously on the ground. They climbed into the taxi, reversed over the remains of the fruit stall and started after me.

"Hannah Harker, what the fuck are you doing?" I thought to myself.

My head was cut but the hot air swirling around me soon dried the blood. I tried to read road signs while twisting and turning through the snarled streets and decided to head towards the Silom area, where I would try to lose myself among the other Westerners in and around Patpong Market.

I heard the sound of sirens and glanced in the mirror again to see that two police cars were now chasing the taxi, which was still following me at breakneck speed. I wondered who exactly the men in the taxi were, whether or not they were armed and what they would do to me if they caught me.

I didn't have time to wonder for long though because up ahead the traffic had stopped for red lights at a busy intersection. The countdown clock at the lights showed they would be red for another 50 seconds so I judged the gap between the rows of stationary cars, pushed the tuk-tuk faster and went for it.

There was a loud crash as my wing mirrors were torn off, but then I was at the front of the queue and my noisy machine darted into the intersection. Traffic was hurtling towards me from the left and the right but I held my nerve, pulled hard on the handlebars and scraped through onto Rama IV Road amid a blizzard of waving fists and flashing lights. I think an oncoming petrol tanker missed the rear of the tuk-tuk by less than a millimetre!

I screamed and whooped as adrenaline exploded through my veins and I checked my rear-view mirror. The taxi chasing me had also negotiated the intersection, as had one of the police cars, but I watched the second police car get smashed side on by an oncoming truck. The car flew through the air, landed on its roof and rolled into another lane of traffic. It burst into flames as two more cars smashed into it, and several more skidded violently into the pile-up.

I didn't want to think about the carnage unfolding behind me, so I concentrated on the road signs and saw that I was approaching the junction of Rama IV Road and Surawong, around which a lot of Bangkok's sex and tourist industry is concentrated. There was finally some distance between me and my pursuers so I pulled over to the kerb, hopped out of the tuk-tuk and slipped into Patpong Market.

While the holiday brochures show Thailand as a country of beautiful temples, idyllic beaches, elephants and smiling children, many Western tourists come to the country for very different reasons. In fact, the area around Patpong is the absolute opposite of the holiday brochure portrayal. It's a bizarre and seedy enclave populated by a veritable freakshow of drunken Western louts, transsexual prostitutes, Go-Go girls, conmen, disreputable traders and pot-bellied sex tourists on the prowl for underage girls or handsome young boys.

I barged my way past stalls piled high with pirate CDs, DVDs and fake designer handbags and ignored the persistent calls from grubby little street crooks to "come watch ping pong show".

I glanced over my shoulder and saw the men in suits standing at the end of the market, their eyes darting around in search of me. I cursed, and ducked into a club and ran up the stairs. At the top of the stairs was a dimly lit theatre with a smattering of single men sat quietly by themselves, their eyes fixed on the stage as a tinny dance track boomed out over the speakers. A well-built "woman" in hot-pants greeted me with a smile, but I brushed past her and ran towards the illuminated fire exit sign I spotted at the back of the stage. On the stage itself, two beautiful girls with long dark hair were kissing and playing with each other's tits. Several audience members shifted excitedly, however, when one of the "girls" peeled off the other "girl's" knickers, knelt down and put her erect cock in her mouth.

I should have been prepared for something like this in Thailand, but the sight distracted me and I collided with a low glass table and fell onto the stage. A sharp agony lanced through my slashed shins and suddenly the two transsexuals were trying to pin me down and slap me. Up close I could see that they were clearly men and I felt sick as one of them thrust his hairy groin towards my face. I grabbed his balls and twisted hard until he shrieked and rolled away from me. The other one made a move for me, but I dodged his grasp, spun round and cracked his eye socket with a spectacular right hook.

Gasping for air, I pushed open the fire exit door and ran awkwardly down the metal steps into the alleyway below. Shouts followed me but I hobbled to the end of the alley and found a taxi waiting. I yanked the door open, threw myself in the back and ordered the driver to take me back to the Oriental Hotel.

Chapter 19

I attracted several concerned looks as I arrived back at the Oriental covered in blood from my various cuts, but I ignored them and ran to my room.

I called Bill Laing at the International Morning Post, hurriedly explained to him about the story and video I had and told him what I wanted for them. He went off to speak to Charles Courtney and I spent ten extremely anxious minutes pacing up and down in my suite before he called me back with the offer of a permanent contract on the newspaper if I gave them the story and video exclusively.

I was desperate to get the hell out of Thailand as quickly as possible, but I downloaded the film and pictures from the camera onto a hotel computer and emailed them directly to Laing, then filed as much of the story as I could.

I showered and changed clothes, patched up my wounds as best as I could, threw the rest of my things in my suitcase and went downstairs.

The worried receptionist called a car for me when I explained that I needed to check out early because of a family emergency back home.

Huddled down in the back seat of the hotel BMW, my heart pounded and my eyes darted out of the windows as we sped out of the city towards the international airport.

I tried not to think about the trail of devastation I had just left behind, but I was terrified that my picture might have been caught on CCTV. If it had been then it was probably being circulated among police in the city and emailed to the authorities at the airport. If Gerald Maybank's people got hold of my picture, they would be able to use their unlimited resources to track me down and block my passport in a matter of minutes!

I had a flash of panic and thought about telling the taxi driver to turn round so that I could flee across the land border into Cambodia. Would the Cambodian authorities be alerted about me if I tried to fly out of Phnom Penh? Maybe I could travel all the way to Vietnam and try to fly out of Ho Chi Minh City?

Signs for Suvarnabhumi Airport appeared up ahead and I realised we were nearly there. I put thoughts of Cambodia and Vietnam out of my head and concentrated on composing myself.

The driver dropped me right outside the terminal building just as a big group of Australian backpackers were walking in, so I tagged onto their heels as best as I could and tried to shield my face.

Inside the building it felt like a million cameras and eyes were looking at me. There seemed to be police and airport security staff everywhere, and it felt like all of them were expecting me.

My return ticket to London was for a flight that wasn't due to depart until the following afternoon, so I went to the British Airways information desk and said I had to get on an earlier flight. The female advisor was apologetic and told me that tomorrow would be the earliest I could fly, but suggested that I try the Aeroflot desk because there was a flight to London via Moscow that evening.

More eyes followed me as I ran to the Aeroflot desk and after a certain amount of confusion managed to book myself on the flight to Heathrow via Moscow Sheremetyevo Airport, which was due to take off in a little over 90 minutes.

My heart was in my mouth as I approached passport control, but I chose the lane with the most bored looking official and he stamped my passport and waved me through without really taking any notice of me.

I slipped through the security checks without incident then found a dark corner in the departure lounge bar and steadied myself with a couple of large vodkas until it was time to go to the gate.

The alcohol had the desired effect and I even managed to relax a bit when I got to the gate. I couldn't help but smile as an endless procession of fat, middle-aged Russian men in gaudy tropical shirts and expensive jewellery swaggered in with their tarty blonde mistresses in tow.

When we boarded the plane, however, it seemed to sit on the tarmac for an age, and with each Russian message that came over the public address system I expected the police to walk on board and frogmarch me off to some Bangkok dungeon.

The minutes ticked by excruciatingly slowly, but then the doors were shut, the aircraft started its taxi and moments later we were hurtling down the runway and climbing up into the night sky.

I was wedged between two overweight Russian men in suits who stank of vodka and I think the stewardess took pity on me because she kept me constantly topped up with my own supply of vodka until I smelt as bad as they did.

It was an almost nine hour flight to Moscow, and by the time we arrived I had managed to strike up a conversation of sorts with the two men either side of me. I have absolutely no idea what they were saying as they spoke in Russian the whole time and knew about five words of English, but they were good enough to help me off the plane at Sheremetyevo and one of them even carried my bag to the transit desk for me, before crushing the life out of me with a bear hug and tottering off.

There was a two-hour wait in Moscow before my connecting flight to London so I had a quick walk around the airport shops then settled down for more vodka.

I had no idea what the local time was and I don't really remember going to the gate when my flight was called or getting on the plane. I either fell asleep or passed out shortly after take off and only woke up as we started our descent to Heathrow, my head in absolute pieces.

Once off the plane, my senses sharpened as I joined the gloomy shuffle of people returning home to miserable England and I realised that I still had to get through passport control before I was in the clear. It had been several hours – I had no idea exactly how many – since I left Bangkok, and if Maybank had managed to identify me there would probably be a red flag on my passport and I would be detained at the final hurdle.

The customs officer raised an eyebrow as I approached his desk and reluctantly handed over my passport.

"Long flight?" he asked.

"Um, yeah," I muttered. I must have looked like shit.

"Where have you flown from today?"

"Moscow. No, Bangkok. I've come from Bangkok via Moscow."

He looked at me without comment as he slid my passport through his scanner and stared hard at something on his screen. His face seemed to darken and he looked over his shoulder and beckoned a supervisor.

Fuck. I was done for. I was too exhausted to run so I just stood there and accepted my fate.

The customs officer whispered something to his supervisor and pointed at the screen. The supervisor studied the screen, shook his head and walked away.

The customs officer handed me back my passport.

"Thank you, Miss Harker. Next."

I stood motionless for a couple of seconds, and then I realised I was free.

I beamed at the officer then ran through to collect my suitcase and got a taxi straight to the office of the International Morning Post.

Chapter 20

While I was in the air another reporter at the London office had managed to track down Mazlan by phone. After briefly sticking to the innocent card game story, the arms dealer came clean and admitted that he had been approached by a girl from the MoD press office - who happened to be having an affair with the minister - and told that a £150,000 backhander would seal the body armour contract for him. To make things even better for the story, Maybank had checked out of the Oriental and gone AWOL – presumably to invest some of his windfall in a bit of local culture – and the MoD confirmed that press officer Gemma Barnes was on holiday, but they couldn't say for certain where she had gone.

When the taxi dropped me off at the Post, I borrowed some make-up from Pandora the newsdesk assistant and spent ten minutes in the toilet trying to make myself look human. I was unsuccessful.

Editor Charles Courtney and news editor Bill Laing greeted me excitedly and we had a meeting in Charles' office. They asked me how I had got the story and I told them I had decided to cover the conference on a freelance basis to try and make a bit of money while on holiday in Thailand. I said I had noticed Maybank and Mazlan being very cosy and when I discovered who Mazlan was I had followed them, eventually winding up at the Thai boxing and getting the video. As a cover story for me it was flaky as hell, particularly as they all knew I had previously stitched up the footballer Jason Brady, but everyone was so excited that it was good enough.

A full-time employment contract had already been drawn up and I signed it there and then, with a very big grin on my face. My starting salary would be £30,000 and Charles' secretary Rebecca gave me a stack of leaflets outlining various staff benefits and other things I needed to know.

I went with Bill and looked over the final version of the story, corrected a couple of factual errors that I spotted, then got a taxi back to Rockingsworth and collapsed with exhaustion.

The following day's edition of the International Morning Post sent everyone remotely connected with British politics into a state of shock and topped news schedules across the world.

MAYBANK TAKES £150,000 'BRIBE' FROM TERROR SUSPECT
'I paid defence minister for army contract,' military supplier claims
WORLD EXCLUSIVE REPORT AND PICTURES BY HANNAH HARKER IN BANGKOK

BRITISH Secretary of State for Defence Gerald Maybank was being hunted by Downing Street last night after he was sensationally filmed taking a briefcase of cash from a Malaysian businessman with suspected links to Al Qaeda.

The film, stills from which are published exclusively in today's Post, were taken at a secret meeting between Maybank and military supplier Mazlan Azmil in Bangkok yesterday.

Maybank, who was officially in the Thai capital for a conference, was last night missing from his five-star hotel in the city.

Mazlan, who is currently under investigation for alleged links to Jemaah Islamiyah, the South East Asian wing of Al Qaeda, told the Post he had paid Maybank a £150,000 bung to secure the contract to supply the British Army with body armour for the next five years.

Mazlan said: "I was approached by Maybank's mistress, a Ministry of Defence public relations officer, and told my company would be given [the arms contract] in return for £500,000. This price was negotiated and we eventually agreed on a figure of £150,000.

"A fake card game was set up between the two of us, where I 'lost' the money to Maybank and then had to pay him in cash the following night at a Thai boxing match."

He added: "I assume somebody must have been on to Maybank and his scam, but I do not consider myself to be any kind of villain. His people approached me with the offer and arranged everything."

The astonishing allegations will send shock-waves through Whitehall and will be a devastating personal blow to the Prime Minister, who has always championed Maybank and was believed to be grooming him as a potential successor.

An MoD spokesman confirmed that a junior employee from the communications department was on three week's leave, but said it was "absolutely ludicrous" to suggest she had brokered a deal with Mazlan or was having an affair with Maybank.

A Downing Street spokesman would only confirm that Maybank was in Thailand for a conference and said he knew nothing of any deals with Mazlan.

However, a senior source at the Ministry of Defence said: "The call from the Post [about the film] has been like a bomb going off here. Maybank has vanished from his hotel, Downing Street has launched a manhunt for him and everyone from the Deputy Secretary of State for Defence to the cleaner is being interrogated about this Mazlan guy and any deals."

Opposition leader Michael Scully called for an immediate investigation by Downing Street, the police and British security services.

He said: "Should this prove to be true, it would be the most shameful abuse of position in living memory and I would expect to see many heads roll."

In addition to this story, the paper carried a piece about Mazlan and Jemaah Islamiyah, a profile of Maybank and his rise to fame and a short article explaining about the body armour contract. The newspaper's leader column also focused solely on the scandal.

When I eventually woke up from a long, deep sleep I drove to the Rockingsworth Informer and handed in my resignation. Tina Karageorghis had seen my name splashed all over the front of the Post that morning so didn't need to ask why I was leaving. I think she was a bit pissed off that I'd been doing shifts on the sly, but she was gracious enough to offer sincere congratulations and I think there was a proud look in her eye.

The other reporters were all thrilled for me, although Phil could have tried a bit harder to disguise his jealousy.

Simon was upset that I was going, but he put on a brave face and seemed relieved when I assured him we would still be able to hang out together and I wouldn't start looking down on him or letting the Post go to my head.

I called Naomi, who seemed to be even more excited than me, and then telephoned mum and dad. Dad wanted to fire a thousand questions at me about the story, but mum was in a sombre mood because at the weekend it was the anniversary of the twins' deaths. I promised them I would go down and visit on Saturday and they were both delighted.

That evening I went for a quick drink with Liam and dumped him, which turned out to be more difficult than I had envisaged.

"You've hardly given me a chance, Hannah," he whined. "You're always working and every time we see each other you're so stressed out I'm afraid to talk for fear of getting my head bitten off."

"Well then, it sounds like this is definitely the right thing to do. I'm sorry, Liam, but I just haven't got the time or the energy to commit to a relationship at the moment."

"Jesus, why don't you listen to yourself, Hannah? Since you started at the Post you've become such a drama queen. You suddenly seem to think you're so damn important."

"Fuck you, Liam. Some of us have ambition."

"What, taking pictures of footballers snorting cocaine? What a massive contribution to society."

"Piss off. You think anyone gives a toss about a village bobby, filling in reports about smashed windows and stolen flower pots? Four kids die in a fire and you're asked to do some real detective work and you fall apart."

"I don't have to apologise to you for what I am, Hannah."

"That's right, Liam, you don't, because I don't give a fuck about you, your little job or your little problems and tantrums anymore."

"Don't make an enemy of me, Hannah, you'll regret it."

"Oh, so it's threats now, is it? How very mature."

"Nobody makes a fool of me, Hannah, especially not a jumped up little bitch like you! I promise that if you walk out of here you will regret it."

"Really? Why, what are you going to do?"

"Don't do this, Hannah. Don't make me your enemy."

"Get fucked."

I coolly got up and walked out of the pub, deleting all his messages and his numbers from my mobile as I walked home. That was one hassle off my back. What a freak!

I had to serve a month's notice at the Informer, but luckily I had a couple of weeks holiday left so I took some time off to be at the Post for the aftermath of the Maybank scandal.

When the errant politician did eventually reappear in London the story seemed to get even bigger. He of course denied any affair or secret deals with Mazlan, but the video of him taking the money at the Thai boxing was there in colour for everyone to see so he had to say something. He rather unwisely chose to present his defence on the BBC's Newsnight programme, and was swiftly taken to pieces by the presenter and left looking like a deceitful criminal. A rather bemused Gemma Barnes returned to work after a pleasant three weeks in the Seychelles and was promptly suspended from her job pending an internal enquiry and criminal investigation.

Clearly furious and suspicious of the whole story, Downing Street's Head of Communications called Bill Laing to question my own credentials and point out what an incredible coincidence it was that I should be sitting there with my camera when Maybank and Mazlan turned up at the stadium. He also told Laing about the chase through Bangkok that had left two police officers seriously injured. He demanded a meeting with me, but good old Bill just told the guy to piss off and concentrate on preparing a response to Maybank's imminent sacking. The video evidence was irrefutable and whatever the circumstances behind it there would be no option but for Maybank to go.

Although this incident didn't worry me unduly, I did get jitters when one of the Post's veteran reporters, an enigmatic alcoholic called Mike Potter, told me he had heard through the grapevine that Maybank was getting some of his closest allies to lean on their contacts in the intelligence services to try and get to the bottom of the matter. Apparently Maybank was popular at both MI5 and MI6 because he was always very vocal in his support of their work and he had effectively told the heads that if he became Prime Minister he would make the war against terrorism a key policy, with generous funding and relaxing of the law to facilitate their efforts.

Eventually, however, not even the Prime Minister could protect his protégé from the onslaught any longer and privately asked him to resign, rather than be sacked. In his resignation speech a clearly furious Maybank said he had been the victim of a "gross scam" which he planned to get to the bottom of. The Prime Minister said that the investigation into the matter would continue and should it prove that Maybank was indeed innocent he would be reinstated immediately. At the present time, however, he had no choice but to reluctantly accept the resignation.

I didn't feel particularly proud to have cost Maybank his career, but the man was a fool who had blundered blindly and greedily into my trap.

Big stories came my way thick and fast in the following weeks at the Post and my phone was always ringing. Shadow Cabinet ministers, union leaders, disgruntled government employees – you name it, they were offering to leak memos or pass on strong rumours over drinks or lunch.

The only negative was that my hitherto successful attempts to abandon obedience, conformity and generally acceptable social behaviour wavered significantly when I was working there.

When I was on duty I was willing, courteous, presentable, supine and, frankly, obsequious. I paid great deference to everyone from the junior reporters to the editor himself and I constantly worried about the impression I was making, what people thought about me and whether or not I was popular and well regarded there.

I simply wasn't myself – not even my old self, let alone the new, convention-shunning me. I was a different character depending on who I was dealing with and I became the person I thought they most wanted me to be. To the junior reporters I was always helpful and praised their stories. To the news editors I was a nodding automaton programmed to say yes to every outlandish request and jump as high as commanded. To the senior editors and Charles himself I was a schizophrenic collection of characters that mirrored their own personalities.

Although I hated the charades, I consoled myself with the knowledge that at least I realised what I was doing. I wasn't blindly following the pack and dressing the same way as everyone else, discussing the same television programmes and chewing the same sandwiches. I was deliberately putting on a veneer of normality to deceive them into thinking I was like them, so they would accept me and I would be able to start slithering up the ladder. In time, more of my true self would be revealed, but for now it was necessary to cloak myself with a Trojan Horse of ordinariness so that I could infiltrate their lair. When my mask slips, Troy will fall.

The remaining days at the Evening Informer were agony. One afternoon I was idly surfing the net when Phil Crichton started laying into one of the trainees, a young girl called Kate. Phil had overheard her telling Simon that she had not managed to get any decent eye-witness quotes when she went down to the scene of a jewellery store robbery earlier that day so she had sat in a café and made a few up.

"And what happens when the police call up and ask for details about these vital witnesses?" Phil asked angrily.

"I'll, um, say they wouldn't give out their details," Kate replied unconvincingly.

I decided to get involved.

"Jesus, Phil, we've all done it. Most of the degenerates you stop in the street can't string two words together anyway, so you have to put a few words in their mouths."

"Putting words in someone's mouth isn't the same as completely inventing stuff. Kate's still got a lot to learn, a hell of a lot, and if she starts getting into bad habits now it'll only get worse. Today it's an invented quote, tomorrow she's inventing whole stories."

I turned away to hide any guilty expression that might have crept across my face.

Phil continued, addressing the whole newsroom now: "Believe it or not, some people do still trust journalists and believe what we tell them, so it's up to us to make sure we don't let them down. Sure, a story is better, more exciting, with nice juicy quotes, but if we can't get those quotes then tough, the story runs without them."

"I hardly think," I said, getting back into the argument, "that creating a little old lady to say 'Ooh, it was like something from a film' is going to destroy the public's faith in the press. Everyone knows half of these things are invented anyway: 'a source said', 'friends of the star commented', 'an onlooker described' - Christ, it goes on in a lot bigger and more reputable media organisations than this."

A hail storm started up outside, the icy stones hammering against the windows and a gloomy drabness descended. Kate had slunk into the shadows.

Phil said: "I personally think all these tabloids inventing stories about so-called celebrities and the like are a disgrace to our profession. The editors should ban them and get their reporters out finding real stories. The trouble is, though, it's not just the tabloids anymore. Some of these hacks that started out making up 'insignificant' eye-witness quotes end up on broadsheets or the television, and when they start making stuff up there people can get killed."

"And this coming from the guy who can't stop bragging about his shifts on the News of the World," I groaned. "Honestly, you're so melodramatic sometimes."

"Oh, you think so do you? Well, when you get sent to some war-zone, Hannah, you might then start to realise the severity of the consequences of making things up. A twisted quote from some army guy, the local militia read it and they massacre a village. It's the old power without responsibility thing, isn't it? Well, we have got a lot of power and it's about time some people started being a bit more responsible with it. And you," he glared at me, "would do well to take that thought with you off to the bloody International Post.

He gave us all a contemptuous look and stormed off to the canteen, muttering to himself.

My last day at the Informer finally arrived and after a rather emotional speech from Tina nearly everyone came down to the pub with me for drinks. I think my moving to the Post served as a jolt of inspiration to many of them, particularly the ones who were in serious danger of resigning themselves to a life of peddling town hall tittle-tattle and residents' rants. People I'd never spoken to before were buying me drinks and grilling me about how best to go about getting shift work. I answered them good-naturedly and promised to keep in touch with people I knew I'd never speak to again, but I suppose it was quite sad to be leaving the place "where it all began".

Chapter 21

With the Rockingsworth Evening Informer now behind me I was at the International Morning Post full time, which often meant all day, every day. My social life was reduced to chatting to colleagues over a Kit-Kat at the vending machine and four hours sleep became a luxury, but I was generally enjoying it.

The Maybank/Mazlan affair went quiet after a while, but my second splash story came not long after. A disgruntled civil servant leaked an email to me from a senior Home Office minister to the Chief Constable of a northern police force urging him to deny to the media that a Pakistani student with suspected links to a firebrand Muslim cleric had been beaten to death during his arrest by two white police officers. The email suggested the official line should be that the man had been attacked by an unknown gang and died despite the efforts of the officers.

Needless to say, the story was dynamite and the repercussions astonishing. More heads rolled and my career was on fire, with rumours circulating that I was in line to scoop several top journalism awards, although this never actually happened.

Most of the contacts I developed were very keen to remain out of the limelight so a lot of my time was spent sitting in dark pubs waiting for these anonymous sources to drop in and slip me a leaked document, a grainy photograph, an intercepted email or occasionally stop for a 30 second off-the-record briefing. I was drinking heavily again and was susceptible to bouts of depression if I spent too long alone.

One scorching Monday afternoon in July I was in a gorgeous country pub on the outskirts of Henley-on-Thames to meet a recently sacked Foreign Office minister who wanted to spill the beans about his back-stabbing former colleagues. I'd already been in the deserted pub for three hours when he sent me a text to say that he'd changed his mind and wasn't now going to say anything. I was a long way through my second bottle of white wine by this point, so rather than head back to London I rented one of the rooms above the pub for the night and stepped out into the garden.

I squinted as the fierce white sun bounced off the low garden walls into my blurry eyes. The warmth on my face and body was delicious and I stood for a moment gently inhaling the jasmine-tinged air as lively sparrows, seemingly oblivious to the heat, hopped and chirruped in the rustling oak trees and a small white aircraft buzzed lazily overhead.

Freshly cut grass had been raked into neat piles and gave off a wonderful summery scent as I started strolling down the narrow twisting path deeper into the garden. Beds of dazzling flowers waved at me as a gentle breeze rocked their stems and a chubby bee flashed past and made a nuisance of itself by zinging and darting around my head. I swiped at it with an irritated flick of my wrist and it hovered at eye-level, perhaps trying to stare me out, before shrugging its wings and diving down to bury itself greedily into the purple embrace of a clematis.

Rather than enjoy the moment, the mood turned sour as I allowed a cloud of melancholy to drift over me. I was lonely; desperately lonely. Although I lived in a fast-paced world of constant communication and interaction, I didn't feel like anyone really cared whether I was there or not. I was part of something too big to be significant and I was really becoming aware that nobody would miss me if I wasn't around.

I needed love but was so hopeless that if someone gave it to me I would throw it back in their face. I just didn't know how to have a stable relationship because all I wanted in life were the things I couldn't have.

One of my many vices was infatuation and so I would often become infatuated with the least appropriate or least accessible people. For a while after I started working full time at the Morning Post I had become horribly and dangerously infatuated with a reporter who was married with three kids. I knew nothing would come of it, but that's exactly what the appeal was: I just wanted something I could never have. If somehow I did manage to get that thing, I would soon grow bored of it and move on to killing myself over the next thing I couldn't have. This is how fucked up my head was.

The guy was a flirt and probably led me on more than he needed to. A few times he came out for work drinks and it was all meaningful looks, lingering touches and innuendo between us. He was gorgeous, witty and smart and I became so desperate for him I vowed that I wouldn't rest until I had him, even if it meant doing something to his wife!

The emails between us went back and forth and there were even a couple of cosy lunches with just the two of us, but all the time I knew really that it was empty and there would be no happily ever after.

The day he quit the newspaper I threw myself at him in the corridor and, in floods of tears, begged him to carry on seeing me. He smiled dutifully and placed a fatherly hand on my shoulder and tender kiss on my cheek. Then he winked at me, turned away and I never saw the bastard again!

Back in the garden of the Henley pub I manage to tear myself out of this dreary reverie and skulked back into the pub and up to my room, only venturing out every couple of hours to buy another bottle of wine from the bar.

The weeks became months and it was only a matter of time before the first offer came in from a rival newspaper trying to poach me. The Telegraph put a very attractive package on the table, but when I "accidentally" let it slip to Bill Laing that they were after me a letter arrived at my house the next day saying that my salary at the Post was going up to £38,000, so I stayed.

As another reward for my loyalty and good work, Bill assigned me to a choice job – covering the Queen's week-long state visit to India, where the press were to be put up in the best hotels courtesy of the Indian government.

India was one of the places where Naomi and I had spent time on our world trip and she begged to come with me when I told her about the job.

"I can't babe," I told her. "It's work."

"Pretend I'm your interpreter or something," she pleaded.

"They all speak English," I laughed.

"I know, I know; I'm just jealous and could do with a change of scenery. I dated one of my neighbours a few weeks ago and he's turned into a bit of weird stalker. I wouldn't mind getting away from him until he moves onto his next victim."

"What do you mean? Is he dangerous?"

"Oh God no," she laughed. "He's harmless, but it's a pain in the arse having to sneak into my own home every night so that he doesn't see me."

"Well listen, why not wait until I get back from India and we can think about getting somewhere together in London."

"Really?" Naomi exclaimed, sounding thrilled.

"Sure, why not. I think I've outgrown Rockingsworth and it's about time I got myself back to London and into the thick of things. Besides, I've had enough of living by myself and having to put up with my own miserable company; I'd love to have you around to come home to. I'm earning decent money now and we could probably get somewhere really nice."

"That would be amazing."

"Why don't you come and house-sit for me while I'm away – it'll give you some breathing space from your psycho neighbour and you can practice tidying up my things!"

"Okay, cool, when are you off?"

"Tuesday. Come over on Monday after work and we can have a night in before I go and think about where in London would be good to move to."

"Brilliant, I'll see you on Monday then."

I was so busy sorting out the Indian trip that Monday came round before I knew it. We had a really nice evening in, chatting about the place we were going to get over a bottle of wine and a curry.

Even though we had been friends for years, I felt something different between us that night. There was a spark, something intimate, and I sensed that moving in together would be the beginning of something very new and exciting between us. We shared a bed that night, as we always did, but this time I pressed my body against hers and we spooned. Her hair was in my face and it smelled of her. I kissed her gently on an exposed part of her neck and she rolled over so that we were face to face, our lips virtually touching.

"Is this right?" I whispered, the question aimed more at myself than at her.

"Yes," she whispered back, "I think it is."

Our lips did touch and we then took it in turns to plant little kisses on each other's faces, giggling as we did so. I wanted to explore her and get to know the rest of her body, but I was so happy that I just pulled her against me and we ended up falling asleep in each other's arms.

I had to leave early for Heathrow the next morning and she got up two hours earlier than she needed to so that she could see me off. Saying goodbye to her that morning I felt a real love for her and I didn't want to leave her. I remember her standing in the doorway in a pair of my pyjamas with a big grin on her face, and then she kissed me on the mouth and I left.

In the horrible insanity that was soon to come, the Indian trip has become a whirlwind of chaos in my memory. The whole week is a jumbled sideshow in my head of heat, noise, crowds, smells, dancing, eating, drinking, polite laughter, clapping, insects, dust, colour, exuberance, poverty, friendship and loneliness. No one day or event is clear in my mind, but there is no need for it to be because the whole thing was overshadowed by such an unbearable turn of events.

I got back to England the following Tuesday afternoon and caught the train from Heathrow to Rockingsworth. I remember being so excited as I struggled back to my house with my cases and ringing the doorbell, but there being no reply. I remember cursing Naomi for being out while I rummaged for the front door key, and then I remember feeling my heart flutter for no apparent reason as I stepped into the hallway. I remember silence when I called Naomi's name and I remember dropping my cases on the floor. I remember feeling my bladder strain and running up the stairs to the bathroom, unzipping my trousers as I went. I vaguely remember pushing the bathroom door open and being hit by a repugnant smell. Finally, I remember looking into the bath tub and experiencing my life disintegrate and my sanity imploding.

PART 2
DECLINE

"When we have lost everything, including hope, life becomes a disgrace, and death a duty." – W.C. Fields

"Death must be so beautiful. To lie in the soft brown earth, with the grasses waving above one's head, and listen to silence. To have no yesterday, and no tomorrow. To forget time, to forgive life, to be at peace." Oscar Wilde

Chapter 22

What I saw that day in my bath tub was the beautiful naked body of my beloved Naomi. It had been hacked, smashed, gouged, burnt and flayed beyond recognition and was bobbing in a puddle of unlit petrol. A slick of blood had congealed on the floor and dotted across it, like hideous islands, were several teeth, fingers and a shredded nose. Draped over the radiator, like leathery tea-towels, were discoloured tapestries of skin.

I will never forget the sound of a veteran detective weeping as a coroner quietly whispered to him the details of her injuries and the torture and agony she must have suffered.

I never knew how deeply agony could bury itself inside a human being. A whole lifetime worth of experiences, memories and history instantly erased and replaced by an excruciating darkness that turned the whole body into a screaming, wretched pulp that wanted to tear itself apart.

Consequence? Destiny? Accident? Coincidence? What is it that squeezes such terrible pain inside? Suicide is not an option; cannot be an option. So what? How does this heart, mind and body explain and deal with the filthy claws that are ripping the head apart from the inside, stripping the skull and laying it bare? White cracking knuckles grind against a paralysed grey balloon that once smiled on the canvas of the mirror. What is this black torment that has raped my gasping insides? Pray for self destruction, but the invader laughs mockingly. Guilt of taking those young lives in a raging fire has become an insignificant speck. This new torture is something quite spectacular, something previously incomprehensible but now the defining characteristic of this new, broken and insane being. Make the agony evolve; create hatred and revenge. Everyone must suffer and endure this. I am reborn.

My beautiful, sweet, sweet, darling Naomi. I adored you with all my heart, and now I mourn you with the fragments of it that remain. Even though I am now quite mad and should take my own life or offer myself for incarceration, I shall instead find those who have done this to you and inflict even greater violence upon them. Did they think you were me? Did they do these things to you for information about me? Did they do this as part of their revenge on me? How long did you suffer, my love? I will suffer equally. I will suffer for eternity. I love you so much.

Chapter 23

Bill Laing and Charles Courtney both said I could take paid sick leave for as long as I needed, but after Naomi's funeral I had to get back to work.

The official investigation into her murder was put into the incapable hands of Rockingsworth Police (luckily not Liam, but an equally inept Detective Inspector called Chris Bedford). I didn't want that lot involved at all, so I set them off in the wrong direction by suggesting it may have had something to do with my story on the Pakistani student being killed by the white cops because I had received death threats after that was published.

I had already decided that Naomi's death was almost definitely linked to the scam I pulled on Maybank and Mazlan. Jason Brady, the coke-sniffing footballer, had honestly believed he had been stitched up by two prostitutes, and the cops who killed the student had been testified against by virtually their whole force and were in custody awaiting sentencing after pleading guilty to manslaughter.

Maybank, however, had made a quick and miraculous comeback as a highly paid consultant to leading defence suppliers and I had heard through the rumour mill that one of his new clients was a certain Mazlan Azmil! Remembering what Mike Potter, the veteran Post reporter, had said about Maybank being in bed with the security services, I decided to use that as a starting point in my own very personal investigation into Naomi's murder.

I collared Mike in the office one afternoon after he had returned from the pub.

"Hi Mike, how are you?"

"Hello Hannah." He looked at me with a sympathetic face. "How are you getting on now?"

"Oh, you know, just trying to throw myself into my work."

"That's probably the best thing," he said, his weathered face flushed from that day's alcohol intake."

"Yeah. Listen, Mike, I need your help."

"Oh?"

"This is just between you and me, Mike, but I think my friend's murder has something to do with that story I did on Maybank and the Malaysian arms dealer, Mazlan. Remember what you told me about Maybank, MI5 and MI6? I think that's where it starts."

"Oh, now Hannah, this is a bit much…"

"Mike, please. I'm worried about my safety, my life, and I can't trust the police on this one. I don't want you to do anything wrong, just have a chat with your contacts and see where Maybank got when he asked MI5 and MI6 for help before. Try and find out if he spoke to Mazlan after the story broke too. I've heard that he's offering the guy consultancy services now. If that's true then this is completely fucked up."

"Hannah, the security services don't go around assassinating British citizens on their own soil. This isn't the movies. And Gerald Maybank, a former Cabinet minister, wouldn't be involved with that sort of thing either."

"Mike, she wasn't just killed – she was methodically tortured to death. No valuables were taken from my house, so it wasn't simply a robbery gone wrong. Whoever murdered Naomi was either after information, or they wanted to send me a very clear message."

"Okay," Mike held up his hands. "I'll make some enquiries. But what would you do if it turns out that Maybank or the security services are behind this? You can't go after these people yourself, Hannah. Who do you think you can turn to?"

"I'll decide that later, when I know if I'm barking up the right tree or not. Just do what you can, Mike. Please."

He didn't seem happy, but he promised he would find out as much as he possibly could and get back to me.

I had been staying in a hotel close to work while I had a new bathroom fitted at home to try and exorcise some of the horrors that had been committed in the old one, but when the work was completed I found I was still unable to sleep in the house alone anymore. Not knowing who else to turn to, I asked mum and dad if they would come and stay with me for a while. It occurred to me that I could be putting their lives in danger by having them in my house, so I got in touch with Detective Inspector Bedford at the police station and he agreed to put the house under surveillance. When my parents turned up two days later, I flung my arms round dad and burst into tears.

A few nights after they arrived mum went up to bed early, leaving dad and I alone in the lounge sipping whisky.

"What do you think this was all about? Really?" asked dad.

"I don't know. I told the police it might be connected to the story I wrote about the Asian boy getting killed by the white cops, but I really think it's linked to Maybank and the arms dealer."

"So why don't you tell them that? They will try to help you."

"I don't trust them not to mess things up."

"Things couldn't be much more messed up than they already are. What's the alternative anyway? You can't be thinking you're going to solve this by yourself."

"They're not used to this sort of thing, dad. I've got better contacts and more knowledge about this."

"Don't be so fucking stupid, Hannah!" He slammed his drink on the coffee table and caught me by surprise. "You've got no idea what you're doing and that's why Naomi is dead. No, don't look at me like that. You're an exceptionally talented girl and you've worked wonders in the last year or so to get where you are, but this time you are out of your depth. It wasn't local yobs who killed Naomi, it was stone cold professionals who had access to confidential information about you and then tortured an innocent girl to death. If you had any sense you would ask for round-the-clock police protection and request a lengthy period of leave from the newspaper and disappear for a while until this is solved. If you seriously think you're going to deal with all this yourself, you're going to wind up like your friend."

"Well, thanks for your confidence and support." I got up to leave.

"Sit down!" he barked. "I've already lost two children and since they died your mother has become little more than a goddamn shell of her former self. You are my family, Hannah, and I'm not going to sit by and let you get murdered."

I hung my head.

"Okay, dad, okay. Just let me tidy up a few things here and then I'll take that paid leave the paper offered me. I'll disappear somewhere quiet until it's safe to come home. Okay?"

He grunted and downed his whisky, looking as if he didn't believe a word I'd just said.

"Well, make sure you do," he growled eventually. "Now, come here and give me a kiss goodnight."

I kissed him on the cheek and gave him a big hug. "Night dad, I love you. Thank you for coming here, I really needed you."

"And I really need you too, darling. You are the apple of my eye and I can't begin to tell you how proud I am of what you've achieved. Whatever this horrific situation is all about, the proper authorities will get to the bottom of it and then you'll be free to carry on with your career. Everything will be all right soon, I promise."

He ran his big fingers through my hair and I held on to him tightly and briefly wallowed in his familiar smell, before heading up to my bed and the nightmares.

A couple of days later I was at work when I got an email from Mike Potter, asking me to meet him in the pub at lunchtime. He was already there at a gloomy corner table when I arrived at 12.30 and he had two empty pint glasses in front of him and a half-drained tumbler of Scotch. I bought him another large Scotch and an orange juice for myself and sat opposite him.

He looked scared and his hands were playing nervously with his glass.

"You're not going to like this, Hannah, it's even crazier than I expected. You've got to take this information to the police, but it didn't come from me."

"What is it, Mike?"

"Okay, after your story broke, Maybank got onto some of his MI5 contacts and asked them to get as much information from MI6 about this Mazlan character as they could. He also asked them for any information they had on you. There was already a load of information on Mazlan that MI6 had compiled, particularly since he was linked to Jemaah Islamiyah, but nothing major on you, apart from your address and that sort of thing.

"Now, according to my sources, that wasn't enough for Maybank and he got them to put you under discreet surveillance, take a few pictures, see who you met, where you hang out, that sort of thing."

"Jesus, can he do that?"

"Don't be naïve Hannah. They do what they want, how they want, when they want to whoever they want."

"Shit. So that means they knew it was Naomi in my flat, and presumably they knew I was out of the country covering that thing in India."

"I guess so."

"And they murdered Naomi anyway!"

"Hey, slow down there." Mike raised his palms. "There's absolutely no proof that she was killed by the Government, and that's certainly not the sort of thing you want to be mouthing off about around the place either."

"Well who did it then, Mike? It wasn't fucking burglars!"

"How well do you know this Mazlan character?"

"Not at all really," I said, not wanting to admit of course that I'd met him in Bangkok.

"Well, he's a really nasty piece of work. Four years ago his main competitor was stabbed to death in the street by 'muggers' and two years later a couple of aspiring defence suppliers died within a week of each other in mysterious road accidents. The link with JI is almost certainly valid and your story abut him trying to bribe Gerald Maybank has inspired the authorities to redouble their efforts in investigating him."

"So you're saying Mazlan killed Naomi?"

"If you want my honest, and completely anonymous, opinion, Hannah, I think Maybank, certain people in MI5 and Mazlan are all working together and this whole thing is completely out of control." He downed the Scotch he had been drinking and started on the one that I'd bought for him.

"But Maybank is soiled goods since the scandal broke," I said. "Surely nobody senior in the security services could risk having anything to do with him on a professional basis."

Mike spluttered into his Scotch.

"Don't you believe it, Hannah. How do you think he ended up as a top consultant to defence suppliers? The bloody Prime Minister is secretly vouching for him left, right and centre. He's telling everyone that Maybank has got to sit out in the cold for a while to keep up appearances with the public and the media, but before you know it he'll be back again. You know how it works, we've seen it before. He's even been invited to Hong Kong in a few weeks to attend the international terrorism conference with all the world leaders."

"Jesus, so this thing goes to the very top then? To the Prime Minister?" A fury started burning inside me and I felt dizzy.

"No, no, I wouldn't have thought complicity in your friend's death goes beyond one or two people, but you must be careful."

I wasn't listening to him anymore. My head was alive with thoughts, questions, plans and rage.

"Hannah? Hannah. Are you listening to me?"

"Yes, Mike, sure. Look, thank you so much for this. I mean that. I'm not going to do anything stupid and your name will not be mentioned to anyone in connection with this."

"Thanks. Jesus, Hannah, I've been in this game for a long bloody time and seen and heard things you wouldn't believe, but this is something else."

"Well at least I know now what I'm up against. Do you want another drink?"

"No thanks, I'd better get going," he said, looking at his watch.

"Yeah, me too."

Mike pulled on his tatty old trench coat and walked to the door, bidding farewell to nearly everyone in the pub as he went. I got up and followed him outside, my eyes unhappy with the glare after the darkness of the pub.

Neither of us noticed the grey Land Rover weaving through the traffic at break-neck speed until it was too late. I had snagged my coat on the door of the pub and was still standing on the pavement, but Mike was halfway across the road when the driver seemed to slam down on the accelerator.

The huge vehicle hit Mike just below the chest and knocked him straight down, under the front wheels.

Everything seemed to move in slow motion and subconsciously I expected to hear a frantic screech of brakes, but instead the driver kept his foot down and the front and rear wheels crushed Mike. The Land Rover whipped around a corner and before I could get a look at the number plate it was out of sight.

Several people were screaming, someone was shouting for an ambulance to be called and doors were opening everywhere as shopkeepers, office staff and café owners raced out into the street. I didn't need to go into the road to know that Mike was dead; that was perfectly evident from the seeping puddle of blood around the cracked and twisted body.

I sat down heavily on the kerb and found myself waiting once again for the now familiar flashing blue lights and wailing sirens.

Chapter 24

"Bastard! Fucking hit and run bastard! One of the few decent men left in this business, killed by a fucking hit and run bastard!"

Charles Courtney put his head in his hands, close to tears I think, as I sat across from him in his office three hours after Mike's death. Charles had just got back from the hospital, where he had tried to comfort Mike's devoted wife, Sandra, while she attempted to identify her husband.

It was unsettling to see a man like Charles in this state and it was Rebecca and Pandora who seemed to be holding it together, dealing with the phone calls and answering questions.

The paramedics had assumed I was in shock when they arrived and found me sitting silently on the kerb, but it was not possible to shock me anymore. I had actually been deep in thought, thinking how there was no way Mike's death was a coincidence. Just seconds after revealing an incredible Government conspiracy, the man gets run down by a Land Rover in broad daylight. It didn't take a genius to put two and two together. I wondered if the fact that the killers knew Mike would be in the pub at that time meant someone at the Post was leaking information. Saying that, however, Mike drank in the same pub virtually every day and predicting his movements wouldn't have been hard. I kept this to myself, of course, and gave only a brief statement to the police.

Back at the office I had told Charles that everything happened so quickly I'd not really seen what happened. Now the editor was close to breaking down in front of me.

"I'll leave you alone now," I said, getting up to leave.

"No, no." Charles waved me back down and recomposed himself with a big sniff. "Christ, it's you we should all be worried about, Hannah. First your friend and now this. Tell me what we can do, what you need, and it's yours. We can find you the best counselling people there are."

I liked Charles, he was a sweet guy. Despite being such a powerful man professionally, he was really sympathetic on an individual basis to his people. Sure, if you fucked up or simply weren't up to scratch he'd take you apart, but he seemed to recognise when someone in the office had genuine issues, like I obviously did now.

Although I had no definite plans in my mind yet, I had already decided my revenge should be swift and unspeakably violent. If Charles was ever going to grant me a favour it was now, so I asked him for one.

"Thanks for the offer, but I don't think counselling is what I need. I need a break, away from England for a little while. I noticed that three weeks from now the world leaders are getting together in Hong Kong for a major conference on terrorism. If it would be okay I'd like to go over to Asia now, get my head together and then cover the conference. I think that would be the best and safest thing for me right now."

Charles was too distraught to think straight.

"Um, okay, sure, if you think that's what you need."

"I do, Charles. I think it will be perfect for me right now."

"Okay then. Let the foreign desk know you're going to be covering it and ask if they can sort out all the passes and paperwork you'll need."

"Will do. Thank you, Charles, I appreciate it."

"No problem, Hannah. You look after yourself now, you hear me?"

I gave him a warm smile and without thinking I reached over and squeezed his hand. "I promise. You look after yourself too."

On the way out of Charles' office, Rebecca stopped me and asked if she could have a word. I followed her to one of the kitchen areas and she turned to look at me with a serious expression on her face.

"I've just had the police on the phone. The Land Rover that killed Mike went into a wall just after the crash and the driver was killed instantly. They said it was stolen and the driver, a young guy, was being chased by an unmarked police car. He must have lost control after hitting Mike."

A grim smile appeared on my face.

"Sure, he must have lost control. Either that or someone caused him to lose control. Very thorough, tidying up any loose ends like that."

"What the hell are you talking about, Hannah?"

"Nothing; don't worry about it."

"You're planning to do something stupid, aren't you?" she said.

"No, of course I'm not."

"Don't take me for a fool, Hannah," she snapped. "Whatever you're into, whoever you're up against, it's time to just tell the police about it before you wind up in the fucking ground!"

"Becca," I touched her arm and tried to give her a reassuring smile,

"I appreciate your concern but I'm fine. I just want to get away for a little while."

"Don't you get it? You're not safe here in this country, so who the hell is going to protect you on the other side of the world? You are going to die! Do you understand that?"

My smile disintegrated and I gave her a cold, dead stare. "Yes, Rebecca, I completely understand what dying is. And I don't care."

She threw her hands up in disgust, called me a fucking idiot, and stormed off.

I went to my desk and got my mobile then I took my company credit card from my purse and booked a one-way ticket to Malaysia.

Chapter 25

After all the horror and bleak days in England, I arrived in Kuala Lumpur and it seemed like some kind of sunny fairytale kingdom where everyone always lived happily ever after. It was a sprawling, wonderfully warm city of colossal department stores, sky-trains, gleaming steel and glass towers, enclaves of intriguing cultural diversity and bucket-loads of money. There seemed to be no pie that this Asian tiger didn't have its sharp claws plunged into. It was a proud advert for Capitalism, where everyone from the Chinese selling fake designer handbags in Petaling Street Market to the executives looking down on the clouds from their eyries at the top of the Petronas twin towers appeared to exist for the sole purpose of making money. It also felt like one of those shamelessly Westernised cities that whores itself to global brands so that you could sit in any McDonald's restaurant or Starbucks and always be able to see another one out of the window.

My mission in the city was violence rather than money, but I did my bit to bolster the wallets of the fat cats by checking into the five-star Shangri-La Hotel in the downtown Golden Triangle district. I felt at home in Asia and was tempted to relax for a while and live it up a little, but I had a lot of work to do in a very short space of time.

Mazlan's company was based in the Pudu area, right next to the stink and noise of Puduraya Bus Station, and I had already been to take a look. While tiny in comparison to many of the other buildings in KL, it was big enough to have two security guards at each visible entrance and it boasted a fair-sized lobby just inside the main entrance, where all visitors had to check in at reception then pass through an x-ray machine before getting scanned with some piece of hi-tech wizardry by more uniformed guards. It was clear that I wouldn't be able to get to Mazlan in his office, so that was the first problem to solve.

The good thing about a city like KL, where money is the be all and end all, is that supply always seems to meet demand, no matter what it is you demand. The young man selling knives, swords and various items of lethal-looking martial arts paraphernalia on a stall just off Petaling

Street Market initially laughed when I asked him if he knew where I could buy a gun. His laugh quickly transformed into a smile when I tossed a brick-sized wad of ringgits, the local currency, in front of him and promised him the same again if he delivered.

I met him that night outside a busy noodle stand and followed him nervously down a nearby alley where I was passed a heavy brown paper bag.

"Colt .45. Very best gun," the dealer said proudly as I tucked the parcel into my jacket. "Full magazine inside. Very easy for lady to use."

"Thanks," I said, handing over another wad of ringgits.

"No problem. You want come have some noodle with my friends?"

"Maybe some other time." I smiled at him and hurried back to the hotel.

The next morning I called Mazlan's office, a plan having come to me during the night.

"Good morning, it's Jane Chau calling from the New Straits Times," I announced when the receptionist answered the phone. "I was hoping Mr Mazlan might be free to join me for lunch today?"

"I'll put you through to his secretary."

I sat on my bed toying with the gun as I waited to be transferred.

"This is Mr Mazlan's secretary, how can I help you, Miss Chau?" The male secretary sounded like the last thing he wanted to do was help me.

"I was wondering if Mr Mazlan was free for lunch today."

There was an audible snort of derision on the other end of the phone.

"Mr Mazlan is meeting very important clients from overseas this lunchtime at the Golden Palace Restaurant. May I ask what this is about?"

"I would like to interview him, to hear his side of the story in response to recent media articles."

"Mr Mazlan has already said everything he wishes to say to the press. Good day, Miss Chau."

The rude bastard hung up, but I already had what I wanted.

It was only just gone 10am, so I had a leisurely breakfast in my room, familiarised myself with the gun, then pulled on a baseball cap to complete my hastily assembled tourist disguise and took a cab to the Golden Palace Restaurant in the Bukit Bintang area of the city. When I got there I found a handy café opposite, ordered a coffee and started watching the cars pulling up outside the restaurant.

It was approaching 1pm when a black Mercedes pulled up and the driver performed an impressive reverse parking manoeuvre to squeeze between an Audi and another Mercedes. I took a deep breath when the driver's door opened and the familiar, giant figure of Mazlan stepped out and bounded up the steps to the restaurant. I had assumed he would have bodyguards with him, so the fact that he was alone was a huge and unexpected bonus.

I guessed he would probably be inside for at least an hour, so I ordered a light salad from the café, slowly ate it while keeping an eye fixed on the restaurant across the road, then paid and went and sat on a nearby wall with a cumbersome city map unfolded on my lap.

At 2.45pm the doors of the Golden Palace Restaurant swung open and Mazlan walked out, again alone, glancing at his watch and taking car keys from his pocket. I pulled the cap low over my face, pushed the gun into my jacket pocket and with the map flapping in my hand I walked towards him.

"Excuse me, sir…"

I waved the map in front of my face as Mazlan beeped the alarm on his car and started to turn towards me.

"I'm in a hurry," he said, opening the driver's door.

"Me too," I hissed. "Get in the fucking car."

"What the hell…" he stammered.

I showed Mazlan the gun, then opened the rear door and climbed in behind him.

"Now, shut the door, buckle up and drive."

"What the fuck is this?" he demanded, obviously stunned.

"Don't you remember me?"

I took off my cap so he could see me in the rear-view mirror as I pressed the Colt against the back of his skull.

"You!" he screamed. "What the fuck are you doing here?"

He tried to turn around, but I pushed the gun harder into the nape of his neck.

"Just drive home, nice and easy. Try anything cute and I'll blow your head away and take my chances in the ensuing crash. I don't really care if I live or die anymore, Mazlan, but I'll sure as hell take you with me. Now drive."

He started the car and pulled away gingerly then kept silent as the

Mercedes bullied its way through the thick city traffic and out towards the northern suburbs. I ordered him to switch his mobile phone off then concentrated on keeping my hand and breathing steady as we entered an area of lavish homes hidden behind foreboding security gates.

"This is my home," he announced as we pulled up outside something of a fortress.

"Is anyone in? Wife? Children? Security?"

"My children live with my ex-wife in Singapore. I live alone and a cleaner comes once a week. That was yesterday."

"I hope that's the truth, because I don't want to have to slaughter your children. Now, drive up to the front of the house, then we both get out and you can turn off all your alarm systems, got it?"

He didn't answer, but drove up the long gravel driveway, parked in front of the two storey house and got out. I followed him as he deactivated his alarms and then told him to go in and walk to the kitchen. All the while I had the gun held to his head.

The house was cold and silent and the bare hallway seemed to confirm that no woman lived here, no one to fill the place with homely trinkets and make it welcoming. His kitchen was predominantly steel and as we went in my distorted face reflected off various rounded chrome surfaces – a face as distorted as my mind and my body.

"Sit on your hands, cross-legged on the floor," I said to him. He did as he was told. "Now, I want you to tell me about my friend Naomi. Tell me about the things you did to her."

"Who? What the hell are you talking about...?"

A deafening boom filled the room as the gun went off in my hand without me consciously pulling the trigger. Mazlan's kneecap exploded in a mist of blood and splintered bone and he fell back screaming. I quickly recovered from my surprise and stood over him with the gun now aimed at his face.

"My friend, Naomi, who was butchered in my bath, motherfucker. My best friend, who was tortured, cut to ribbons and left to die in a bath of petrol! Fucking remember that?"

"God, I had nothing... I'm going to fucking pass out. Maybank must have done..."

"Maybank must have done what?" I shrieked, the gun nearly going off again in my rage.

"Maybank contacted me after your story came out and asked me what I knew about it. Please, my knee."

"What did you tell him?" I demanded, ignoring his pleas.

"He emailed a picture of you to my office and said you were the reporter who had written the story. He asked if I recognised you, so I told him it was you who had come to me with the offer in the first place. Please Gemma, or Hannah, whatever your fucking name is; I didn't hurt anyone over this."

"So Maybank did it, did he?" I asked incredulously. "I'm supposed to believe a former Cabinet minister broke into my home and murdered my best friend?"

"I don't know, maybe he had nothing to do with it, but there are people who do these things, people who are employed very discreetly by Governments. You British, like the Americans, think your society is so superior to others that you have the moral right to throw your weight around, when in fact your Governments are as corrupt as many of those you seek to judge."

"Spare me the newspaper editorials, Mazlan. You're a corrupt fucking arms dealer, and that's all I'm interested in now. I want you to put me in touch with your friends at Jemaah Islamiyaah."

He laughed, despite his pain, and gave me a bewildered look. "What the hell for? Do you have any idea who these people are?"

"They're terrorists, not unlike my so-called Government. I want a contact number, or a meeting arranged."

"You stupid bitch! It's not like that; you don't just look these people up in the telephone directory."

"Mazlan," I said calmly, "since you last saw me I have lost my mind, or rather it was stolen from me by the British Government when they slaughtered Naomi. I have a whole new perspective on violence now and, to be honest, I'm just aching to test how far I'm willing to go. Looking around this rather dull kitchen of yours I can see at least eight ways of torturing you and if you don't tell me what I'd like to know by the time this hob heats up," I turned on one of the hobs on his electric cooker, "I will melt the fingers on both your hands. After that, I've got a couple of ideas for the cheese grater."

The hob was already starting to glow orange and Mazlan was staring at me with a resigned look.

"Okay, okay," he said, "it's your funeral. I go through a guy called Lee at a restaurant in Singapore. He contacts the JI people and either arranges discreet meetings or comes back with shopping lists from them and details of where shipments are to be dropped, and how payment will be made."

"How high up is this Lee?"

"I don't know; probably not very. He's just a messenger. He probably has to go through two, three, four more people."

"How can I contact him?"

Mazlan shook his head despairingly and reeled off a telephone number, which I wrote down on a notepad.

"Right, I want you to call him from your mobile and put him onto me."

The cowering Malaysian switched his phone on, pushed some buttons then held the phone to his ear.

"Lee?...It's Orca...I know, I know, but I've got someone here who wants to speak to you."

Mazlan passed me the phone.

"Is this Lee?" I snapped.

"Who is this?" asked the Oriental male on the other end, sounding annoyed.

"I'm the person in Mazlan's kitchen holding a gun to his head."

There was a brief pause, then: "So what. I don't think that's a problem for me, or my friends."

"Don't be so sure. Mr Mazlan has been in contact with the authorities again. They are very interested in his connection to JI and may be prepared to offer him leniency, perhaps even immunity, in exchange for information."

Mazlan started to protest, but I trained the gun on his groin and he shut up.

"What do you want?" asked Lee, now sounding distinctly alarmed.

"I want to meet your bosses, the very top people."

"Not possible. They don't meet people. Who are you?"

"I am somebody who can make Mr Mazlan vanish. I can also offer Jemaah Islamiyah its very own 9/11 – an opportunity to make a statement so big that the world will not be able to comprehend it."

There was silence on the phone and then Lee spoke again.

"Okay, one hour from now somebody will call back on this same number."

I ended the call and Mazlan started going mad again.

"Have you lost your fucking mind? What the fuck are you doing?"

I stared at him nonchalantly for a moment then lunged forward and smashed him across the temple with the butt of my gun. His eyes rolled back and he toppled over with blood streaming from his head.

I felt surprisingly calm but knew my nerves would start to jangle as I waited for the return call, so I poured myself a large Jack Daniels and perched on one of the kitchen stalls. As I looked down at Mazlan's body and felt the warmth of the bourbon inside me, my mind drifted.

I started to wonder what would happen if I was successful in my mission to avenge the death of Naomi by bringing death to those who had killed her. What would my purpose be after that? What would be the point of my existence?

I had set out on my journey to cure boredom, and in that respect I had certainly been successful. But the consequences had been beyond anything I ever could have imagined. People had died, more were set to die, and the effect on me personally had been devastating. I had postponed the grief and guilt of Naomi's death, and to an extent that of Mike Potter, so that I could focus on retribution, but that grief and guilt couldn't be suppressed forever. And besides, there were other, more dangerous, changes happening within me.

It was increasingly starting to look like I would either die in my pursuit of revenge, or would have to take my own life after I had achieved my goal. As my eager thoughts of dying in a plane crash suggested, death was not something that particularly frightened me. It certainly seemed to be an infinitely preferable alternative to growing old after a dull, average life and either being left a prisoner at home with television and medication for company, or moving into a leafy lodge to play scrabble with piss-drenched husks turned senile by boredom.

But the thought of killing myself was a whole new scenario. How would I do it? Would I do it with a clear mind and savour the moment, or would I intoxicate myself and do it? Would I go for something quick and violent, a bullet in the brain perhaps, or something slower, so that I could experience that ultimate feeling of dying? Perhaps I would choose an agonising exit; a way of punishing myself for the suffering I had caused. The possibilities were endless.

The one thing I knew for certain was that when my life ended I would also put an end to the unhappiness that had lived with me like a birthmark and had evolved into greater and greater despair as each new tragedy played out. It was worth dying just to be rid of that.

My morbid musings were brought to an end by the mobile phone ringing.

"Yes," I answered, focusing my attention back on the task in hand.

"Come to the front door." The voice was not Lee's, but the caller hung up before I could reply.

Mazlan was still unconscious so, picking up the gun, I cautiously went to the front door and peered through the spy hole. Distorted slightly through the tiny circle of glass was the stony face of whoever had just called me. His eyes had an Oriental slant but his skin was dark, like an Indian. His nondescript black hair could have come from anywhere between Mumbai and Tokyo, but the thin moustache above his even thinner lips gave him a look that suggested his origins were from the Indo part of Indo-China. He was staring blankly at the closed door and he continued to stare as I swung the door open and pointed my gun at his head.

"Mazlan," he simply said, looking past me and the gun into the house.

His hands were empty and the immaculate charcoal suit, white shirt and black knitted tie he wore gave him a look of authoritative respectability.

"In the kitchen," I said, letting him brush past me into the house.

I followed him silently into the kitchen and watched nervously as he examined Mazlan on the floor, then turned to me.

"Can I borrow your gun," he asked matter-of-factly, his accent indistinguishable.

"Not a fucking chance," I hissed, gripping the weapon tighter.

He shrugged, pulled a long knife from his inside jacket pocket, knelt beside Mazlan and slit his throat from ear to ear. My mouth fell open and my stomach churned as his neck split open and blood started pumping from the gaping black wound. Mazlan regained consciousness long enough to register shock and the fact that he was dying, then his body spasmed, twitched and he was dead.

The killer casually wiped the bloodied blade on Mazlan's suit and slipped the knife back into his pocket. He stood up and looked at my horrified face, then an arm shot out and a powerful hand clamped around my wrist. The gun fell to the floor and as I writhed in vain against his grip, I saw his other hand draw back, clench into a fist and then swing forward into my face.

Pain burned my head and a dark grey mist started dancing in front of my eyes as I fell to the floor, struggling to retain consciousness. My hand touched something warm and wet. It was resting in the puddle of blood growing around Mazlan, but my shocked brain couldn't decipher the signals it was getting to move it.

There were a few seconds of complete darkness, then the hazy light again. The killer was straddling me, a long spike in his hand. He moved the spike to my bare arm and pushed the cold steel through the skin, through the flesh and into a vein. My arm tingled, burnt, and then went completely numb. The same thing happened to my left shoulder, left side of my body, left leg, right leg, right side of body, right shoulder and right arm. Finally my head became paralysed and the grey mist I had been fighting gave way to complete blackness. I was gone.

Chapter 26

Black. Not painful, swirling blackness, but sharp, patterned black. Symmetrical and deliberate.

And white. This also precise, almost mathematical. Black and white. White and black. Nothing else except cold. Yes, very cold.

AGONY! Whole body burning; incredible, incredible pain. Muscles hard, bursting. Then soft, limp.

Blackness.

Black and white. Cold. Fuzzy. A sound – then the pain again! Arching! Burning! Bursting! Snapping!

Blackness.

Just black and cold. Pain! Stops. Trembling, shivering, cold and silence. Pain! Stops. Trembling and wetness.

Blackness.

White. Pain! Long pain – no end. Sharp and focused. Twitch.

Blackness.

Black and white. Cold. Dull pain. Different. This is body, this is head. Eyes. Look and see. Black and white is room. Big, cold chessboard room. Long walls, very high ceiling, no windows, no sign of doors, all black and white checked.

This is my body, it is sitting. Chair is cold, hard, metal. Steel bands are clamping arms and legs to this chair. My body is shivering and naked. On the chessboard floor are crumpled white knickers. Knickers look wet and are stained yellow and have flecks of red.

Next to knickers on the chessboard floor is a white metal box with black wires coming from it, like the legs of a giant insect. Brain is starting to work again, the lights coming back on and senses starting to function.

My name is Hannah Harker. I have been kidnapped and tortured mercilessly. Where am I?

At the far end of the room a section of the chessboard wall suddenly opened inwards and a figure stepped through carrying a black stool and a white bathrobe. As he walked towards me, his black shoes making a loud noise on the floor, I saw he was of the same appearance as the man who had killed Mazlan and taken me: Oriental eyes, dark skin, thin moustache and neatly combed black hair. He was wearing a black tunic buttoned to the top and white trousers. He looked to be about 40.

He placed his stool directly opposite me, sat on it with one leg crossed over the other and placed a cigarette in his mouth. He took a deep drag as the orange flame from his lighter licked the end, leisurely exhaled a thin jet of plum-coloured smoke and glanced at the metal box with the wires on the floor beside me.

Shaking his head and looking at me sadly he spoke without an accent: "Such a primitive tool, but Mr Serrasalmus – my friend who you met at Mr Mazlan's house in Kuala Lumpur – insists it is most effective for the purpose of taming a wild animal like yourself in preparation for a more docile and relaxed conversation. Used on the nipples and genitals of a man it produces a stunning effect, but applied to the same areas of a woman the effects are nothing short of phenomenal." He paused and glanced at the box again, then at the ugly wounds on my chest and between my legs. "But I'm not telling you anything you don't know, am I?"

I told him to fuck himself, but it came out as little more than an aggressive gurgle.

"Now then," he continued, knocking some ash on the floor, "during the three days that Mr Serrasalmus has been entertaining you – yes, it really has been that long – we've been doing a little investigating and come to a puzzling dead end. As far as we can tell you're not military, not affiliated to any secret service or intelligence agency, not one of those vulgar mercenaries and not even a humble police officer. Yet, there is nothing we have learned about you to suggest you would have the slightest interest in our cause, let alone joining us.

"According to our sources, less than a year ago you were nothing but an innocent little girl writing for a small English newspaper. Then you came across a couple of big stories, one involving the unfortunate Mr Mazlan, and made it into the 'big time'. A few months after that, you turn up in Malaysia, torturing Mr Mazlan in his own kitchen and demanding to meet

Jemaah Islamiyah! So, Hannah Harker, what on earth do you want with us? An interview?"

His voice had remained calm and composed throughout and now he was silent as he studied my eyes, apparently eager to hear my reply.

It took me a few moments to compose my thoughts before I could answer him. Yes, the bastard had tortured me, I was in real danger of being killed, and I felt hopelessly vulnerable strapped naked to the chair, but I had come looking for them. I had sought them so they could help me get my revenge on the people who had tortured and killed Naomi. That was more important than my own suffering because Naomi had gone through a million times worse than me, and all because of me. I had come looking for ruthless terrorists and that's exactly what I had found. My sole motivation in life was now revenge, and perhaps after Gerald Maybank and others were dealt with I could go after personal vengeance against the sadistic motherfucker Serrasalmus and the prick in front of me, but for now I wanted their help.

"What's your name?" I asked, instilling my voice with confidence.

"A little impolite of you to answer my question with a totally unrelated question of your own," he said, "but since you ask, my name is Guntur. To pre-empt your next two questions, I am the regional commander of Jemaah Islamiyah and we are in the bowels of JI's Singapore headquarters. It's a rather modest building by all accounts and far too near those fat, beer-swilling morons who parade up and down Boat Quay for my liking, but it is conveniently close to the harbour." His mouth twitched the briefest of smiles. "Now, as I have accommodated your queries, perhaps you would be so good as to answer my original question."

"Okay, I want you to help me blow up the International Terrorism Conference in Hong Kong," I said, staring straight into his eyes.

He looked hard at me, then leaned into my ear and whispered: "There are worse tortures than electric shocks, Hannah, and the consequences can be a lot more severe and permanent than soiled underwear and a few burns." He placed a hand on my bare thigh, his warm breath tickling the hair follicles in my ear. "We have a man here who has been with us for three years; a pet project of Mr Serrasalmus. Every day for those three years he has been sexually abused, tortured to the brink of death and then given just enough food and medicine to ensure he lasts the night and is conscious the following morning. Can you even begin to imagine how much pain he could inflict on your delicate little body? I suspect you won't want to even think about it. No, Hannah, you must be totally honest with me and tell me really why you are here."

"I told you why I'm here," I spat back defiantly. "I want you to help me destroy that conference because those people murdered my best friend."

I went on to recount the entire story to him. I was honest about setting up Mazlan and Maybank, I described what they did to Naomi, and I told him of my determination to get revenge on her killers.

He listened carefully, thoughtfully and without interruption as I spoke, and then sat in silence for a good couple of minutes after I'd finished while he analysed what I had said and considered his response.

"I believe you, Hannah," he finally said. "I believe you are telling me the truth." He lit another cigarette. "Unfortunately, there are very many issues, problems that lead me to think your mission has been fruitless.

"Firstly, there are less than three weeks to this conference, and an attack of this magnitude takes months, if not years of planning. Secondly is the fact that being an international conference on terrorism bringing together all of the world's leaders, security will be absolute. There would be no way of breaching the measures in force, short of detonating a nuclear bomb.

"As you may or may not be aware, JI has been hit hard in recent years by various crackdowns. Indonesia's counter-terrorism squad, Detachment 88, has been given funding, equipment and training by the Americans and Australians, and as a result they have been successful in capturing or killing a great number of our leaders. Our goal of uniting the nations of Indonesia, Brunei, the southern Philippines, Malaysia and Singapore into a fundamentalist Islamic state, something we refer to as Daulah Islamiyah, remains the same but our resources are being stretched thinner all the time and an operation on the scale you are proposing requires significant investment.

"We are going through a period of great change, Hannah. Our philosophies and goals are essentially unchanged, but the death of Osama Bin Laden has sparked a real debate among Islamic Fundamentalists about whether our strategies need to evolve. The world is changing and people are thinking differently, so we are wondering if we need to think differently too.

"As a final point, if all of this doesn't convince you, Hannah, then I have one more concern that I think will put paid to your fanciful plan: I don't believe you have the strength or the will to go through with it. I believe you when you say that you want to do it, that you wish to have your revenge, but I fear that when the moment came to 'push the button' your determination would falter because your heart is not so strong. You know I speak the truth, Hannah; you know you do not have the faith or strength to destroy yourself for a cause…"

He was going to continue but I couldn't listen to him a second longer, and I cut in with frightening calmness.

"Listen to me, you motherfucker. You know nothing of me. You know nothing of what is inside me, what I am capable of doing. I am a machine now and all I care about is killing the people at that conference.

"To take your first and second points together, there is more than enough time and the security issue will not be a problem."

I proceeded to explain to him in detail exactly how I intended to go about exploding a bomb inside what would be one of the most high profile gatherings of world leaders in years. He listened and nodded as I spoke, appearing to agree with me when I explained solutions to various problems. Of course, my plan was not without risk or expense, that was why I needed his organisation, but it was extremely plausible and I figured it had a more than 50:50 chance of success. The short time frame could also work in our favour because the intelligence services wouldn't know anything about it in advance.

"As for your reluctance to go into this project as an organisation," I continued after explaining the technicalities of the plan itself, "I cannot think of a better way of declaring the seriousness, competence and sheer size of JI than an attack on this scale. Before September 11, 2001, hardly anyone outside of intelligence circles had heard of Al Qaeda, but since that day it has become a name on the trembling lips of every man, woman and child on the planet. Just imagine what this attack would do for the name of Jemaah Islamiyah and its leaders! Bin Laden is dead and jihad needs a new face, so why not make it yours? Just as he was, you would become synonymous with the Islamic struggle right across the world.

"You want to unite fundamentalist Muslims by playing on the global intolerance and oppression of Islam? The people at this conference are the very people who dictate and cultivate that intolerance and oppression, forcing it upon their uneducated citizens until it becomes an accepted truth. You know that the West, led by America, will move from one Islamic country to the next waging war, just as they did with the Communists. The old enemies were Russia, Vietnam and Cuba, now it's Libya, Afghanistan and Iran. Who's to say Indonesia won't be next, or Malaysia, if they can come up with a half decent excuse to invade?

"Destroy this conference and you are not killing innocent civilians indiscriminately, you are specifically targeting the warmongers of the West. The media will call you terrorists, but we all know who the real terrorists are. It will be the ultimate rallying call to Muslims everywhere: dancing in the streets of Jakarta, Kuala Lumpur and Manila, jubilation in Tehran, Damascus and Kabul, confusion, panic and doubt in Washington and London."

Guntur was smiling now and gently nodding.

He said: "Okay, Hannah Harker, you are an eloquent advocate of jihad! I'm not sure that you believe what you are saying to me – I think you will say anything to secure my support – but I am willing to sanction this strike provided our leaders approve it and on the provision that you lead it. Your proposal does represent an opportunity for Jemaah Islamiyah to make a bold statement of intent and if you are successful then JI will publicly claim responsibility. If you fail then we will deny any knowledge of the plot."

"I will die for this," I assured him. "I will do everything in my power to ensure it is a success."

Guntur leaned forward and pushed something beneath my chair, which catapulted the steel restraints back and freed my hands and legs.

"I want you to do one thing for me," he said, his tone completely different now, almost respectful, "and then you will shower and have food and clothes and we will talk more."

"What's that?" I asked, standing up and rubbing my wrists.

"Come."

He passed me the white bathrobe, which I gratefully pulled on, and then he led the way across the chessboard floor and out into a long, completely white corridor. A staircase leading upwards was at the end of this corridor, but before we reached it we stopped at a door that I didn't see until we were standing right next to it. The door was on a slide and when he pulled it to the side there was complete blackness beyond; blackness and a terrible smell. A smell that I had last encountered when I had found Naomi's beautiful body mutilated in my bath.

Guntur flicked a switch and the room was instantly thrown into a blinding white light as if a thousand halogen bulbs had suddenly been turned on. It was an almost divine light, but this was not heaven, this was hell.

Only two things were in the room, which was as white as the corridor outside: a rusty black bed and the twitching, bleeding man chained to it. The remains of the man's face turned to look at us, the eyes expecting fresh agony. Was this Serrasalmus' "three-year project", I wondered?

As if hearing my thoughts, Guntur spoke: "A rather lowly JI member who we recently discovered was on the payroll of Australian intelligence. God knows what they offered him, but it has already led to a great deal of suffering for him, and his family."

"Great," I said sarcastically. "Can I have some clothes now?"

"Not just yet. You have one more thing to prove to me."

"What?"

Guntur pulled a ceremonial dagger from the folds of his tunic and handed it to me.

"I want you to prove to me that you really will kill when the time comes. I want you to kill this man."

I looked at the dagger, then the wretched figure on the bed, then at Guntur.

"This man is not a part of my plan. I have no issue with him, and nothing to prove to you."

"Wrong, Hannah, you have everything to prove to me. Many innocent lives will be lost if your Hong Kong plan is successful – press, security guards, interpreters, assistants, catering people – so I want to see you actually kill someone, just to reassure me that you won't back out at the last minute."

"Suppose I kill you!" I said menacingly.

"Then you will wander around this maze until our security people catch you, take you to Mr Serrasalmus and you get skinned alive and thrown into a pit of salt, or whatever takes his fancy. Please, just kill this man and we can continue to more important matters in much more agreeable surroundings."

I turned and looked once more at the man on the bed. His eyes met mine and I tried to read them. In the end I decided that they were saying: "Kill me! Please, spare me from any more torture."

I wanted to kill him quickly and didn't know whether to stab him or cut him. I'd killed four boys in a fire, but that was an accident in a lifetime

180

quite distant from this. I walked to the bed and placed the point of the dagger over his heart. Our eyes met, and I quickly looked away. In my head I counted very slowly to three then pushed the dagger down.

I screwed my eyes shut, then opened them again and saw that the knife had done little more than prick the skin. Shit!

I took a deep breath and raised the blade. It hovered in my hand and then I switched off my thoughts, shut down my mind and tried to focus on nothing as I looked blindly at the white wall. I flexed my bicep then brought the knife crashing down into the man's chest. This time, the cold steel tip of the blade sliced through his body with ease and punctured his heart, causing almost instant death.

I let go of the handle, tore my eyes from the wall and turned to the grinning figure of Guntur.

"You passed," he chuckled. "Welcome to Jemaah Islamiyah. You have now lost your murder virginity!"

I've lost more than that, I thought. I've lost everything I ever was. From this point on, I was a cold-blooded killer.

Chapter 27

The gun pressed against my temple was a Browning Hi-Power 9mm. The finger on the trigger was decorated with a thick jade ring and the tattoo on the man's forearm was a stamp of allegiance to the Wo Shing Wo, one of Hong Kong's most notorious Triad societies.

The air was almost unbearably humid and the case I carried ridiculously heavy, but my mind was cool and calm as I spoke to the hood.

"I am here to see Kwok Lai. He is expecting me."

The man spoke rapid Cantonese into the small radio on the lapel of his jacket and there was a crackle of static before a voice replied in the same language. The man lowered the gun he had been pointing at me and I was allowed through a thick steel entrance door into the barely noticeable club on Fife Street, between Sai Yee Street and Fa Yuen Street in the Mong Kok area of Kowloon.

It was a wholly inauspicious venue for an event where millions of Hong Kong dollars were due to be bet on an illegal cricket fighting tournament that afternoon. While cricket fighting was not in itself illegal in Hong Kong, betting on it was and the whole thing was kept under close scrutiny by the dominant Triad Societies: the Wo Shing Wo and the 14k.

The scent of sweat and jasmine tea clung to the humid air as I was led across a grimy concrete floor to a large table, where the man I assumed to be Kwok Lai sat, flanked by two suited bodyguards.

I knew that he was 87-years-old and was astonished by how well he looked. He had a thick head of neat grey hair, inquisitive and appraising grey eyes and a once handsome face tarnished by time and stress. He was wearing a tailored navy blue suit, a crisp white shirt and sky blue tie.

Lai had recently been elected as the dragonhead – leader – of the Wo Shing Wo despite complaints from many members that he was far too old for the role and would lack the spirit and resolve to battle against the dual enemies of the police and rival 14k.

The concerns were completely unfounded, however. Lai had been born into violence and lived with it all his life. As a teenager in World War Two he had joined the East River Column, a guerrilla movement fighting against the brutal Japanese Imperial forces who had seized control of Hong Kong following the surrender of the British Governor, Sir Mark Young, on Christmas Day 1941.

After the war he joined the Wo Shing Wo and spent most of his life running prostitution, gambling and drugs rackets on the streets of Hong Kong, until he finally moved up into the organisation's hierarchy and started dictating the rules rather than enforcing them.

My meeting with him had been set up through Guntur's contacts in JI and I knew that I was only granted this very rare audience by virtue of the fact that I was going to offer him a large sum of money.

A plastic tub with a cricket inside it was on the table in front of him and as I sat down in the chair opposite he started to speak in lightly-accented English.

"For $30HK I buy this ugly insect at the Bird Market. I feed it, tease it and make it angry with bamboo sticks, train it to become aggressive, and in the space of a single five minute fight it can make me many, many thousands of dollars.

"When I was a young man cricket fighting was so popular that people would devote their lives to hunting down the wildest, most fierce crickets. It was not just about money, but pride. To win meant honour for the cricket's owner, to lose meant humiliation.

"Of course, nothing so popular could be allowed to survive in this pitiful modern society of ours. The police won't let us bet our money on the fights, the use of chemicals on the land is destroying the crickets and the young people of today would rather inject drugs into their bodies or stick knives into one another than spend time patiently coaching a creature like this."

He looked at me directly for the first time, his grey eyes almost misty with melancholic nostalgia.

"But we will defy all these obstacles, young lady," he continued, "and continue to enjoy our sport, just as we enjoy many things outlawed by those who deem themselves morally superior to us.

"I think maybe you don't really understand though. How could you? You are young and, perhaps, innocent while I am a sad, cynical old man." He smiled and opened his palms in a c'est la vie gesture. "But you are not here to listen to me lament the past, are you. I understand that you have business you wish to discuss with me today. Would you like some tea?"

"Yes, I would like some tea, thank you, Mr Lai. My name is Hannah

Harker, it is an honour to meet you."

He dismissed the compliment with a slight snap of the wrist and sat back as a pretty Chinese girl filled two cups with jasmine tea from a porcelain teapot, which she left on the table between us and then retreated into the shadows. Lai drank noisily from his cup, then looked at me and spoke.

"I will tell you now Miss Harker that I have a great dislike for the people you represent. They are a dangerous mob of animals with unrealistic goals and a sickening indifference to innocent life. However, I am a businessman so I will listen to your proposal impartially and make any decision based on whether or not I judge it to be in the interests of my organisation."

I nodded respectfully. "I fully appreciate your feelings, Mr Lai. I personally feel exactly the same way about them, but they are a means to an end for me. They have provided me with the US$1 million I have in this briefcase, which I am offering to you in return for your organisation causing a major disturbance outside the Hong Kong International Conference Centre on the final day of the forthcoming terrorism conference. Another US$1 million will be paid after the conference."

"A disturbance?" he said, eyeing me suspiciously.

"Well, more of a riot to be precise."

"Presumably to create a distraction, but for what purpose?"

"That isn't important," I said.

His fist smashed against the desk, making me jump.

"Don't take me for a fool, little girl," he hissed. "I don't want my group associated with international terrorism. We have enough trouble taking care of the police as it is, without that sort of attention on us."

"Nobody will think that this is Triad related," I said. "These conferences attract disturbances all the time. There will be so many anti-Capitalist, anti-war, anti-everything protestors there already that it will be a time-bomb waiting to go off. All we need is for your organisation to send a few extra people down there to light the touch paper and ensure that a riot does indeed happen. I'm sure that for $2 million you can persuade some of your men to throw a couple of petrol bombs."

Kwok Lai scowled at me, clearly unimpressed with my disrespectful tone, but able to see that a lot of money was being offered for a relatively simple task.

He took a long slurp of tea and stared at his cricket for the best part of two minutes, clearly lost in deep deliberation as he made up his mind.

Kwok Lai never made hasty decisions, which is why he was still alive after nearly a century of fighting.

Finally he looked at me, reached for the briefcase I had placed on the desk, and said: "Give me the exact details of what you want and when you want it."

Chapter 28

I had been told by Guntur and the JI team who had worked on the plot with me to stay in Hong Kong after my meeting with Kwok Lai, but I disobeyed them.

I knew it was a risk to leave because they were probably watching me, but the conference was still three days away and I wanted to go back to Thailand. I had a strong feeling that I was going to die in Hong Kong and I just wanted to be somewhere tranquil for a while to reflect on my life, try to get my head a bit straighter and prepare for the end.

Bangkok Airways operated a three-hour direct flight from Hong Kong to Koh Samui, so I booked myself on the first available one. Upon reaching the island of Samui I joined the throng of excited young backpackers on the pier and boarded the overcrowded ferry to Koh Phangan. I found a seat below deck but the stench of engine fumes and the choppy waters of the Gulf of Thailand started twisting at my stomach so I went and sat outside where the carefree travellers around me were cheerfully swilling Chang beers, flirting, reading and talking about the upcoming Full Moon Party.

The ferry eventually chugged into Thong Sala pier and while most of the passengers jumped onto songthaew taxis bound for the beach huts around Haad Rin I went in the opposite direction to a small, quiet resort near Mae Haad Beach where I had stayed with my beautiful Naomi while we were travelling together.

I recognised the owner, but she didn't recognise me and I handed over a few hundred baht and strolled across the blistering sand to one of the little wooden huts sitting in the shade of a wind-battered palm tree close to the seashore. I kicked off my flip-flops, stepped over the little pile of coconuts at the foot of the creaky steps, and dropped myself into the well-used hammock without even bothering to unlock the hut or unpack.

After weeks of physically, mentally and emotionally suffocating work it felt good to relax and spend some time leisurely thinking through the logistics of what I would have to do in Hong Kong.

After killing the unfortunate man on the torture bed in Singapore, Guntur the JI chief had treated me completely differently and I was allowed to shower, given expensive new clothes and then we ironed out the details of my plan over drinks in his study. An architect's map of the International Conference Centre had been procured from somewhere and two other JI members had joined the discussions to give their views on how best to proceed. It was eventually decided that during the Triad riot on the final morning of the conference, I would dash in to the building with the explosives strapped to my body, having made my face well known to security guards during the previous three days. I would transfer the explosives to my handbag in the toilets and then in the afternoon, when all the heads of state would be gathered in the main hall for the closing speeches, I would slip out to the toilet again, this time leaving my handbag under the chair, and remotely detonate the explosives.

The US President was going to appear on the third day of the four day conference and give a speech before returning immediately to the States. We discussed at length how we may be able to penetrate security and bomb the conference while he was there, but after hitting a series of dead ends we reluctantly conceded that the security would simply be too tight that day. Instead, we would wait until he had left, and the security significantly slackened, before taking out the remaining world leaders the next day.

If by some chance I did survive the whole thing, it had not escaped my notice that I would probably be the only journalist left alive, or at least not seriously injured, in the building to report this incredible story as an eye-witness. I wasn't giving myself very good odds for survival though.

I still didn't know how I was going to receive the explosives. Guntur simply said that somebody would make contact with me in Hong Kong once the conference got underway, give them to me and explain how to use them. I wasn't happy about leaving it so late, but I couldn't exactly argue that I was experienced in this area so I reluctantly had to bow to his experience.

I tried to think more about how the plan would unfold, but even though it was still early morning the sun was already hot and I soon slipped into a deep sleep as the rolling waves played a lullaby and a gentle breeze rocked the hammock.

The big orange sun was kissing the horizon when I awoke several hours later and a quartet of leather-faced fishermen were dragging their nets and colourful long-tail boat up onto the beach after a hard day scouring the sea for anchovies and other pelagic fish to sell to the local markets.

My head was groggy so I went into the hut, stripped off and stood under a sporadic cold shower while a pair of geckos clung to the wall eyeing me suspiciously.

It was hot inside the hut so I didn't bother drying myself, instead laying down on the small bed and enjoying the chill as the overhead fan swished the air over my wet body. I remembered the litre of vodka I'd bought at the airport in Hong Kong and guiltily took it from my case, tipped a generous measure into the glass beside my bed and swallowed it in one go. The liquid burnt my throat as it went down, but the feeling was good, and I followed it up with two more shots. After that, my head was in a more familiar place so I pulled on a clean bikini, slipped some cash into the zipped pocket on the bottoms, wrapped a sarong around myself and took the remainder of the bottle back out to the hammock.

The beach was now deserted and the sky streaked with orange, red and violet as the sun melted into the sea and a near full moon rose to take its place.

I tried to gather my thoughts but couldn't focus, so I just sat there for a while enjoying the moment before taking the vodka and going to find a comfortable spot on the beach.

A slight chill had picked up so I sat down and hugged my knees to my body. Ahead of me, the moon shone its eerie light onto the inky sea, creating a twinkling pathway to the shore, where exhausted waves licked the jagged line of seaweed and shells.

Nothing stirred on the surface of the water.

I suddenly began to cry uncontrollably. I just fell apart in that spot and laid all my emotions bare before the moon and the sea. The tears streamed out as I twisted my face to the sky so the winking stars could watch my pathetic collapse.

Misery, loneliness, guilt and self-pity poured from my wretched little heart and the sea began to whisper to me. It called me closer, said it would listen to me, hold me tight and wash the sorrow away.

In a daze I hauled myself to my feet and started to stagger to the shore. The dusty sand became harder and moister, while the reassuring lap of the waves grew louder and the white orb in the heavens grew larger.

Warm froth tickled my ankles and then a colder wetness began slapping at my shins.

I gulped another mouthful of vodka and spun the bottle out towards the murky horizon.

The floor was soft and the water lifted my sarong and stroked my sunburnt thighs before gently feeling my bikini bottoms and flicking cold kisses on my abdomen. I never imagined the end could be so calm and beautiful.

A charcoal wall was rising ahead of me and then collapsed just below my neck. I gasped as the floor disappeared and my head was swallowed by the bubbling swell. Everything was suddenly spinning and looping, and it felt like a siren and a drum were clashing deep in the centre of my skull. My eyes were rolling and I had the sensation of being trapped in a giant washing machine. Round and round, up and down, in and out, side to side, back and forth.

My fingers scratched uselessly at water and my limbs flapped like those of a rag doll. I choked as my lungs begged the sea to let them live.

I wanted the end now. I lost all control as my body was rolled and spun by the ocean and I just wanted it all to be over. There was no life flashing before my eyes – just panic and fear.

I struggled in vain to break the surface, but I was too weak. There was a sensation of utter peace and contentment and then everything ended.

Something was scratching my face and ice was running through my veins even though my skin was burning. A dull pain shrouded my body and my head wanted to burst. I opened an eye and saw sand. I opened the other eye and a bolt of excruciating sunlight lanced it. Consciousness began to seep through me and I realised where I was.

The sea had spat me out. Not even the vast ocean wanted my contaminated soul and it had vomited me back onto the shore to continue my eternal misery.

My sarong was gone and my exposed skin was raw from the sun. I got to my knees and expected to see my beach hut, but the tide had dragged me a long way down the coast before dumping me in a rocky bay with no obvious signs of life. My feet and legs were cut and I limped painfully along the shoreline back towards my resort. En route I passed a small shop and pharmacy and went in to buy my supplies for the day. The elderly woman behind the counter was understandably concerned about a western tourist staggering in covered in blood, but I gave her a cold stare and she reluctantly sold me two bottles of SamSong rum, a tube of Savlon and a pack of Tramadol.

When I eventually got back to my resort the beach was alive with crowds of beautiful, bronzed young people and I attracted a few looks as I walked up to my hut and fell into the hammock. Ignoring them, I dropped four Tramadol pills with half a pint of SamSong, which swiftly erased all memories of last night's suicide attempt. As a calm wave flowed over me I looked out at the beach and started to surreptitiously masturbate over a group of gorgeous Israeli girls and boys who were playing a game of volleyball in their skimpy shorts and bikinis.

That night I repaired the physical damage as best as I could and went down to Haad Rin to find sex.

My trip to Koh Phangan had coincided with the monthly mayhem of the infamous Full Moon Party. Nobody ever really needed an excuse to get wasted and party here, but this was the one night each month when Haad Rin Beach became a fluorescent river of SamSong, Red Bull and coke and 30,000 painted ravers twisted and gurned from bar to bar, illuminated by the kerosene-scented glow of swinging fire sticks and poi, until the sun cautiously poked its head back over the beach the next morning to reveal a sandy graveyard of plastic buckets, lost flip-flops and broken humans.

I found what I was looking for in a grimy den of crunching techno, epileptic strobes and writhing flesh just back from the main beach.

Already wired from SamSong and Tramadol, I took another pill that I was handed by a stranger in the toilet and went clawing for sex as my mind dissolved. I didn't care about race or gender; I just wanted non-violent physical contact.

The first boy I found was young – maybe 18 – and small. He looked Mediterranean but I glared at him when he tried to speak and forced my tongue into his mouth. A clumsy hand crawled up under my skirt and I led the boy over to a seat in a darkened corner and urged him on as he childishly jabbed his fingers between my legs.

Angry beats punched the walls around us and screeching distortion tore at our faces.

I unzipped the boy and took his stiff cock out. His eyes were wide with drugs and excitement as I peeled off my knickers and climbed onto his lap, facing away from him as he slid into me from behind.

Whatever pill I had taken in the toilets kicked in and the music drilled into my cerebrum as I bounced up and down on the boy's lap. Hands touched and squeezed me and I shut out everything except the music and the sex before building up a quick rhythm and finally allowing a fucking mind-blowing orgasm to nuke every sinew of my twitchy being.

Hot semen filled me and the boy fell back. I climbed off him, glared at him, and slid off to be consumed by the heaving crowd.

I sneered and jerked my limbs aggressively in time to the beats in the middle of the dance floor, trying to make eye contact with people I wanted to fuck. Bodies and faces came close to mine, and I closed my eyes and let them press and grind against me. My mouth fell open in a silent scream as several hands probed and explored me, fingers crawling into my underwear, digging into my flesh and sliding into both my holes. I ignored the disgusted stares from pretty tourists and just let it all happen as my tongue skipped from mouth to desperate mouth.

Fuck you all, I thought. *Fuck you all to hell.*

I woke up sometime the next day on top of a sleeping bag on a sandy wooden floor. I was completely naked and my clothes were in a bundle in the corner. There was a bed next to me and a hairy arm was hanging over the side of it. I got to my feet and surveyed the rest of the scene. I was in a beach hut – not my own – and there were four bodies in various states of undress on the double bed, two men and two girls. Empty beer bottles, spirit bottles and spliff butts littered the floor and bedside tables.

I felt sore as I pulled my clothes back on and a flick-book of pornographic images flashed across my mind: my mouth buried in a sandy blonde pussy, a cock pumping the back of my throat, a hand twisting into my pussy, and fingers squeezing into my arse.

Giddy, I checked that I still had my purse and passport, then left the hut and got a *songthaew* taxi back to my own hut. I quickly packed my things, checked out and started making my way back to Koh Samui.

Fun time was over and the end was near. It was time to return to Hong Kong and avenge the death of Naomi.

Chapter 29

Hot water scalded my body as it burst from the shower head, so I turned it down a notch and wallowed in the steaming torrent for nearly 20 minutes before grabbing a towel and rubbing myself dry.

I'd been avoiding mirrors recently but stopped in front of the one in the bathroom to see what the last few months had done to me. The face that stared back wasn't actually as bad as I had feared. I looked older certainly – I looked like a woman instead of a girl – but the alcohol, insomnia, stress, grief and violence hadn't been as cruel to my face as it had to my head and heart. There were heavy black bags under my eyes and hints of grey in my hair, but the Thai sun had given me a tan and the few spots that had gathered on my chin could be easily concealed. I hadn't eaten properly for a long time so ribs were starting to show on my body and my arms and legs looked skinny, but it hadn't yet got to the stage where people would find my body disgusting.

Satisfied, I walked naked from the bathroom, picked up a glass of neat vodka and stood by the window of my room high up in Kowloon's famous Peninsula Hotel on the junction of Nathan Road and Salisbury Avenue. It was dark outside and beyond the twinkling lights of the ferries, junks and other vessels bobbing in Victoria Harbour the panoramic span of glass and steel skyscrapers on Hong Kong Island was being bathed in gaudy neon and dancing green laser beams for the benefit of the tourists below me in Tsim Sha Tsui. I looked across at the area called Admiralty, where the low, comparatively inconspicuous building that housed the International Conference Centre was located. This was a new building that the conference organisers had ironically chosen because it was set back slightly from the harbour and so was thought to be less vulnerable to a potential terrorist attack. The much more famous Hong Kong Convention and Exhibition Centre in Wan Chai North, where Governor Chris Patten had handed Hong Kong back to the Chinese on behalf of the British Government in 1997, was directly on the edge of the harbour and so presented more of a risk from attack by water.

As I watched I knew that inside the conference centre it would be a hive of activity as security people searched every inch for explosives, catering staff prepared food and organisers put the final touches to the terrorism conference, which would get underway at 10am the following morning.

Feeling too excited and anxious to relax, I slipped on a T-shirt and shorts and went out into the humid craziness of Kowloon. Not wanting to walk too far in the heat, I took the clean and efficient MTR from Tsim Sha Tsui a couple of stops back to Yau Ma Tai and went for dinner at the Chinese Garden Restaurant, an almost hallucinogenic arena of bright lights, bubbling tanks of live seafood, rapid fire Cantonese, chopsticks clattering against bowls and plenty of beer guzzling. Pretty little Chinese waitresses with earpieces in bustled around the tables like excited presenters on the set of a children's television programme and I was soon tucking into beef and bamboo shoots with oyster sauce, crispy duck and a couple of cans of Heineken.

After dinner I walked round the corner to Temple Street, where I unhurriedly explored the famous night market. I bought a couple of pirate DVDs, a copy of Chairman Mao's Little Red Book, resisted the urge to buy a nine inch vibrator and watched some atrocious karaoke with a blind guy on a fiddle. Haggard old women and men at wooden tables beckoned me with wrinkled fingers to have my fortune told, but I already knew my destiny and I didn't want to share it with strangers.

By the time I reached the end of the market it was starting to get late so I walked back to the Peninsula and slept like a log.

I woke early the next morning feeling refreshed and relaxed. After a light breakfast in my room I dressed in a smart black suit and walked the short distance to the bustling Star Ferry terminal, where I joined hundreds of other people on the brief but noisy ride across Victoria Harbour to Central.

Gazing up at the awe-inspiring buildings around me like a small child, I picked my way along the crowded streets to Admiralty and presented my press pass at the police barricade on Harcourt Road before being allowed to join the queue of people waiting to run the gauntlet of security.

I felt eyes on me everywhere and in every corner stood suited men in dark glasses with conspicuous wires running into their ears and even more conspicuous bulges under their jackets. Sniffer dogs were prowling up and down the queue of hot and harangued media people and everyone was being herded through metal detectors, having their clothes scanned for traces of explosives and photographed for a security pass.

Nobody was taking any notice of the small crowd of banner-waving protestors that had gathered outside to bemoan the greedy, war-mongering leaders of the West and for the first time I felt really nervous. Would the Triad riot in a couple of days cause enough of a distraction for me to smuggle in the explosives?

When I reached the reception desk I showed my press card to the impassive security guard and gave him a friendly smile.

"Hey, how's it going?" I said. "Bet you'll be glad when all this is over."

He didn't reply or even look at me. He pushed my identification back across the desk and motioned for me to walk through the metal detector.

Jesus, how was I ever going to get past these robots with a bag of explosives? The security made JFK airport seem lax. I had to hope that everyone was just extra tense because it was the opening day and that they would relax a bit as the conference wore on.

I finally made it to the main hall, where scores of print reporters were battling with the TV and radio guys for a prime spot near the stage. The stage itself was bare apart from a long table with a dozen or so chairs lined up in a row behind it and huge bunches of microphones in front of each seat: CNN, Sky, BBC, Fox, the Chinese networks, etc. Hanging above the stage was a screen displaying the name of the conference, in case anyone had forgotten why they were here.

I got a seat six rows back next to a girl who seemed to be enjoying watching an escalating battle for positional supremacy between a CNN anchorwoman and an NBC reporter.

"Stupid Americans," she said with an accent I couldn't quite place as I sat down. "Just look at them. They've got to be seen to be sitting in the front row when their dull little reports go out tonight."

"They're never happy unless they're at war with someone, eh," I replied, turning to look at her. "Hannah Harker. I'm with the International Morning Post." I offered a hand. She was cute. Really cute.

"Simone Ryan, I'm with the Guardian." She shook my hand warmly and returned my look. "Well, it certainly beats trade union disputes back in London. A few days in the sunshine, bit of shopping and then some fairly straightforward copy to file at the end of the day."

"It certainly could be worse," I agreed, my eyes reluctantly leaving hers, scanning the room and coming to rest with disgust on two men chatting amiably in the front row: Sebastian Barr, The British Prime Minister's official spokesman, and Gerald Maybank!

Maybank threw his head back, laughing at some joke or other, and I wanted to run over and plunge a knife into his face. It confirmed to me, too, that the bastard was still very cosy with the Government and that strengthened my resolve to blow the lot of them to hell.

The conference eventually got underway with a bland and predictable opening speech from the UN Secretary General followed by a more inflammatory speech from China's Minister of State Security, who spent nearly two hours flicking through colourful charts and graphs and waving a laser pen over a projected image of a world map.

Lunch was big enough to feed a small African country and the highlight of the afternoon was a cautionary 30-minute speech from the French President, followed by a lengthy and dull translated lecture from the Japanese Prime Minister and a few lacklustre words from the German Chancellor. The US President wasn't due to arrive until the third day and the British Prime Minister looked slightly lost without his buddy, sandwiched as he was uncomfortably between the Russian President and the Italian Prime Minister.

There was a flurry of questions from journalists at the end of the day, then everyone started filing stories from laptops and shooting pieces-to-camera before piling out of the conference centre for a much needed drink.

I went off with Simone to nearby Lan Kwai Fong, the small enclave of bars with names like The Bulldog where homesick ex-pats congregate each night for bangers and mash, English football and overpriced lager.

We found a bar that didn't seem to be quite as packed as the others, bought vodkas and took them to a quiet booth tucked away at the rear. I had been chatting to Simone throughout the day, but as we sat down I was able to properly look at her for the first time. I suppose that was the moment when I knew my life was going to take yet another emotional detour, probably for the worse.

Quite simply, she was the most attractive girl I had ever been in the company of. She wasn't necessarily the most beautiful or the sexiest, but there was something about her that instantly set my hormones bouncing and I knew I would do everything in my power that evening to take her to bed.

She was a bit older than me – perhaps in her early thirties - but height and build wise we were about the same. Her hair was almost black and was tied back in a ponytail and her long thin nose and mouth weren't dissimilar to mine either. What made her truly beautiful though were her eyes, which she later told me she had inherited from her mother, a schoolteacher from Alcobendas, a working class town located a few kilometres north of Madrid. They were deep, dark and beautiful and everything she did and said was reflected in them. They were constantly alive and it took a lot of effort not to become completely lost in them as they reeled you in. She was dressed unfussily in tight black trousers, black sandals and a white shirt and the only make-up she wore was a smudge of concealer on a couple of spots and a little mascara around the eyes.

She was smiling at me.

"Are you all right?" she asked in her intriguing accent, which I had learnt during the lunch break was a mixture of Spanish and Irish. Her mother had married an Irish journalist and moved to Galway when Simone was eight.

"Um, yeah, fine. I think the heat's frazzled my brain a bit, I've not been with it at all lately."

"Tell me about it. I've been having about four showers a day and my body still seems to be dripping with sweat all the time."

A mini volcano started trembling between my legs. Was she fucking flirting with me? Was she keen?

"Come and sit over this side if you want," I said as coolly as possible. "The fans seem to be getting me and missing you."

She pushed her glass across the table then came round and sat next to me, twisting so her knee was pressing against the outside of my thigh and her face was close to mine. I took a long gulp of vodka to muffle a little whimper of excitement.

"So, Hannah, what's waiting for you in London?"

"What do you mean?"

"Do you have a husband? A boyfriend? A girlfriend?"

"Oh, um, no; I'm not seeing anyone right now. You know what this business is like, the hours and the lifestyle make relationships very hard, unless you're going to get together with another journalist, and we all know what arseholes they are. What about you?"

"No, nothing either really. Kind of makes you wonder if there's even any point going back, doesn't it?"

Her eyes were trying to lock mine.

"Yeah, things certainly seem to be a bit more, erm, interesting out here," I replied feebly.

"It does look that way from here."

She grinned and casually let her hand rest on my thigh, just an inch too high for it to be simply a friendly gesture. I was sweating a lot and I pressed my leg a bit harder against her knee and turned to look her properly in the eyes.

"Where are you staying?" I asked.

"Some shit hole up in the New Territories, with a bed barely big enough for a cockroach, and there are plenty of them. What delightful little hostel did the Morning Post manage to find for you?"

"The Peninsula." I grinned sheepishly. "A reward for good behaviour."

"I say," she arched her thin black eyebrows at me. "You must have been very good to someone."

"I'll be as good or as bad as I need to be if it means getting something I want."

"Hmm," she smirked, ran her tongue quickly over her top lip and looked hard at me again. "What else do you want, Hannah Harker?"

"In life, or tonight?"

"Let's start with one thing at a time. What do you want tonight?"

Simone's glass was empty and I looked down at it to avoid her burning gaze.

"Why don't we discuss it over another drink," I said. "Back at my place."

"At the Peninsula? Do you think they will let a peasant like me in?" she joked.

"They probably won't let you into the bar," I said with a playful frown. "I'll have to distract the doorman and smuggle you up to my room."

Her lips parted a fraction and she reached for her handbag. "Let's go."

The MTR train from Central back over to Tsim Sha Tsui seemed to last an eternity and it was so packed that Simone and I had to stand on opposite sides of the carriage, catching each other's eyes occasionally and smiling. We eventually got off and walked hurriedly to The Peninsula, pushed through the busy lobby and went to the lifts.

The lift ride up to my floor was torture. She moved as far away from me as she could in the tiny box and started sucking a fingertip, pretending she was nibbling a fingernail. I could see she had a big smile on her face, but she refused to look at me.

The lift mercifully reached my floor and I pushed past her as the doors parted and walked to my room. I fumbled with the key card and felt her breath on the back of my neck as I eventually got it to work and pushed the heavy door open. I switched on the lights and she followed me in.

"Wow," she said, taking in the surroundings, "you really are the little princess up here in your castle."

"One mustn't grumble, dear girl."

She smiled and walked towards the bathroom.

"Call down for some champagne will you," she called over her shoulder. "I'm going to take a shower, if you don't mind?"

"Be my guest. Are you hungry?"

"Yes I am," she said, pushing the bathroom door closed with her foot as she started unbuttoning her shirt. "But not for food."

My heart fluttered as I stared at the closed bathroom door and heard the shower start. I called down to room service and ordered a bottle of Moet with two glasses, then rummaged around in my suitcase for the nicest underwear I could find – matching black satin panties and bra from Agent Provocateur that had been delivered to me at the Jemaah Islamiyah headquarters in Singapore.

There was a knock at the door and I let the room service boy in to drop off the champagne, ice bucket and two glasses. I thanked him, slipped him a bank note and then shut the door as Simone reappeared from the bathroom with one of the towelling robes tied around her.

"That's better," she announced. "Why don't you jump in while I get the champagne open?"

I shut myself in the steamy bathroom, stripped off and stood under the shower, taking extra care to clean myself thoroughly, then got out and brushed my teeth. My hands were shaking as I checked my face in the mirror and pulled on the underwear, then pulled on the other towelling robe and went back out into the bedroom.

Simone sat on the edge of the bed with a glass of champagne in each hand, one offered towards me. I sat right next to her, took the glass, chinked with her and took a long drink before placing the glass down on the floor.

"So," I asked quietly, "what are you hungry for?"

She gave a little cough and leant forward to put her glass on the bedside table. As she did so, her dressing gown parted and I saw she was wearing no bra. She turned back, put her right hand on my thigh and with her left hand she gently but firmly pushed me onto my back on the bed and lay down next to me so that our faces were almost touching.

"I am hungry for you, Hannah."

Her lips met mine and she planted three tiny kisses on my mouth – one on each corner and one in the middle. As she kissed me the third time her mouth opened and her tongue slid out to start licking my own parted lips.

I was suddenly aware of being damp between my legs and I closed my eyes and pushed my tongue out to meet hers. They playfully flicked at each other and shyly danced, before our mouths locked firmly together and the kiss became altogether more passionate.

Her hand reached down to undo the belt around my robe and goose bumps seemed to break out across my body as her fingers started making little circles and crawling across my stomach and chest.

I removed her belt too and when her robe fell open I saw that she was completely naked underneath.

"You're beautiful," I murmured as I looked at her firm breasts, gorgeous tanned abdomen and the thin black strip of hair between her legs.

"Thank you," she whispered and rolled on top of me.

She started kissing me even more furiously and her breasts and groin were pushing against mine as her foot stroked up and down my shin.

I reached down under her robe and placed my hands on her amazing little arse, grabbing a cheek in each hand and squeezing hard.

Her mouth worked away from mine and started kissing my chin and then my neck and throat. I loved having my neck kissed and I arched my back to expose more of the flesh for her to run her tongue over. She also used the opportunity to reach under me and unclip my bra, then pulled my robe off and tossed it on the floor. She then sat up on me and shook off her robe.

My body, naked apart from the little satin knickers, was quivering with excitement and I watched the stunning woman sitting astride me take a hair band from around her wrist and tie her hair back into a pony tail. She then winked, grinned and began agonisingly slowly pulling my knickers off.

My heart was pounding with anticipation as she pushed my legs apart and an orgasm threatened to escape when she touched her lips against the inside of my thighs.

I threw my arms up behind my head submissively and lifted my arse off the bed to push my groin towards her. She pushed her hands face up into the space under me and I let myself drop back so that my arse was resting on her warm palms. She then kissed my pussy and a trillion volts of electricity surged through me.

I writhed with utter joy as her tongue teased the outside of my pussy and then pushed inside and greedily lapped my wetness.

Simone did things to me with her tongue that no man had even come close to doing. It was so incredible that I could barely stand it and when she slid in a finger as well I simply let out a huge shriek and came hard in her face. She moaned herself and tried to put a second finger in, but I wanted to have her too.

"I can't take anymore," I whimpered pathetically. "Let me have a go on you."

She crawled off me and while she was still on all-fours I pounced on her, pinning her legs to the bed and kissing the base of her spine. She giggled and buried her face down into the pillow so that her arse stuck up in the air. I kissed it and playfully bit at it while running my fingernails down the back of her thighs to the crease at the back of her knees.

Her muffled voice said something into the pillow, but I just stared at the gorgeous sight before me and clamped my mouth against her pussy. She was already soaking and I felt yet another orgasm grumbling through me as I tasted her cum mixing with my own saliva.

I kept my mouth locked against her for several minutes until, gasping for air, I swapped my tongue for my fingers. She squealed and urged me on as I pushed two fingers deep inside her and used my thumb to rub her clit. Her breathing grew heavy and I could see she was biting the pillow as I worked my fingers deeper, faster and harder to try and tease an orgasm from her. With my spare hand I ran my fingers across her back and then put them in her mouth so she could suck on them.

Finally her whole body shook and I felt her pussy tighten around my fingers as she came.

She collapsed onto her back and we started kissing again and hugged each other tightly, squeezing our bodies as close together as was humanly possible. We intertwined our legs and it was amazing to feel our hearts pounding against each other as the intense sex gave way to tenderness and affection.

Our faces were glistening with sweat and each other's juices, and I happily closed my eyes and let her kiss me as I gently played with her hair. I whispered that I loved her and she gripped me even tighter. We just couldn't get close enough to each other, so we got under the covers and hid there, holding each other until dawn.

Simone left my room early the next morning so she could collect a change of clothes from her own hotel before the conference started for the day.

Almost as soon as she had gone I missed her. I remained in bed and wondered what the night before had meant for her. I had told her at one point I loved her, and even though I knew how vulnerable I was to extreme infatuation perhaps I had meant it. What were her feelings though? Would she be awkward with me today? Would she come back tonight? I struggled for some reason to vividly recollect her face and this set me off on a typically melancholy train of thought about unrequited love and rejection, which I struggled to snap out of. Eventually I just closed my eyes, relived the memories of the night before and brought myself slowly to orgasm with my fingers.

Chapter 30

The next day security at the conference was just as tight visibly, but the tension seemed to have eased a bit, presumably because the first day had gone without a hitch.

The protestors were still chanting outside the building and the police and security agents were still eyeing everyone suspiciously, but the nervous edge that had been palpable the day before had definitely lessened.

As I made my way to the reception desk I was pleased to see the same security guard on duty and even more pleased when he returned my smile and said "Thank you very much, Miss Harker" when he returned my ID and conference pass.

In the hall the Americans were still fighting for the best seats, but I took the same spot next to Simone, my heart fluttering when I saw her again. Her hair was down today and she was wearing a tight red shirt, unbuttoned to show off her cleavage, and a short black skirt. She had bright red lipstick on her mouth and heavy black mascara around her eyes. I wanted to fuck her there and then.

"Hey." I let my fingers brush against her bare thigh.

"Hey back, gorgeous." She stroked the back of my hand and shuffled closer so that our hips pressed together.

"Did you get back to your place okay this morning?" I asked.

"Yes. The receptionist gave me a very dirty look for being a filthy stop-out though."

She looked at me and winked.

"I had a little solo session after you left," I admitted.

"Did you indeed? I had better confess in that case that I thought about you while I was in the shower this morning. It's a shame you weren't in there with me."

We both giggled and held each other's gaze.

"Are you coming over tonight?" I asked.

"We'll see. I expect so."

I grinned, I think more out of relief than anything else, and settled back in my chair as the conference got underway.

The main speech today was from the British Prime Minister, who kicked off proceedings with a selection of sound-bites about Al Qaeda and the Taliban to ensure he made the following day's front pages but didn't actually say very much of interest at all. He was followed by the Russian President, who spent a dire hour describing through a translator how he would crush rebels in the north Caucasus region, where the insurgency had spread from Chechnya to neighbouring Dagestan and Ingushetia.

I filed some copy back to the Morning Post during the lunch break and then in the afternoon sat through speeches from the Italian Prime Minister and Indian Prime Minister, before the day finished early.

On the way out I asked my security guard at reception for directions to Kowloon's Lady's Market, just for the sake of getting him to remember my face, and we shared a joke before I left and returned straight to the hotel.

I ate a light meal alone in my room before Simone came round again, this time with an overnight case. I struggled to hide my delight that she would be staying all night.

That evening there was none of the urgency of before and we both took our time in our love-making. We undressed each other slowly and touched and caressed with care, responding to each other's bodies. We kissed like familiar lovers and we used our fingers, mouths and tongues much more gently, patiently bringing each other to orgasm. For several hours we played together like this, taking it turns to pleasure each other, and once we were both satisfied we laid in each other's arms and chatted until the sun came up.

The following morning – the third day of the conference – was all about the arrival of the US President.

Simone and I had ordered breakfast in bed, but our tender words to each other were drowned out by the sound of helicopters trembling and buzzing outside the window.

We showered and dressed together then took the lift downstairs and stepped outside to find treble the number of Hong Kong police on the streets and a conspicuous US military presence.

A security checkpoint had been set up on the Kowloon side of the Star Ferry terminal and we had to show our press passes and submit to a search before being allowed to board the ferry.

On the ride across Victoria Harbour we watched a police patrol boat stop a suspicious looking junk and a posse of armed officers jumped on board and started roughing up the crew. A black speedboat with a US flag fluttering on the stern swept up alongside the junk and four divers dropped into the water to carry out a search of the hull.

When we got over to Hong Kong Island we found that an exclusion zone had been established which effectively blocked off the whole of Central and Admiralty. Armed security people prowled everywhere and snipers were visible on rooftops.

We were practically dragged off the ferry by police and once again had our press passes checked before being frogmarched along deserted roads to the conference centre.

The protesters were nowhere to be seen (they had been penned off several blocks away from the conference centre) and more helicopters hovered overhead as American secret service agents snarled at reporters. Simone and I were pushed through a metal detector and had to empty our handbags, before being roughly frisked by some bitch in a suit who made sure she had a good grope. My friendly security guard had returned to being a robot and when I eventually made it into the hall even the American TV people seemed to be on their best behaviour.

As most people expected, the day was little more than a platform for America to assert its right to detain, bomb and torture anyone who doesn't know the words to Star-Spangled Banner or who has a beard. The British Prime Minister looked much happier sat next to the President and the pair of them clapped loudly at the vitriolic rant from the US Defence Secretary and the weary lecture from the head of the CIA.

At lunch I filed an updated story back to London and then was talking to Simone when one of the conference centre staff came trotting over and told me I had a call at reception. I followed him to a desk where he handed a phone to me.

"This is Hannah Harker, who am I speaking to?"

"Stop fucking around with your dyke friend, you have work to do."

I didn't recognise the voice but instantly knew it was someone from Jemaah Islamiyah. He was right and so I decided not to argue and let him continue.

"Tonight you are to be alone at your hotel, in your room. Someone will collect you at 9pm. If you miss the appointment you, your girlfriend and both your families will disappear."

"I'll be there," I growled, thumping the phone down.

I walked back to the lunch area and found Simone.

"Who was that?" she asked.

"Bloody office, checking up on me."

"Other side of the world and they still track you down."

"Yeah, I know. Listen, babe, I'm not feeling too great. Do you mind if we don't spend the night together?"

"What's up?"

"I don't know, just tired I guess, and all this heat and weird food is starting to play around with me. I'll be fine after a good night's sleep."

"Oh, okay."

She looked hurt so I let my fingers touch hers and I told her it was fine and that I wasn't making excuses not to see her.

"Sure?" she asked.

"Of course. I promise I'll go to sleep thinking about you. I'm going to miss you like hell."

"I'll miss you too."

We looked into each other's eyes, desperate to kiss one another but knowing that was impossible where we were.

The afternoon session was given over to the US President's speech and the American media people greeted his arrival at the lectern with thunderous applause, while the rest of us sat there with rather bemused smirks. His speech held no surprises and I had trouble writing some of his bullshit down with a straight face.

He eventually finished and everyone stood aside as he was whisked away in an armoured procession to Chep Lap Kok Airport, where Air Force One was waiting to rescue him.

After the President left there was almost a party atmosphere at the Conference Centre and the remaining security people could be heard making sarcastic comments, joking with the press and visibly winding down. A whole group of us – minus Simone who had gone straight back to her hotel - headed over to Lang Kwai Fong for drinks and I stayed for a couple of vodkas to calm my nerves.

From Central I went back to the Peninsula and waited in my room for a phone call from reception, which came at precisely 9pm.

"You have a visitor in reception, Miss Harker."

"Thank you, I'll be right down."

I had to stop myself holding my breath in the lift down to reception, and when the doors pinged open I had to suppress a gasp: Serrasalmus, the bastard who had tortured me for three days, was standing there in a charcoal three-piece suit with a big grin on his face.

Before I could react he stepped towards me, embraced me firmly and kissed me on the mouth.

"Hello, Hannah," he leered. "How's your cunt?"

In a flash I reached between his legs and crushed his balls in my hand. He didn't so much as flinch.

"I have a car waiting outside, my darling. Come."

I reluctantly let him lead me outside, where a chauffeur was waiting beside a black Bentley with the back door open. I climbed in and Serrasalmus followed, shutting the door himself as the car pulled out onto Salisbury Avenue and turned up into the kaleidoscopic chaos of Nathan Road, heading away from the harbour.

The driver expertly manoeuvred the big car through the jungles of neon, concrete and glass that were Tsim Sha Tsui, Jasper Road, Yau Ma Tei, Mong Kok and Prince Edward out towards the New Territories. As we approached Yeun Long, where the pace of life tangibly eased, Serrasalmus picked a satchel off the floor and placed it on the seat between us.

"Now, listen carefully," he said, taking out a large oblong package wrapped in brown paper. "This is Composition A, a plastic explosive that contains RDX. I don't expect you to know anything about this but RDX is the most powerful and brisant explosive. Brisance, Hannah, is the shattering capability of an explosive and this guarantees that your efforts tomorrow will be as messy as possible. "

"This," he said, taking a black plastic box from his pocket and extending a steel aerial, "is a remote detonator, which will trigger the explosives. It has a powerful signal so you can leave the explosives shut in a handbag and still detonate them from several rooms away, which I suggest you do if you want to keep your pretty face in one piece."

He put everything back into the satchel, handed it to me then continued. "The riot that has been arranged will reach its peak at 9am, so this is when you are to arrive at the conference centre with the explosives and the detonator taped to your beautiful body. Now, you will be delighted to hear that I will already be inside the centre by this point…"

"What! How the hell are you going to get inside?"

"Oh, don't you worry about that, it's all taken care of. When I see you dashing through the riot to safety I will be able to guide you through security, with the approval of your friendly guard on the reception desk, and get you past all the dogs and detectors."

"And then what are you going to do?"

"I'm going to stick around and watch how you get on, from a safe distance of course."

I could feel my chest pounding, both with revulsion at being so close to this maniac and the thought of him watching over me tomorrow.

"I warn you now," I said, "that if you try to fuck with me in any way tomorrow, I will kill you."

"Hannah, my angel, I'm just going to be there to make sure things run smoothly for you. Think of me as your new daddy."

I ignored him and noticed that the Bentley was heading back towards the harbour, the billboards and shop-fronts of Nathan Road becoming gaudier and the crowds thicker. I was dropped right next to the famous lion statues outside the entrance to the Peninsula and clutching the satchel tight against my chest I hurried passed the smart little doormen, through the lobby to the lifts and went straight up to my room.

Later that night, sitting alone on my bed with a half empty bottle of vodka, I gently wept as I considered not going through with the bombing.

My change of heart had nothing to do with the bombing itself or the fact that the leaders of some of the world's most powerful nations would be killed. No, it was because of my irrational crush on – love for? – a girl I barely knew.

It had hardly crossed my mind previously that Simone would be in the hall when I blew it up, but now I had the explosives in my room it really hit me. What spell, what fucking curse, had the girl put on me in such a short space of time that this was happening to me? Was she some kind of angel perhaps, sent by a God somewhere to stop me and protect the world? She had chained herself to the inside of my head and wouldn't let a second pass without rattling those chains and reminding me that she was there.

Drunkenly, I hit myself hard on the head with the bottle, called myself a weak dyke bitch and called her an ugly slut whore, but the face in my head smiled back sweetly and those eyes just pushed their love deeper into my heart and I was back to square one.

I forced images of Naomi's corpse into my head to remind me why the bombing had to happen. The love I had for Naomi was so deep and was forever inside me on so many levels that I couldn't betray her by not going through with it. Christ knows I had made enough sacrifices to get to this point, and Simone would just have to be my final sacrifice.

But what if she didn't have to be?

I let out a little cry and swore at myself. The girl just used you for a fuck, I told myself, because she loves the attention. What a boost it must be for her ego to have someone like me chasing her around and hanging on her every word. She would go off with another man or woman, probably right in front of me, without a second thought. There's no fucking way she was laying pissed in her bed right now thinking about Hannah Harker. She was probably in an alleyway with a cock stuffed in her mouth, or with some hostess girl's fingers up her! My whole body was clenched in rage, but then the images scattered and I completely broke down in hysterical sobs.

No matter what I told myself, I couldn't erase the memories of the way she had looked at me, the sincerity with which she had used her hands and mouth on my body. At first it may have just been sex, but after the first night the warmth and pleasure I had shared with her was love.

I was in love with her. It had been love at first sight. It happens. Maybe it hadn't happened to me before, but now it had.

My head was throbbing and my face clammy with tears. Was there any way I could detonate the bomb without hurting her? There had to be. No matter what happened to everyone else at the conference, I knew that I mustn't hurt Simone.

I felt sick and terrified. I had finally found love, but fate despised me so much that it had made me fall in love with someone I might have to murder before the week was out. It was such an insanely cruel twist I almost felt I should smile.

The whole room was spinning and it was so hot I was burning up. I took a swig of vodka and nearly threw it straight back up.

I wanted her there with me at that moment. I buried my face into the pillow in the hope of catching her scent, but the bed had been changed. If I could blow up the building without hurting her, would we live together? My heart skipped at the thought, but then my head took me to the scenario where she died and down I went again.

Finally something took pity on me and I passed out.

Chapter 31

The sound of an agitated mob reached my ears the moment I stepped off the ferry at Central the next morning. As I neared the conference centre the noise became a deafening fury and when I actually saw the riot I was absolutely stunned at the performance Kwok Lai had arranged.

The Chinese Prime Minister was due to give the closing speech today and outside the conference centre was maybe a thousand people – men and women, young and old – screaming in Cantonese and Mandarin what I guessed to be pro-democracy slogans. Rocks were being hurled at riot police, who held an unconvincing line behind shields, and as I approached the scene a petrol bomb flew through the air and smashed against a police van, setting the vehicle alight.

Under my jacket and shirt I felt the explosives strapped around my waist press against my body and I started to sweat. I had no idea how stable the explosives were and what it would take to set them off. With petrol bombs, rocks and bottles flying around me, I had horrifying visions of my top half separating from my bottom half with a very loud bang.

Men in military uniforms – soldiers from the People's Liberation Army - were shouting into loud speakers and I had to dive for safety as an armoured car with a mounted water cannon hurtled past.

Cameramen and reporters were starting to come racing out of the conference centre to capture the action and I saw one of the CNN journalists fall to the ground clutching his bloody head after being hit by a stone as he tried to do a piece-to-camera in front of the mob.

As I ran to the doors of the conference centre, half a dozen sweating men in vests started chasing after me bearing an assortment of sticks and bottles. The doors swung open and a hand pulled me inside, then a voice screamed for help to keep my pursuers at bay. I realised the hand and the voice belonged to Serrasalmus, dressed in a security guard's uniform, and his orders were soon obeyed as the cops with sniffer dogs and explosives detectors ran from their posts to the main doors to keep the rioters from storming the building.

My friendly guard at reception was stood behind his desk with a very concerned look on his face as he watched the glass doors rattling under a barrage of fists and bars. He glanced in my direction, recognised me and waved me through towards the main hall before returning his attention to the assault.

Deftly avoiding the metal detector, I scurried straight to the toilets, gratefully transferred the explosives from my sweat-drenched body to my handbag and then threw up with relief.

The heads of state were already in the building and several journalists were already in the main hall, sending their photographers outside to snap the chaos while they took advantage of the absent television crews to get seats at the front. There was no sign of Simone and I thought for a moment that maybe my prayers had been answered and she had come down with some sort of sickness, but then I saw her walk in talking to one of the cameramen.

I sighed and walked to the front row too and sat centre stage, tucking my handbag packed with explosives under the chair and taking out a notepad.

A combination of water cannons and police brutality eventually subdued the mob outside and as the ringleaders were taken away in wailing police vans the journalists and cameramen started drifting back into the hall.

Just under an hour late, the final day of the International Terrorism Conference got underway. The first speaker was the Australian Prime Minister, who had a hell of a job keeping the interest of the people in front of him because everyone believed the riot was a far better story than any dull speech. I was the only one amongst them who knew that by the end of the day there would be a story so huge, so utterly incomprehensible, that September 11 and July 7 would pale into insignificance. A news event was about to happen which would change the world forever.

I scanned the line of smug, overfed faces on the stage in front of me and stopped to stare at the British Prime Minister, who was sharing an unspoken joke with Gerald Maybank, sat seven spaces to my left in the front row between press secretary Sebastian Barr and Donald Keyes, the man who had succeeded Maybank as Britain's Secretary of State for Defence.

I hadn't yet decided when to detonate the explosives, but seeing them all sat there having a laugh while my Naomi's mutilated body was buried under the ground made me want to push the button right there and then.

I decided I would go after the Australian Prime Minister's speech. Simone had taken a seat right at the back of the hall and I thought there was every chance she would be unscathed in the explosion.

The speech seemed to be winding down and I felt my heart start to beat faster and my hands began to sweat. I genuinely needed the toilet, such were my nerves, and as the speech ended in muted applause, I got up from my seat and walked as calmly as possible to the toilets, leaving the handbag pushed out of sight under my chair.

Gasping for air as I reached the toilets, I locked myself in a cubicle and sat trembling on the toilet seat. I blocked out any thoughts that might have been trying to invade my mind, took four deep breaths and reached into my jacket pocket for the detonator.

But it wasn't there.

It wasn't fucking there! Frantically I hunted through all my pockets until I was sure. I'd left the fucking thing in my fucking handbag! Fuck!

Wanting to hit myself for such stupidity, I returned to the main hall, smiling sheepishly at the Indian Prime Minister, who had just begun his talk as I sat back down. I wanted to go straight back to the toilet, but I knew that would arouse suspicion, so I sat there in turmoil waiting for the lunch break.

Lunchtime eventually arrived and I shuffled out to the buffet area with a growing sense of dread rolling around in the pit of my stomach. I saw Simone standing alone by a plate of sandwiches and walked over to her.

"Hey, babe," I said, giving her a smile.

"Hey." She didn't return my smile.

"Did you get caught up in that riot this morning?"

"I managed to miss the worst of it."

"Good, I'm glad you did." I bit my lip, looked at the floor then looked back at her. "Look, Simone, there's something really important I want you to do for me."

"What's that?" she asked, frowning at me.

"When we go back into the hall after lunch, I'm going to get up halfway through one of the speeches and go to the toilets. I need you to come with me."

"Hannah," she sighed and looked away, "let's just do our jobs while we're here, okay. I can come over to the hotel tonight, maybe."

"No," I said firmly, grabbing her arm. "Simone, this isn't about sex, it's something extremely important. You absolutely have to come with me when I go out."

She shook her arm free and scowled at me now.

"What the hell is it, Hannah? What's this about? Look, we've had a lot of fun, I really like you and I'm sure we can have more fun, but if you're going to get weird this isn't going to work."

"It's nothing to do with us, or sex or anything else like that," I said with growing frustration. "Just follow me to the toilets when I get up to leave."

I walked away leaving her looking puzzled, angry and frightened and went back to the hall early to make sure I could regain my seat in the front row.

The Spanish Prime Minister kicked off proceedings in the afternoon and I sat patiently, the detonator now definitely in my jacket pocket, while he had his say, and then handed over to the Chinese Prime Minister who was closing the conference.

The Chinese leader – officially the Premier of the State Council of the People's Republic of China - was addressing the crowd through an interpreter and I knew he was likely to go on for some time, but my nerves were out of control and barely five minutes into his speech I found myself rising from the chair. This time I felt several eyes, including those of security people, follow me and my footsteps sounded like hammer blows on the wooden floor as I trotted towards the exit door with a pained expression on my face, hoping to give the impression that I was suffering from diarrhoea.

I caught Simone's eye and she looked to the heavens, but then said something to the man next to her and got up too.

The exit door opened with the sort of slow creak usually reserved for horror films and then I was out, into the carpeted corridor that led to the toilets. I smiled as best as I could at the two security men outside the door and made another show of trotting down the corridor to the ladies toilet, hoping they wouldn't realise it was strange for a woman to go to the toilet without her handbag.

I pushed the heavy toilet door open and walked inside then waited for Simone to come in.

"All right then, Hannah," she said as she walked through the door, "what game is this? You do realise how suspicious we look coming out here together."

As I had been walking out to the toilets I realised I had absolutely no idea what I was going to say to Simone, or how I could possibly explain to her what I was about to do. I decided the only thing to do was try to disable her while I set off the explosives, and then worry about explanations later. I was sure I could make her understand, given a bit more time.

I took a step towards her, grabbed her wrist with my left arm and in the same movement swung my right elbow round and hit her hard against the temple with it. Her face creased with surprise and pain, then her eyes rolled back and her legs crumpled. I caught her so that she didn't fall hard, then knelt down beside her to check she was still breathing, which she was.

I looked at her prone body sadly and then, with my stomach in knots, I pulled out the detonator and extended the long, thin aerial.

The single red button stared at me unblinkingly and accusingly, daring me to push it, daring me to commit the ultimate crime, daring me to kill perhaps several hundred people, myself and Simone possibly included.

My heart was thumping violently and I could feel my pulse tearing through my limbs. I was drenched in sweat and shaking hard.

There was a moment of hesitation. A moment of clarity. A brief moment of sanity. Then a perfect image of Naomi's destroyed body in my bath snapped in front of my eyes. I saw every cut, tear, burn and bruise. I saw the way agony had twisted her body into impossible positions. I could hear the blood-curdling shrieks, the begging and the whimpers as she pleaded with her torturers to end her suffering. I recalled the horror, the sorrow, the pity, the guilt and the anger I had felt when I found her. Above all, I recalled the deep, deep love I had for her, love that I would never be able to tell her about again. Love that I took for granted until she was taken from me.

I wanted to destroy everyone who had taken her from me.

With tears rolling down my face I pushed the red button on the detonator.

Chapter 32

At first there was nothing, just silence. Something had gone wrong. It was a dud. It hadn't worked.

Then the whole world exploded.

I felt the bathroom walls shake, then the ground rumbled and then the noise came. It was a noise like nothing I had ever heard before: a million gunshots, a billion fireworks. It was the sound of everything ending forever.

Water started spurting from sprinklers and ruptured pipes like rain and I was soon soaked. Beyond the toilet door I could hear an unholy roar of suffering and destruction. It sounded like hell.

Nervously, I opened the door and stepped out into the carpeted corridor. The plaster had come off the wall bordering the main hall and the doors that I had walked through just minutes before were gone, with a gaping, burning hole in their place.

The two guards I had just seen lay burning on the floor, not quite dead.

I walked towards the main hall, being drawn into the horror I had created by the growing heat and the hideous shrieking and screaming. A body hurled itself into the corridor, its clothes and hair alight, mouth screaming. It hit a wall and dropped to the floor, bouncing in spasms as the fire tormented bare skin, before it stopped moving.

I reached the doors, paused and then looked into the main hall of the Hong Kong International Conference Centre.

Hell was a playground in comparison.

I retched and stood frozen to the spot as I took in the scene before me. The whole place was on fire and stank of burning flesh. Grown men were rolling around shrieking like babies as fire ate them. Women with no faces were rummaging in the flames for God only knew what. Blackened objects – bodies – were twisted over chairs. Hands, feet, arms and legs were strewn everywhere.

The Chinese Premier ran past me in a ball of flames and I watched two security men with shredded stumps for arms collide with each other and fall onto the blazing body of a cameraman.

Shielding my face from the heat, I picked my way through the flames and devastation to the front of the hall - the worst hit area - and stared at what was left of the stage. Most of the dignitaries had been fused to their seats, their heads and bodies unrecognisable. Where the British Prime Minister had been sat was the bottom half of a torso and legs. On the wall behind his remains was a lumpy brown syrup.

I heard moaning above the roar of everything else and looked to my left. Gerald Maybank was sat bolt upright in his chair, a look of agony on his face. As I walked towards him I saw that the leg of a camera tripod had pierced his gut and nailed him to his chair. I knelt in front of him and smiled.

"Hello, Gerald, how are you feeling?"

"Fuck...fucking help me will you. Jesus. Fuck!"

"Don't you recognise me, Gerald? Hmm, come on now, try to think."

"What the fuck are you...talking about? Fucking help me. Please." Blood started pumping from his wound and he tugged desperately at the tripod leg.

"Do you remember a gentleman called Mazlan Azmil? A case of money in Bangkok? Is that ringing any bells, Gerry? Do you remember the name of the reporter who set you up? Hannah Harker – remember that name do you?" Maybank groaned and I slapped him sharply across the face. "Do you remember going to her house and finding her best friend Naomi there? Do you remember slashing and burning her, pulling her teeth out, cutting her fingers off, tearing her face apart?"

"What the fuck are you talking about? I...I...of course I remember Mazlan, and I know who you are too, Harker, but I don't know anything about another girl."

"Don't lie to me, Gerry."

"I swear to you, I don't know what you are talking about! I don't know anyone called Naomi."

"But you gave the orders to torture her to death, didn't you."

"I didn't tell anyone to do anything!" he squealed.

"But you did, Gerry. You gave the orders to kill her."

"I'm begging you, please don't do this. I don't know what you are talking about. I can give you money if that's what you want."

It was that last comment which triggered my fury. On the floor next to me was a human leg, burning. I untucked Maybank's shirt and as he screamed protestations I held the burning leg to the tails until they caught light. Pinned to the chair, Maybank could only watch in growing terror as the flames crawled up his shirt and starting tickling his chin.

"This is for Naomi, Gerry. This is for stealing from me the one thing in my life that ever mattered. You destroyed a beautiful, innocent girl and now this is your turn. I only wish I could make you suffer for longer because you deserve to spend an eternity in pain for what you've done."

He was screaming like an animal as his skin blistered and fell away. His hair curled and disappeared and soon he was simply a human torch, his screaming something I was not able to comprehend. I stared into his eyes until they burst.

"Nicely done, Hannah," said a familiar voice behind me.

I spun around and found myself face to sweating face with Serrasalmus.

"What the fuck do you want," I snarled. "It's done."

He grinned. "And you thought we were going to let you just walk away at the end did you?"

"Why not? You've got what you wanted. Fuck off back home and take credit for all this."

"Oh, don't you worry, I will do exactly that. But first I have my prize to collect."

"What are you fucking talking about, psycho? This place is going to cave in at any minute. I'm getting out of here."

I went to push past him but he grabbed my arm. I twisted out of his grip and spat in his face.

"Just get out of my fucking way!"

"No, Hannah, you are my prize. You are my trophy for organising this wonderful event and I am going to fuck you, kill you and burn you."

He lunged at me, but I managed to swerve out of the way and he landed in the inferno that had engulfed Maybank. He roared as he burnt his hands and then swung at me again, this time catching the side of my face.

I fell against the stage and suddenly he was on top of me. I went to ground under his weight and he tried to pin my arms with his knees while he tore at my shirt. My fists pounded his chest and I stabbed my fingernails into his face, tearing off strips of flesh, but he was relentless.

"I'm going to fuck you with fire!" he screamed, punching my face as he had done in Malaysia.

As my head flew to the side, consciousness slipping away from me, I saw a jagged chair leg, just beyond my reach. I needed to get an arm free.

I could see Serrasalmus was aroused now and he was rambling insanely about what he was going to do to me. I took three sharp breaths, flexed my stomach muscles as tight as I could and sat up as much as possible under his weight. It was enough. I sunk my teeth into his face and tore off most of his nose.

He reeled backwards clutching his face in agony, and I rolled to the side, grabbed the chair leg and stabbed it down hard into his bulging groin. There was an awful sound of crunching and cracking bone and then a crimson fountain of blood erupted from his punctured crotch. He made a noise like a little girl and I wrenched the metal rod out and pushed it through the side of his face so that it went in one cheek and came out the other, shattering teeth. He clawed towards me but he was nearly unconscious. I got to my feet as he toppled onto his back and with an ear-piercing cry I stamped on his head over and over and over again until it was a spongy pulp and he was dead.

There was a creaking noise and the sounding of tearing metal as the ceiling started to give way. I had one last satisfied look at the remains of Maybank and Serrasalmus and started to run to safety, but then remembered Simone.

I frantically picked my way through the bodies and burning debris, ran back to the toilets and flung the door open.

She wasn't there.

Panic gripped me and I started smashing open all the cubicle doors, but she had gone!

"What the fuck have you done, Hannah?" said a voice behind me.

I shrieked and spun round to see her emerging groggily from behind a pillar with blood pouring down the side of her head and face.

"My poor darling," I said, and started to move towards her.

"Keep away from me. What the fuck have you done?"

There was no love in her eyes now; she was looking at me with anger.

"Baby, it's nothing…"

"You knocked me unconscious! What the fuck have you done out there in the hall? What's that noise?"

"Later, it's not safe in here. We need to get out now, my love."

"I'm not going anywhere with you, you crazy bitch."

The words were like knives being punched into my body, but I told myself she was just dazed and not thinking coherently.

"Simone, something awful has happened and the whole place is on fire. We've got to get out of here now and I'm not leaving you."

I reached out for her hand but she backed away, the expression in her eyes now unmistakably one of fury.

"Please, Simone," I pleaded desperately. "Come with me."

"I don't know who or what you are, but I want you away from me."

"You're hurt, you don't mean that. It's the shock. Let's get you to a doctor."

"Fuck you, psycho."

More daggers cut my body, my heart in particular.

"But, but what about what we did? You love me, Simone, and I love you."

I smiled at her with every grain of love and affection I possessed and there was no way she could mistake the tears in my eyes as anything other than the tears of someone losing an argument with a lover for the last time.

"You mean nothing to me," she spat. "You passed the fucking time. It was spend the night with you or sit in my room watching Chinese television. If you hadn't shown up there was a BBC cameraman I've had before who would've done the job. How I wish now I'd just gone with him, you insane cunt."

My heart shrivelled, hardened into a black rock and crumbled. My whole body was shaking with a new, desperate emotion that not even I had experienced before. Every last shred of love, compassion and humanity was wrenched out of me with her words and I was left with a void. There was simply nothing left inside me and I didn't think I would be able to live anymore. I had known her for a fraction of my life and she had taken me to one of the happiest high points, and then destroyed me in barely the blink of an eye. What can be more painful than love that isn't returned? It is surely the most crushing, devastating thing we can know to give your entire self to someone, and receive nothing in return; less than nothing. I had wanted to give every atom of my body, every second of my life and every beat of my heart to Simone – just as I had to Naomi - but she just stood there and told me that I meant nothing to her, that I had simply passed the time. How could anyone be so cruel?

The only way to survive this was to hate with equal intensity. Hate, hurt and destroy. Retain the depth of feeling of the love, but twist it upside-down so that it becomes a consuming hatred. God help the one in the way.

It was her. She was the devil.

I lost control and pounced on her, clamped my hands around her throat and pulled her to the ground. I don't recall hearing any noise she made, any sense of feeling as my fingers crushed her neck, or any smells. I was on top of her and she may have been punching and scratching me, but I don't remember. I have unstructured memories of her face changing as she moved from life to death: different colours of the skin, eyes bulging and reddening, veins bursting and the mouth contorting. I think I might have pounded her head against the floor tiles and smashed her skull, but I couldn't be sure. It's possible that I cried as she convulsed and twitched beneath me, but this is speculation. I don't think I was ever aware that I was using my bare hands to kill someone who had given me one of the happiest times of my life, who I was in love with just a few moments before. In the end, I don't believe I knew who it was, who either of us were.

My head becomes a new place. For a long time now it has been uncharted territory, but this is something completely different, something terrifying. I don't think the inside of me is human anymore. Things are happening in here that can't be human, and putting this into words is not going to be possible because I can't understand what it is.

Utter detachment and isolation from the previous. Sinking confusion. Gliding opaqueness. Abstract irregularities. Humming warp.

A child again. Newborn. Clammy and cold, roaming eyes. Discovery and terror, new.

In a dark carriage, rolling blackness, distant flames lick up. Ice cloaks lens. It's momentary.

Something else lives here. It watches. Buzzes. Snaps. Boing, boing, boing. Gone. What next? Tickling shards? Too much. A brief silence.

Now the haunting returns. Inside and out. Ingenious. An eternal disciple, loyal beyond this existence. Transparent yet obscured, a transcending phantom. My hideous companion, how I cherish you. Please die.

Hot.

Really not right.

Leaking chimney tarnish me with brushing turbine. No, that's not it. Can you not see, it's inside you. Enjoy and wallow, this is life – feel different and alive.

Chaffing disc. 2, 7, 3, 46, 1. It's that random in here.

Almost lost now. Shutting down. Getting S-L-O-W-E-R. Slowing. Slowing. Slowing.

Bye bye.

Quiet, slow, quieter, slower. So near, please. Almost there. Verge, edge, tip, teetering, slipping. All systems down and back-up failed – but oh Lord, no!

You can't scare me.

Can.

Re-insert and proceed. Sharp skewer. Flashback smile. Rub and twitch. Pounding and a quick click. Click is buzz is tone is sound is word.

Lick flames melt lens ice cloak.

Up and dizzy, going to fall. Bright and scorch. Terrible sound. Grating shriek. White heaven light, gates open onto new dawn.

Welcome. Thank you – it's a beautiful life, a darling world. Smiles and happy cooing, so warm and snug, back in the womb. The best thing ever. Such joy it's heartbreaking.

Explosions of light burst all around. Jib jab, jib jab, jib jab. Flashing lights, lots of movement, colour, sound.

Someone is crawling through back of head, tearing through inner skull, ploughing through tissue and brain.

It's me!

You're here, Hannah.

Who the hell are you?

You've done it.

What?

You're out. Now, address them. Speak and inform. This is you and this is your time. You are somebody at last. You are the most important thing in this world.

Epilogue – a confession by James Howell

Everyone remembers where they were on the day that many of the world's leaders were murdered in the Hong Kong terror attacks.

I was in a bad place, both literally and mentally. I was a struggling freelance writer attempting to put together a feature about the politics of Colombia's various guerrilla factions. I had been living out of a rucksack in a filthy hostel near Popayan for the previous month and earlier that week I had been robbed at gunpoint by two men who burst into my room in the middle of the night.

I had come to the capital Bogota to begin the process of replacing my stolen valuables and drown myself in as much rum as I could consume while the Colombian authorities slowly ushered me through various bureaucratic hoops.

The bar I had chosen for the day was just off Avenida El Dorado and it had a small television above the bar. As reports of the explosion in Hong Kong started getting out, a special breaking news bulletin appeared on the television, with the Colombian anchors excitedly relating the reports that were coming in from various wire agencies.

The Colombian news channel managed to get access to live video footage from the scene and I remember watching intently as a camera zoomed in on a tiny dot of a figure that appeared to be walking out from the centre of a hellish inferno. As the figure grew larger on the television screen I saw that it was a young woman. Her face was blackened and bloodied, her clothes were torn and she looked to be in a state of extreme shock. She was also the most beautiful woman I had ever seen.

In the days following the bombing I watched every television report and read every online news story as I tried to find out more about the atrocity, and more about the mysterious woman who appeared to be the sole survivor.

I soon discovered that her name was Hannah Harker and that she was a British-based journalist with a sensational story. Less than a year prior to the Hong Kong bombing she had been a nobody treading water on a provincial newspaper in a dreary English backwater town. She had hit gold while on a holiday to Thailand with an exclusive story about the British Defence Secretary Gerald Maybank and his civil servant mistress selling military contracts to a Malaysian arms dealer with suspected links to Al Qaeda. She had sold the story to the International Morning Post, who rewarded her with a contract, and she broke a couple of other major stories before tragedy struck. Her best friend Naomi Knowles was brutally murdered in Hannah's own home while Hannah herself was on assignment in India. Shortly after this, a colleague from the Morning Post was killed in front of her in an apparent hit and run accident. Nobody was ever arrested in connection with either death. Hannah was sent by her editor to Hong Kong to recuperate and cover the International Terrorism Conference. Little did any of them know that the conference would end in such complete and utter carnage, with Hannah the only person left alive to tell the tale.

I wanted desperately to meet her, listen to her story and write about her life. For the time being though, nobody could get close to her as she was apparently under heavy sedation in a securely guarded private hospital in Hong Kong. The image of her emerging from the shattered conference centre adorned the covers of newspapers and magazines across the globe – it was instantly iconic – but the story that the world was waiting to hear could not yet be told.

My replacement passport and other travel documents eventually came through and I took the decision to give up chasing Colombian guerrillas and return to England.

Just over a month after the bombing Hannah was released from hospital, flown back to London and gave a world exclusive interview to her own newspaper, the International Morning Post. It was powerful stuff, but everyone knew she was holding back on a lot of the detail. She had already appointed Britain's top publicist to negotiate a television deal and the channel that made the highest bid – reportedly £2 million – aired a dramatic two-hour interview with her.

I watched the interview a dozen times and each time I became more and more besotted with her. She was jaw-droppingly beautiful and spoke with such confidence and vividness, but I also sensed a real vulnerability about her and felt there was something not quite right about the things she was saying. I suppose it was her eyes that gave it away. I'm no psychologist or psychiatrist, but I just saw something dark behind them and instinctively knew that she was hiding the truth.

I racked my brain for something I could do that would allow me to meet her, get to know her and listen to her true story. I knew she was hurting inside and I wanted to hold her, look after her and tell her everything would be all right. She obviously had no idea that I even existed, but I was sure that if I could just spend a short while with her she would open up to me and let me in. Reluctantly, however, I had to admit that access to her was still controlled by her publicist, and I didn't have the money or the influence to secure an official interview, so I would just had to bide my time. While I was waiting for an opportunity to present itself I would occupy myself with researching her story and her relationships and trying to uncover who she really was.

Four months later, the ramifications of the bombing itself were still being painfully felt across the planet, but Hannah Harker had dropped off the news agenda and was no longer being courted by publicists and feasted on by the media. She was now only working part-time on the Morning Post, and spent the rest of her time writing columns for other publications and doing a bit of television work. There was a lot of speculation in media circles that the horrors she had witnessed on that fateful day had left her with deep emotional and mental scars and she was drinking heavily to try and heal them.

I was also freelancing in London again by now and had caught my first sight of her in the flesh jumping into a taxi outside Murdoch's News International headquarters in Wapping. It had been a bitter winter morning and she was wrapped up in a thick dark coat while the ice-laced wind whipped her hair across her face. She looked troubled and lonely and the fleeting incident inspired me to redouble my efforts to make contact with her.

A few days later a terrible opportunity arose when I learned from a friend of mine that Hannah's father had just died of prostate cancer. I quietly cursed my friend for passing on this information and swore to myself that I wouldn't use it to meet Hannah, but I'm ashamed to say that's exactly what I did.

I found out where the funeral was to take place and drove down to the cemetery on a foul Tuesday afternoon two days before Christmas. There were well over a hundred mourners at the service, their faces mostly hidden by black umbrellas as the rain pelted down, so I was able to blend in without arousing suspicion. Hannah and her mother stood side by side, both wearing black but neither showing any emotion, as Peter Harker was lowered into the ground and his coffin covered with wet earth.

Hannah laid a wreath on her father's grave, then gave her mother the briefest of hugs and walked away to her car without once looking back.

My mind was racing as I followed her back home and every instinct told me to leave the girl alone, but I had become so obsessed by her that I couldn't let the chance slip by.

She pulled into the driveway of a very large detached house just outside the M25 in Lingfield, Kent, and I parked up opposite so I would be able to see if she left again. I waited there for over six hours and was just about to try and get some sleep when her front door opened and she stepped out onto the porch, a security light momentarily silhouetting her face before she walked off down her drive and out into the street.

I got out of my car and felt the cold slice through my bones as I took off after her on foot. It was just gone 10pm and I had no idea where she could be going, until I spotted the glow of a pub in the distance and correctly predicted that this was her destination.

I waited outside the pub for ten minutes after she had gone in so it didn't look so obvious that I was following her. When I did walk in she was sitting alone on a stool at the bar with her back to the entrance. There were a couple of old boys sitting next to a cosy log fire supping pints of cloudy ale, and another old boy sitting by himself at a table with a Guinness, but otherwise the pub was dead. The bearded landlord in the thick jumper asked me what I wanted and I ordered a large straight vodka.

I sensed Hannah flicking her eyes in my direction as I walked in and placed my order – she was drinking the same as me – and I sat on another stool at the bar, let out a deep sigh and massaged my temples with my fingers.

"Why were you at my father's funeral today?"

The question took a second to register, but once it did my stomach turned.

"Excuse me?" I asked with mock surprise, trying to buy myself time.

"Why were you at my father's fucking funeral, and why have you followed me home?"

She hadn't turned to look at me yet, she was focussed solely on the glass in front of her on the bar.

I knew it was useless lying, and trying to pretend that she was mistaken. I was wearing a black suit and black tie, and looked ever more out of place in this rural pub than she did. I decided to come clean and be completely honest with her.

"I know that Gerald Maybank had your friend murdered for the stitch-up job you did on him and Mazlan. It's no coincidence that you were there in Hong Kong is it? You had something to do with it all?"

Hannah finally turned to look at me and for the first time I was able to look directly into her beautiful eyes. She didn't say a word and not a flicker of emotion showed on her face. She just looked at me for a few seconds, downed her drink and walked out of the pub.

I followed her outside and jogged to catch up with her as she started walking back to her house.

"I'm sorry that I chose today to do this," I said.

"What are you?" she grunted. "MI5? MI6? A little policeman?"

"I'm nothing like that. I just wanted to meet you and listen to you and hopefully find out the truth about what has happened to you."

"Why the hell would you be so interested in me?"

"I'm a writer and think you have an incredible story to tell."

"I've already told my story."

"No, you told a story. You told a certain version of events that I don't believe. I think the truth is even more amazing and I'd like to hear it."

"I'm tired of talking."

"Look, if I managed to find out about Maybank killing your friend Naomi I'm sure it won't be long before the authorities figure it out too and start to piece together what really happened in Hong Kong. They won't risk a trial and having you tell the world how the British Government murdered Naomi, they will have you silenced. You will disappear, Hannah, and nobody will ever hear the truth. Please tell me what happened and let me write your story."

We reached her house and stopped at the front gate. Finally, the stony expression on her face eased and she looked at me properly for the first time.

"What's your name?"

"James Howell."

"How is it that you know so much about my life?"

"I've been researching you, talking to people and making enquiries.

To be blunt, I've been obsessed with you since I saw the pictures of you walking out of that conference centre."

She let out a quick, sharp laugh. "So you're a stalker!"

I smiled back at her and looked at the heavens. "Yeah okay, if you like. Come on, either tell me to fuck off so we can both get on with our lives, or invite me in for a drink."

She invited me in for a drink.

During my research of Hannah I had often wondered what her home would be like.

As I became aware of the horrors and anguish she had been through, I came to imagine that she would live in some cold, dark cave of a place shut behind heavy locked and bolted doors. I pictured her sitting scared on a hard floor, surrounded by shadows, too afraid to open the curtains.

The reality was, of course, a lot less sinister but there was still nothing particularly welcoming about her home. Pictureless, white-washed walls rose up from the dark wooden floor and as she led me through the house to the lounge area I could see no sign of any furniture, clocks or mirrors. The lounge itself was nearly as barren: just two leather armchairs sat in the middle of the room with a low coffee table between them, no other furniture. There was, however, a picture in this room; a large, framed print that had been hung very carefully above the empty, yawning fireplace. I recognised the two people in the picture instantly as Hannah and her friend Naomi.

"That was one of the happiest days of my life," Hannah said, seeing that I was looking at it. "We were in Thailand and neither of us had a care in the world. We were so young and innocent and had our whole lives ahead of us to look forward to. How things change."

She waved for me to sit in one of the armchairs.

"What do you want to drink?"

"Vodka."

"I'll bring the bottle."

As she left the room I looked at the coffee table and saw that there were two empty vodka bottles on there, an empty glass and half a dozen empty packets of the anti-depressant drug Citalopram. I was wondering what sort of diet the poor creature lived on, when she re-entered the room and answered the question for me.

"Most days I'll have three cups of coffee and 100mg of Citalopram for breakfast, as much solid food as I can physically stomach for lunch and then a bottle of vodka or more for dinner. It keeps the weight down, if nothing else." She smiled but I didn't see the funny side.

She tossed a blank A4 pad of paper onto my lap along with a handful of pens, poured me a huge glass of vodka, then lit a few candles around the room and fell down into the armchair opposite.

"What are your plans for Christmas?" she asked, slipping off her jacket and crossing her legs to get comfortable.

"I hadn't really given it any thought," I answered honestly.

"Why not? Don't you have a wife, kids, family?"

"No."

"Then stay here with me."

"Turkey and crackers?"

"What do you think?"

"I think I'd love to stay here with you."

"Good. I don't really sleep much so I should be able to tell you my story in a few days. When I do need to sleep, you can come with me."

I avoided eye contact, swallowed the rest of my glass of vodka and refilled it.

"And what will happen when you've finished telling me your story?" I asked. "Is there going to be a happy ending?"

"Not for me."

"Why not? Maybe I can help you."

"Don't get involved with me, James." It was the first time she used my name. "We will spend time together over the coming days, and we will sleep with each other because we need physical comfort, but you cannot allow yourself to fall for me. Everyone I have ever cared for in my life has been taken from me. My dad was the last person left alive who I loved, and now he is gone I have nobody left to lose. As you said, my time is running out and one way or the other I am living on borrowed time."

"Don't say that..."

"If you can't accept that, then you had better leave now because you have not even begun to hear a fraction of the truth yet. Whatever you think you know about me you should forget about it. When I've finished telling you my confession you will look at me in a whole different light. You will be scared of me. You will hate me. You will understand why all of my suffering has been deserved."

The dead, stony expression had returned and I realised she was crawling back into a place where I would never be able to follow her, a place I would struggle to ever even comprehend.

"I have been walking on a tightrope of sanity but have lost my balance and will fall at any moment now. The anti-depressants had helped to steady me for a while, but they were just delaying the inevitable. I have been taking a higher and higher dose, but they have been having less and less of an effect. There is blood on my hands and evil in my heart and I can't expect chemicals to conceal that anymore. Just listen to my story, James, and then run as far away from me as you can."

Run from her was the last thing I wanted to do. I wanted to reach across and hold her, kiss her and reassure her that everything would be all right. She didn't want that though, and I was starting to get the feeling that she never would.

"Fine," I said, picking up a pen and the notepad. "Tell me your story."

I lost track of time during the first session because there were no windows in her lounge and no clocks on the wall. We drank, she spoke and I wrote. Occasionally I would ask her a question to get more detail or clear up a confusing point, but generally she recounted her story eloquently, chronologically and clearly.

At times it was harrowing though. When she described how the boys had died in the fire at Venna Mansions and how she had fallen to pieces after that, she seemed to be on the verge of losing control. I pressed her for detail and to tell me how she felt and she obliged, but I could tell that it was taking its toll on her.

On a couple of occasions she asked me to leave the room so she could write things down in her own words. I did as she asked, and sat drinking in her kitchen until she called me back in. Each time I returned she was flushed and trembling and I knew she had been crying.

Sometime later, several hours after she had begun her story, she just stopped speaking and told me that she was tired.

"Go and get some rest," I told her. "I'll sleep down here."

"No," she insisted. "Come with me."

I too was exhausted and gladly followed her upstairs to her bedroom.

For so many months and I had been obsessed with her and had, sadly, fantasised about what it would like to sleep with her. That night, though, we were both drunk and tired, she was emotionally exhausted and I was trying to get my head around some of the things I had just heard her say.

We showered in her en-suite bathroom and did have sex, but it was strange and awkward. I was submissive and let her take control. There was nothing loving or erotic about it – we simply went through the motions and then fell asleep with our backs to each other.

We tried again the following morning and it was better, but I knew the whole time that she was holding back. She wasn't going to make love to me because she wouldn't let herself become emotionally attached to someone again in such a reckless way.

I persuaded her not to have antidepressants for breakfast and we instead drank coffee together and forced down some toast, before returning to bed where she continued her story.

She told me about the night she and Naomi pulled the sting on the footballer Jason Brady and we both laughed. She was also smiling when she told me about the day she and Naomi had gone out and blown the money she had been paid for the scoop. She was starting to relax a bit and when she described the night that she had sex with the stripper Mei we both got excited and spent a good couple of hours enjoying each other under the covers.

It was late on Christmas Eve when we emerged from her bedroom and we went downstairs hand in hand and called out for pizza. The delivery boy had tinsel on his scooter and we joked with him, gave him a £100 tip and went back up to bed where we scoffed turkey pizza and guzzled a bottle of champagne she found in the back of her drinks cabinet. That night we fell asleep in each other's arms with big grins on our faces and I started to think that everything was going to work out.

I was horribly wrong.

During the night I became restless and after an hour of tossing and turning I decided to get up. I had not been given a tour of Hannah's large house and thought I would have a harmless little snoop around some of the upstairs rooms. Her bedroom was at the end of a long landing that had more rooms coming off it and a closed door at the other end.

The first room I looked in was completely empty, and in the second room I checked there were just a few cardboard boxes in the middle of the floor of books, clothes and trinkets that she had never unpacked.

As I moved further up the landing towards the door at the end, I started to notice a foul smell.

The next room I peered into was bare again, and as I came out the smell had grown stronger and more grotesque. When I got even nearer to the door at the end I found myself retching.

A floorboard squeaked noisily under my foot and I told myself to stop being stupid, turn around and go back to bed, but the next thing I knew I was reaching for the door handle and pushing it down.

The door creaked open and I was enveloped by a smell so repulsive that I threw up on the spot.

It was a small bathroom with a little window that let in a thin shaft of amber light from an outside street lamp. Most of my vomit had splashed over the toilet seat and wash basin in front of me, but it was the bath that I was looking at. I could see it was full of liquid and there were things floating in the liquid. As I leaned in closer, holding my breath to block out the stench of chemicals and rotting meat, a black football bobbed to the surface and slowly turned around.

I recoiled in horror as the dim yellow light revealed the decomposed remains of a human head. The image instantly seared itself into my memory for eternity: empty eye sockets, a chewed-up nose and a gaping mouth with the teeth smashed out.

A light bulb suddenly burst to life above me and the nightmare was revealed in full.

"This was how I found Naomi; mutilated in a bath at my house."

I swivelled around and Hannah was standing naked in the doorway of the bathroom, staring right through me with dead eyes.

"Hannah," I spluttered in terror. "What have you done?"

She shifted her gaze to the bath as a hairy torso and foot floated to the surface.

"His name is Liam King. He was a policeman who thought he was better than me."

"But...I don't understand. You killed a policeman? When? Why?"

"We slept together for a while in the past. He bored me so I left him and he took it badly. He decided he wanted to take revenge against me for humiliating him so he started to dig around in my past and see if there were any skeletons in my closet that he could use against me. As you can imagine, he didn't have to dig far."

I sat down on the toilet seat, not wanting to look in the bath, and let her continue.

"He found out that I'd attacked Ruth Chapman at school and remembered that the same girl had been brutally beaten in a park a few years later – he had been involved in the investigation as a junior officer. He tracked Ruth down and asked her if it was possible that I had attacked her in the park as well. Initially she stuck to her story about the Eastern European rapist, but then admitted to Liam that she had been knocked unconscious from behind and had never actually seen who the assailant was. She apparently couldn't believe that I would hold a grudge for so long and take such violent revenge, so she threw Liam out of her house and slammed the door in his face. I hope she does know that it was me."

"So this cop came here to arrest you for beating up a girl at school and you killed him!" I shook my head incredulously and she sat on the edge of the bath.

"No, finding Ruth was just the beginning for Liam. After putting two and two together with her, he obviously came to the conclusion that I had some kind of psychotic tendencies and he reopened the case files on the Venna Mansions fire. He knew that I'd been there on the night of the fire, but there was nothing unusual in that because I was a reporter and had every right to be there. He interviewed all the firefighters he could find who had fought the blaze and asked them if they had noticed anything strange about me that night, but it had been such chaos that hardly any of them could even remember me being there.

"Despite this dead end he knew I was behind the fire so the smart bastard got hold of my bank records and found that I'd made a £5 payment at a local petrol station on the day of the fire. As luck would have it, the garage stored all their CCTV tapes on site and it took him just a few minutes to locate the tape from that day. At 5.43pm there was clear black and white footage of me filling up a petrol can and putting it in the boot of my car.

"It wasn't the sort of evidence that would secure a conviction in court by itself, but he knew then that I had started the fire. In hindsight I'm astonished that they hadn't checked the CCTV footage from local petrol stations at the time, but then Rockingsworth Police and Detective Inspector Liam King were never the most competent investigators."

She reached for a towel and wrapped it around herself with a little shiver.

"Did he then find out about Maybank and what they did to Naomi?" I asked.

She looked at me with a hollow expression, as if she didn't understand the question. She looked at the mess in the bath, and then she looked at her fingers.

"I was wrong," she muttered.

"Wrong about what?"

"Everything."

"What are you talking about? I don't understand; what were you wrong about?"

"I got everything wrong. Maybank wasn't lying; he really didn't know."

A tear escaped from her eye and she blinked it away and looked at me.

"I had used my own passport to travel to Malaysia so Liam was able to trace that and place me there at the time of Mazlan's murder. I then dropped off the grid while I was in Singapore with Jemaah Islamiyah before resurfacing in Hong Kong at the beginning of the conference. He correctly surmised that I had set off the explosion to kill Maybank for Naomi's murder."

"And so," I said, "he came here to take you in? I suppose there must be a big reward for whoever provides information leading to the arrest of the conference centre terrorists."

"No," she shook her head, "that's not why he came round here."

I was confused. "Then why?"

"I was wrong about Liam. I was so wrong about him. When I got together with him I just thought of it as a fling. When I later got bored and split up with him, I didn't think it would be any big deal, but he took it badly. He made these threats and said I would regret it, but I never really thought it was anything more than bitterness. I just assumed I'd damaged his ego."

"So what happened?" I pressed her.

"On the night my dad died I had been at the hospital to say goodbye to him and got home here very late. I was inconsolable so I don't really know what time exactly it was, but I suppose it was gone midnight. I had my key in the front door when he appeared from nowhere, held a knife to my throat, and told me to go into the house.

"I remember that he was very calm, and when we got into the house he took a pair of handcuffs from his coat pocket and cuffed me to the radiator. He helped himself to a glass of vodka from the kitchen, then sat cross-legged on the floor in front of me, slapped me around a bit and said he had a story to tell me.

"When I was on the Evening Informer a teenage girl had been abducted, and was later found raped and murdered. Liam was put in charge of the murder investigation but no arrests were ever made. I had assumed that, just as with the Venna Mansions investigation, it was because of his incompetence that the girl's killer was never caught, but I was wrong. There was a very good reason why Liam never arrested the girl's murderer."

She stopped and took a deep breath. I suspected what was coming but let her say it.

"Liam killed her. While I was handcuffed to the radiator downstairs he explained to me how he had seen her walking home from school one day, followed her and then dragged her into his car when she reached a quiet back road. He took her back to his house and, in his own filthy fucking words, 'enjoyed her delicate little body for two wonderful days', before strangling her and dumping her body in a skip."

I looked at the remains of the monster in the bath with renewed disgust.

"A week after that, he told me that he had driven to Portsmouth, abducted a young woman as she walked home from work and drove all the way back to Rockingsworth with her in the boot. This time he said he was particularly cruel and tortured her for several days before killing her. He described to me the things he did, but I don't want to think about them again so please don't ask me. When he had finished with her he drove all the way back to Portsmouth and dumped her body in a ditch."

Hannah all of a sudden burst into tears and I got up and hugged her.

"Come downstairs, darling, let's get out of this room."

"I haven't finished telling you what happened."

"It's fine, tell me downstairs. Go and sit on the sofa and I'll fix us both a drink."

She went to the lounge while I poured us large vodkas and went and sat next to her. She was rocking and shaking so I held her hand and asked her to tell me the rest.

"When I dumped him he said he had gone into a wild rage and beaten a random man unconscious on the way home from the pub that night. He said that he vowed he would get revenge on me for humiliating him, no matter how long he had to wait.

"He followed me and watched me for months, but because I was at the Post my movements were completely unpredictable and he never had a chance to put a plan together.

"That is until I went on my assignment to India."

I closed my eyes. Oh God, I thought, don't let it be true.

"He knew who Naomi was because I used to talk about her all the time when we were going out together. He knew that she was my best friend and he knew that I loved her. As soon as I left for India he knew exactly how he could get revenge on me.

"When it dawned on me what he was about to say, I nearly tore the radiator off the wall trying to get to him. I couldn't bear to hear it and I tried to cover my ears, but he punched me and leaned in close so that he could speak directly into my ear. I screamed and screamed and tried to bite him, but he held my face tightly between his hands and spent the next 20 minutes whispering to me what he had done to Naomi for the five days that he was at my house."

Hannah went silent, presumably reliving the pain in her mind.

We sat there without saying anything for several minutes, before another terrible fact dawned on me.

"Everything that you did after Naomi's death was for nothing."

She looked up at me and nodded, her face bright red and streaked with tears. "That's right. I was convinced that Maybank was responsible for her death and it was all a huge Government conspiracy, but I was wrong. Mike Potter getting run down in the street was simply a random hit-and-run, not an assassination. Mazlan knew nothing about it when I confronted him in Malaysia and he just suggested that Maybank was responsible to save his own skin. Maybank himself, even when I was burning him alive, protested his innocence and said he had nothing to do with Naomi.

"I slaughtered 314 people when I blew up the conference centre in Hong Kong, including Simone who I killed with my own bare hands. I expect thousands more have already died around the world because of the fall-out and reprisals following the bombing. All those lives have been lost because of two psychopaths – Liam and me."

"Don't say that about yourself," I said, but we both knew that she was. "What happened with Liam then? How did you escape and kill him?"

"After he finished telling me about Naomi he was triumphant. He knew that he had destroyed me and had his revenge for being humiliated. I tried to stay defiant, to take some of the shine off his moment of glory, so I called him a pathetic little cunt and said that he could never take away my memories of Naomi.

"He hit me and was suddenly on top of me, pulling my clothes off, and he forced himself inside me. I kicked and screamed, but it was useless because I was handcuffed to the radiator so I knew I had to do something different.

"I relaxed, kissed him and started to pretend I was enjoying it. He hit me again and I told him I wanted him to fuck me one last time. He said I really was insane, but he took the handcuffs off, dragged me upstairs by the hair, threw me on the bed and raped me. What he didn't know, of course, was that since I got back from Hong Kong I have slept every night with a kitchen knife under my pillow. I was pinned on my front and couldn't move until he was finished, but the moment he rolled off me I took the knife and stuck it through his eye. I bit off his bottom lip as he screamed and then stuck the knife through his other eye. He was crying torrents of blood but wouldn't die so I opened his belly up and pulled his intestines out for him. Even then the bastard laid there sobbing and convulsing for ten minutes before he finally gave up.

"I dragged him into the bath and poured all the household chemicals I could find over him to try and dissolve his fucking body.

"The next morning I had to go out to start making the arrangements for my dad's funeral and when I got home the bastard had tried to crawl out of the bath! I thought he was already dead when I put him in there, but he obviously wasn't. I suppose he'd been too weak and had slipped back down face first into the chemicals and choked to death on drain cleaner and bleach.

"I've started to chop him up now, but I've been so busy with dad's funeral that I've not had time to finish the job."

I was pale and she gave me a friendly smile. "Come back to bed for a while," she said. "I need comforting."

"Okay," I replied, not sure how I was even going to begin to make sense of everything I had heard.

"By the way," she said as we walked upstairs together. "Happy Christmas."

We had strange and awkward sex together and then I drifted off to sleep. When I woke up later in the morning she wasn't in bed.

I went downstairs and found her in the lounge, a bottle of vodka in her hand and tears on her face. Pages and pages of barely legible words lay in a pile at her feet and she shook her head at me. I went to cuddle her, but she pushed me away and told me to write.

Over the course of Christmas Day she filled in the gaps of her story as best as she could. It was a nightmare for me, so I can scarcely imagine what it was like for her.

For large parts of the day she ordered me out of the room and scribbled down her own version of events while I loitered in the kitchen or bed, trying not to think about the decomposing body in the bathroom. Every time she called me back to the lounge I would find her a twitching and sobbing wreck.

Hours later I was laying in bed when she called for me from downstairs again. It was still Christmas Day so I hoped she had got everything she needed to off her chest and we could spend some time together again at last. I was going to suggest getting the hell out of the house for a bit.

Halfway down the stairs I stopped in my tracks and realised that it was all over.

The front door was open and Hannah was standing on the porch with a folder full of papers in her hand. It was the story we had written together. The moment I had been dreading had finally arrived.

Painfully, I walked down the rest of the stairs to the hallway and she came and stood in front of me so that the tips of our noses were touching. We both reached out our hands and placed them on each other's hips. I started to open my mouth to speak but she pressed a finger to my lips.

"Don't say it," she whispered. "Don't say anything. Please."

I tried to hold her gaze as manfully as I could, but then blinked and a single tear smuggled itself out the corner of my left eye and slipped vertically down my face. She reached her hand up again and carefully wiped it away with the back of her little finger.

I leant forward to kiss her one last time, but she backed away and turned her head. She didn't love me. Of course she didn't. Why would she? After everything she had told me did I still not get it? I was nothing to her. I had invaded an inconsequential fraction of her life and now my purpose had been served she wanted me gone.

I stepped out onto the doorstep and took a deep breath of air to try and calm myself. It was frosty but sunny; an inviting day.

I wanted to be strong and just walk away, but I turned for one last look at her. She was looking at me. Our eyes locked and the faintest smile flicked at the corners of her mouth. I held my breath and for a second thought she was going to laugh, drag me back into the house and tell me that she loved me and that she wanted me to stay with her forever.

It didn't happen though. The momentary smile she had shown me dissolved and with a final blank look she pushed the door closed in my face.

I never saw her again.